DEVIL'S
WAKE

ALSO BY STEVEN BARNES

Streetlethal
The Kundalini Equation
Gorgon Child
Firedance
Lion's Blood
Zulu Heart
Far Beyond the Stars
The Cestus Deception
Great Sky Woman
Shadow Valley

ALSO BY TANANARIVE DUE

My Soul to Take
Joplin's Ghost
The Good House
Freedom in the Family
The Living Blood
My Soul to Keep
The Black Rose

BY STEVEN BARNES AND
TANANARIVE DUE
WITH BLAIR UNDERWOOD

Casanegra
In the Night of the Heat
From Cape Town with Love
and forthcoming
South by Southeast

DEVIL'S WAKE

A Novel

Steven Barnes
and Tananarive Due

ATRIA PAPERBACK

New York   London   Toronto   Sydney   New Delhi

ATRIA PAPERBACK
A Division of Simon & Schuster, Inc.
1230 Avenue of the Americas
New York, NY 10020

First Atria Paperback edition July 2012

ATRIA PAPERBACK and colophon are trademarks of Simon & Schuster, Inc.

For information about special discounts for bulk purchases, please contact Simon & Schuster Special Sales at 1-866-506-1949 or business@simonandschuster.com.

The Simon & Schuster Speakers Bureau can bring authors to your live event. For more information or to book an event, contact the Simon & Schuster Speakers Bureau at 1-866-248-3049 or visit our website at www.simonspeakers.com.

Designed by Jacquelynne Hudson

Manufactured in the United States of America

10 9 8 7 6 5 4 3 2 1

Library of Congress Cataloging-in-Publication Data

Barnes, Steven.
Devil's wake : a novel / Steven Barnes, Tananarive Due.
p. cm.
I. Due, Tananarive, 1966– II. Title.
PS3552.A6954D48   2012
813'.54—dc23   2011033779

ISBN 978-1-4516-1700-9
ISBN 978-1-4516-1701-6 (ebook)

To Nicki Barnes
and
Jason Kai Due-Barnes

"Well, if there's that many, they'll probably get us wherever we are."

—*Night of the Living Dead*

Before:
First Warning

ONE

August 12
3:23 p.m.
I-5 Freeway, Southern Washington State

—ongoing concerns over scattered reports of violent, perhaps drug-induced behavior in the Seattle area," the newscaster's voice boomed from the BMW's Sony speakers, filling the car as trees and farmland zipped past on either side. *"While yesterday's bizarre rampages at a boarding school in New Brunswick, New Jersey, and a diet clinic in West Palm Beach, Florida, did involve some individuals who have received the Amsterdam flu inoculation, the CDC says there is no relationship, as the vaccine has been thoroughly tested. But as a cautionary measure, further vaccinations have been halted until the nature of this—"*

"Do you hear that?" Kendra Brookings asked. "Flu shot's making people crazy."

"Kendra, don't exaggerate," her mother said, weary of the

argument. Cassandra Brookings had the cheekbones and carriage that said "runway" even if she'd opted for owlish glasses and a family therapist's credentials. "These are just rumors. There are always rumors about the unknown. Millions of people have taken the flu shot, and there have been reports of, what? A handful of cases that probably aren't connected at all? These people were probably deeply disturbed from the beginning. Do you have a mental disorder we don't know about?"

Parents are a mental disorder—does that count? Kendra thought. Grandpa Joe, her mother's father, had always said Mom had a naive streak a mile long. Kendra figured her mom had moved to Washington State to be closer to her father's cabin up near Centralia, but Mom would never admit it. Stubbornness ran in the family, and forcing Kendra to get a flu shot on her sixteenth birthday was a perfect example.

"I know you're nervous, sweet pea." Devon Brookings was a big man in his mid-forties, a college athlete who now enjoyed couches more than wind sprints. He and Cassandra ran a family therapy/life coach business that did very well, thank you, but he was totally chair-bound: his waistline was still solid, but expanding nicely.

Dad switched radio stations, trying to cheer her up. A staccato hip-hop rhythm boomed through the speakers. "Don't be. Doc Thorpe has overseen thousands of vaccinations, and never had a problem. Not once. A few folks faint when they see the needle, but . . ." He winked into the rearview mirror. Smiling. This was Dad's idea of a joke.

"You're not funny," Kendra said.

"Don't look so sour. It's not a big deal. We're lucky to get this shot. I didn't want to scare you, but there's a study . . ."

"Yeah, yeah, I heard about that," Kendra said. "In school, Mr. Kaplan had told us that 125,000 people might have died

4

from the new flu in Asia and Europe. But it's not happening here. Pizza, burgers, and fries might be saving our butts." Kendra herself looked too much like a typical Disney Channel Sassy Black Teenager for her own comfort: short, cute, chipmunk cheeks, perfect teeth, and eyes as bright as stars.

"I think Burger King is responsible for those rumors," Mom said. "I wouldn't trust Mayor McCheese if I were you."

"That's McDonald's," Kendra said. Her mother was practically a vegan, and Dad's cooking skills topped out at pan-fried SPAM, so mealtime was an adventure.

Kendra gave up on her pleas, settling for the view as the car crossed the Interstate Bridge into Portland over the Columbia River. Portland wasn't L.A. even in its dreams, but it was cute, like a huge small town. Dad switched off the radio so they could hear the quiet. One thing the Pacific Northwest had over L.A. was raw beauty. All Kendra remembered of grasslands and mountains in L.A. was shades of thirsty brown.

"It still rains too much," Kendra said to her window.

"Got that right," Dad said. "The state flower is mildew."

"But it makes everything look so *alive*," Mom said. "Remember spring?"

The last thing we talked about on the way to Portland was how pretty it is in springtime, Kendra would write in her journal later. *Spring was just another season in the world's long list of wonders I was foolish enough to take for granted.*

IF YOU HAVE FLU SYMPTOMS, PLEASE PROTECT OTHER PATIENTS BY WEARING A MASK. The sign was waiting inside the hospital's electric double doors, beside a cardboard dispenser half full of blue paper face masks. Mom quickly whipped out three masks like they were tissues and passed them around.

"But we're not sick," Kendra said.

"That's right," Mom said. "Let's keep it that way."

"Haven't you heard that hospitals are the perfect place to get sick?" Dad said. As if Portland General had been *her* idea. "If you ever hear the word 'iatrogenic,' you know you've been screwed." Kendra hadn't been to an emergency room since she was four, and she didn't watch hospital shows, so she had no real knowledge as to how crowded and depressing ERs could be. It was a den of the unfortunate, people who were coughing, dazed, or bleeding. There were at least twenty people waiting, enough to fill all but four molded plastic seats.

While Dad checked them in at the front desk, Mom and Kendra found two chairs together in a corner of the waiting room, leaving Dad to fend for himself. To Kendra's right, an old man was nodding to sleep, a glistening snail trail dribbling from one corner of his mouth; on her left, a five-year-old boy with a home-made bandage around his head whined softly to his mother. As soon as Kendra sat down, the kid coughed up a mouthful of vomit. Some of the buttermilky glop splattered the tip of Kendra's sneaker. She stared at the orangish flecks, horrified.

"Are you *kidding* me?" Kendra whispered to her mom after the kid's mother apologized, rushing her son off to the bathroom.

"Adjust," Mom said. "Sometimes little kids have tummy trouble."

Yeah, big kids too, Kendra thought, her throat pinching tight. Except for the dozing old man, everyone nearby stood up to move away from the stench, giving up their seats. Despite the smell, by the time the cleaning crew arrived, newcomers had swarmed the empty seats. Kendra swore she would never visit a hospital again.

When Dad joined them, he motioned them in close for a huddle, checking to make sure no one was listening. "Twenty minutes max—maybe thirty. Then we're in." He sounded like they were planning a bank heist. Kendra felt sorry for the patients who really needed doctors.

Kendra hadn't noticed the mounted television set playing overhead until someone turned up the volume, and suddenly all eyes were on the screen. *Los Angeles—LIVE,* it said. On TV, a street full of shoppers and Armani-clad executive types were screaming and running.

There was some kind of commotion on a street lined with palm trees and Mercedes SUVs. People fleeing. A car was on fire in the middle of a street lined with boutique windows. Kendra's heart slammed her chest. She *knew* that street!

"Oh my goodness!" Mom said, alarmed. "That's Rodeo Drive, Dev. Around the corner from your first office!"

On TV, a man swung a full-size naked mannequin like a baseball bat, slamming it into the face of a silver-haired lady clad only in a nightgown, who'd been running barefoot on his heels. The old lady flew backward like a roller skater hitting a clothesline, her legs splayed in a Y. The entire ER gasped in unison.

"We got out just in time!" Dad said. "See? Rat City. When urban areas get overcrowded—"

"That ain't it!" A voice spoke up. The old man, at last, was awake. He smeared drool from his chin and pushed himself to his feet, leaning on the chair. "My brother's down in a little flea of a town outside El Dorado, Arkansas. Said the same thing happened there yesterday—a nurse went batshit, biting people. Next day, folks who got bit lost their minds, trying to bite too. Says they locked 'em all up in the jail and kept it quiet. But you don't think the government knows?"

If not for what was on TV, the old man would have sounded like a nut job.

On TV, Kendra watched a woman in a nightshirt sink her teeth into the bare forearm of a beefy jogger as he sprinted past her. She held on, teeth clenched tight, even as he yelled and tried to fling her away. The woman hung on like a pit bull, her bright red hair flying back and forth as the jogger struggled to shake her off.

Then it looked like the video camera fell over—or the man carrying it did. With one voice, the ER gasped again. All those who could rose to their feet. The TV screen went black, then returned to the newsroom. The blond Anchor Barbie looked shaken, her lips working without producing words.

"I need to call Willie," Dad said, reaching for his cell phone. Uncle Willie was Bill Brookings, Dad's younger brother, a television producer who lived in Bel Air, minutes from Beverly Hills. He and Aunt Janine had two kids, including Kendra's favorite cousin, Jovana. Kendra saw her father's hand trembling—something she'd never seen before—and felt her first shiver of terror.

Mom was shaking her head. "Mass hysteria? Look at them, Dev. What kind of delusion is this?"

The next scream wasn't from the TV. A piercing sound, midway between human and some kind of jungle cat, came from beyond the waiting room, beyond the nurses' station—past the double doors marked EMERGENCY PERSONNEL ONLY. Someone on the other side of the doors was in a lot of pain. Dying, perhaps. A slow, hard death.

"The damned circuits are busy," Dad said, the only voice in the room. He was so preoccupied that he probably thought the scream was on TV.

All eyes turned from the TV to the double doors at the emergency room entrance. The three nurses at the station put away their charts and phones, staring with the rest of them. *What are we waiting for?* Kendra wondered, holding tightly to her mother's arm. When the main lobby doors slid open, the rest of them found a reason to scream.

8

TWO

Considering the commotion behind the nurses' desk, Kendra might have ignored the gentle mechanical *whooshing* of the lobby doors on the opposite end as they opened and closed, opened and closed. But Kendra couldn't ignore the sturdy, sixtyish woman standing in the doors' path as they swatted her on the back and then opened again. Open, closed. Open, closed. The woman stood in a wide stance as if she didn't feel the doors trying to push her inside, her wispy, snow-colored hair splayed across her face as she stared at everyone staring at her. She swayed right to left in an odd counterrhythm that looked like a dance with the doors.

She was barefoot, dressed in blue silk polka-dotted pajama bottoms and a too-big lumberjack shirt that was halfway unbuttoned. Since she wasn't wearing a bra, the open V across her chest showed far too much of her sagging, freckled bosom.

The woman's eyes were mostly hidden beneath swaths of her hair, but a glimpse was enough to turn Kendra's skin to gooseflesh: The woman's eyes were red-black, a color that wasn't human. Her lips parted to display blood-slimed teeth. Someone was yelling outside, and Kendra made out a guy in a business suit crawling across the driveway's asphalt. The portrait of the woman in the doorway and the yuppie on the ground collided in a way that slowed everything down to syrupy slow motion.

When Kendra blinked, the woman was lurching inside.

One man in the waiting room, himself as big as a lumberjack, jumped to his feet as if she looked like she needed rescuing. "Ma'am?" he said. "Are you all right?" He reached for her elbow, ready to guide her to rest and safety.

The room seemed to vanish, shrouded somewhere in the memory of the woman's teeth, the businessman crawling outside, and the still unidentified screams from inside the ER. When Kendra's eyes focused again, the Amazon's teeth were clamped into the meat of her rescuer's hand. He howled, trying to shake her off. But the Amazon wouldn't let go, even after he lost his chivalry and pushed against her with all his might, a hard *thud* sounding as they both fell against the wall beside the doors.

A yard to the right and they might have broken through the glass door, but Kendra didn't think the woman's teeth would have budged even if they had.

"Get this bitch off me!" The man's eyes rolled back as he screamed.

Several people ran toward them at once. The Amazon let go of the first man to bite the ear of the old man with the brother in Arkansas. Kendra closed her eyes when she saw more blood in the tangle of arms and legs. Closing her eyes didn't keep her from drowning in a soup of red and black. Was this what fainting felt like?

"Kendra, come on!" Devon Brookings barked, and she realized her parents were dragging her toward the door while she pulled against them with all her strength. *That woman* was near the door!

Kendra wasn't thinking—her brain had shut down, body reduced to primal drives—but one glance over her shoulder in search of another way out gave her instincts a jolt. The doors to the ER burst open, emitting a frenzied stampede of doctors and nurses. Their faces told a story Kendra didn't want to hear.

Her limbs were jelly. Her parents had to keep her upright.

"This way!" Dad said. "Hurry!"

They had just reached the doors, squeezing past the wriggling mound of confusion, when her father yelled out an epithet she had never heard from his lips or even realized he could fathom. His leg had been caught as he tried to scramble past. When he shook himself free, he was limping. "She *bit* me!" he said, outraged at the idea.

"Dev?" Mom said, distraught. Kendra barely heard her over the noise.

"I'm fine, I'm fine!" Dad said, urging them on, because they didn't know yet how far from fine they all were; fine was a distant planet away. "It's just my ankle."

Ankle-biters. The term floated nonsensically into Kendra's mind, a memento from a bygone world, as her parents helped her escape into the day's last light.

THREE

Seattle, Washington

Exit 165 off the I-5 was Seneca Street, and a left turn at Pike headed them toward the biggest open-air market Terry Whittaker had ever seen, a warren of little stores, restaurants, venders, and bakeries abutting Puget Sound. He loved the smells and sights, and was reminded that one of his favorite bakeries was just a few dozen feet away. There, hidden among the cakes and crullers, were the largest, fluffiest buttermilk bars he had ever tasted. His mouth watered at the very thought, and he knew that one way or another, he was bringing a bag of the soft, sugar-frosted delicacies back to Skokomish with him.

That would please the other members of the Round Meadows Five, the kids who, like Terry, had had a choice of either Washington's juvenile justice system or a summer herding brats at summer camp. Lockup was a bitch, so it was weenie roasts and sack races for the duration.

Their boss, Vern Stoffer, parked in a little merchant's lot next to a restaurant advertising fresh lobster tamales, and the big black kid called Piranha was the first out. Guy moved fast. Hard to believe he was brainy enough to be a hacker and the short con master of Plaza Park. He was such a jock that it was easy to underestimate him.

It was 3:13 in the afternoon. Only twelve minutes remained before this very normal day became something quite unnormal indeed. Vern was a bulbous sunburned guy who resembled a chubby version of his hero, Bill O'Reilly. Vern walked them up a narrow stairway to an office above one of the larger fish markets. The door said Sal Overton, Manager. Vern opened the door without knocking, admitting them into a small, cluttered office. On the walls were calendars depicting brave sailors risking the Alaska glacier fields to bring back fish sticks, or something.

"Vern," the tubby guy in the swivel chair said. Terry could believe they were cousins, from the same logging family before, as Vern put it, "the Obama recession" had sent logging into the crapper. "You need to call Mom."

"Phones out at the camp aren't right. Been busy."

"Too busy to call your aunt? You know she's going in for her biopsy, and she's scared spitless. You was always her favorite, you know. Step up, Vernie."

Vern shook his head. "I'll be there, Sally."

"Sally" opened his top desk drawer, and pulled out a manifest. "Anyway, like I said, we've got a great deal for the camp. We can give you a price on the salmon because the Jesuits over at Seattle University decided to play footsie with Parker's market instead of mine. Damn mackerel snappers."

Sally looked at Terry cannily. "You ain't Catholic, are ya?" Terry shook his head. And noticed that he didn't bother asking Piranha. "Good. Not that I got nothin' against Catholics, y'understand. Just they tend to stick to their own. Stick to-gether like a buncha used Kleenex. Anyway," he said, grin-ning at what he seemed to consider great good humor, "we got twenty crates, Alaskan crab and salmon, can let you have 'em for fifty a pop."

Vern tilted his head and shook a Camel out of its wrinkled pack. He didn't smoke in front of Molly, his wife and the camp nurse. Not that she didn't know he smoked. It was just a little game they played. "Forty."

"Forty-five."

"Deal. Net sixty?"

"Works for me. See you brought some strong backs to help out." *Now* he looked at Piranha, who was busy cleaning his fin-gernails with a toothpick, studying the results as if they were far more important than anything Sally might have on his mind.

"Anyway . . . let's get to it." He leveraged himself up from the desk and headed with them back down the stairs. The market was bustling, and would be for another three hours until the shops closed for the day, and only the restaurants would stay open. Terry was wondering when he'd have time to grab that doughnut. Those doughnuts, actually. If he didn't bring back a half dozen, he'd catch holy hell from the Twins.

In glass display cases, rows of dead fish gaped into the great beyond, glassy eyes staring at the customers. There was an odd sense of surprise in that expression. As if to say: *A net? It was a net? How did* that *happen?*

The room beyond the display cases was an ice cave, a kind of dry cold that felt exactly like walking into a refrigerator, which it was. "The red stack," Sally said, pointing out a flat loaded to the ceiling with red boxes.

"I'm going back up. Get us some coffee for the drive back," Vern said. Then the cousins went back upstairs and left them in the cold. Piranha took the first dolly, and pushed it out through the double doors and down the sidewalk.

Terry took the second, a stack of six boxes packed with ice and fish, and levered back on the handle. Had to weigh two hundred pounds, but he managed to find the balance point, and was strong enough to steer.

He and Piranha stacked the fish into the van, came back, made another run while Vern loafed about in Sally's office and smoked Camels.

On their fourth run, Terry guessed that they were almost done. He was just thinking about those buttermilk bars again, savoring the first spongy bite, when he heard the first scream.

It was high, wavering. Disbelieving. A woman's voice. Pain.

Terry and Piranha looked at each other. Piranha acted like he didn't give a damn about anything, but Terry knew different. He'd watched the way the big guy had picked up the little girl who broke her toe in the Friday-night talent show a month back. Carried her as gently as a glass doll. He acted hard, but Terry suspected it was just that—an act.

A woman was running along Pike Street, one hand clasped to the side of her neck, or perhaps at the juncture of neck and shoulder, as if trying to hold something in place. She was a thin woman, a "whisper," as Terry's dad used to say, wearing a T-shirt that said HODAD'S OPEN 24 HOURS!

That shirt, gold letters against black, was stained red. And red leaked between the fingers pressed to her neck. Piranha had taken a few steps in her direction when there was another scream, and then another, and people were running in all directions.

"Holy—" Terry didn't get the rest of the thought out, because something was coming down Pike Street, and it was, as Terry's father had often said, bigger than a butterfly and hotter than hell.

The guy was the size of a pro fullback but dressed like a cop.

Terry had never actually *seen* a pro fullback, except on TV, but his chest and back swelled out of his torn blue uniform. The face above the muscular chest was distorted with rage, or pain, or . . . something.

His eyes were crimson. And by that, Terry didn't mean like his old man after a night down at the Lancelot. No, it was as if those eyes were *bleeding*. The big cop was grabbing people as they ran, pulling them close—

And then taking a bite. Just one bite. Arm, face—people were stunned, fleeing in all directions. Terry saw Vern rumble down the stairs carrying a big silver thermos—curious, not alarmed, just wondering what all the fuss was about—and turn the corner, coming face-to-face with the big man with the bloody eyes.

Vern's back was to him, but he imagined that his black eyes must have gone wide.

"Mr. Stoffer!" Piranha screamed, running now, and damn, he was fast, flying, even though he really didn't care much for Stoffer, and not at all for his redneck cousin. But it didn't matter. Before the big kid was even halfway there, the cop had his hands on Stoffer's arm, and yanked him around. Now he could see Stoffer's face, and the expression was such pure shock, such *what-the-hell* that it was almost comical. The cop stared at him, red eyes to black eyes, and then those bloody teeth snapped forward, tearing at the upper arm.

Stoffer screeched and tried to yank his arm away, and his cousin Sally jumped with astonishing agility, hitting the big guy from the side. The cop staggered, but didn't go down. Then Piranha was there, and he saw the grappling and tussling and the blood and seemed uninterested in joining the mob. Instead, he picked up a mop someone had been using to wipe up a spreading stain of melting ice, and smashed it across the big man's neck.

17

Then Terry was there, and managed to get ahold of one of the muscular arms. *Damn* he was strong! Sucker had three guys on him, but the cop was still almost upright, as if he was on crack or meth. For a moment his leg buckled, and it seemed as if he was going down, then he turned his face to Terry, and at this range he could clearly see the thread of little red veins . . . more like little vines, really . . . all over the whites of his eyes.

Then the man convulsed, throwing them off, and got up. He seemed to be distracted, disoriented, as if uncertain where . . . or even who . . . he was.

The cop staggered out into the middle of Pike Street just as a car speeding the other way, slewing to avoid one of the fleeing pedestrians, slammed into him, sending him cartwheeling into that Great Doughnut Shop in the sky.

"Jesus. Jesus . . ." Vern moaned, holding his arm, and looking up at them through the shock. And then, just as if the third time was the charm, he added another fervent "Jesus."

Cousin Sally was blubbering, his hands covered with blood. "What the hell—get him out of here!" People were still running in all directions. There was another disturbance about fifty feet away, more people screaming, and Terry didn't need another invitation. They got Vern to the van, buckled in, and took off as sirens began to howl from the other direction.

Terry drove fast. Without the tie-downs, the flats of frozen fish in the back of the van bounced and swayed in response to the road. Vern sat in the back, holding his arm, as Piranha did a pretty decent job of sponging out the semicircle of nasty bite dimples. It was bleeding, but not rapidly. No arteries, then. "Damn it! Damn it," Vern murmured, laying his head back against the seat. "I want to get back, clean this up, hit the sack. Then first thing,

Molly's a nurse. She can take care of me." He closed his eyes. "I'm sleepy. Tired." He closed his eyes.

Piranha nudged him with his elbow. "You stay awake until Molly says it's all right for you to sleep. Deal?"

"Tomorrow. We got to get the fish back," Vern moaned. "Damn."

Piranha and Terry exchanged a dubious glance. "I don't know, but maybe you've got a little concussion or something," Piranha said. "Have some coffee," and offered him a drink from the thermos.

"I'm scared," Vern said quietly. "Something's wrong. I feel it."

Vern drank coffee the whole way back, and Piranha kept him talking. They were listening to the radio, and the usual rants against socialist liberals were being interrupted by news broadcasts suggesting that while Pike Street had been terrible, there were at least ten other incidents across the city and south to SeaTac, involving at least twenty bug-nuts biters. It was suggested that anyone bitten should seek medical attention.

Well, Terry supposed first thing in the morning would be good enough. And Vern said to see a doctor within the next couple of days, maybe get a tetanus shot. And after all, Molly was a nurse. All in all, heading back to Meadows sounded like a fine idea to Terry.

He cursed to himself.

Dammit! He'd forgotten the doughnuts.

FOUR

I **have** to write this down because Mr. Kaplan says writers should capture the moments in our lives, good and bad, and this is a day in history like 9/11, but worse, because it happened right in front of me.

I'm writing this in my room. The door downstairs is locked but there is shooting outside. I smell smoke from houses only a few streets away. My hand is shaking so much I can barely write this, but I'm afraid NOT to write this because somebody has to. People are going crazy. At first we thought it was just in L.A., and then just in Portland, but on the news they're saying it's happening all over the country and nobody knows why.

I had to stop and take a nap. They're saying not to let bit people go to sleep, but I wasn't bit. Hope it's all right if I just curl up and let the world go away for a while. When I'm awake, I only cry or stare at the ceiling. No appetite, and Mom thinks if I keep writing I might not be so scared and depressed like the people on the radio talking *about Portland General. Or maybe I should say Portland in general. The country in general.*

I'll write about what happened at the hospital one day, but my hand starts shaking every time I think about it, so I'll start with how we got the hell away from there.

Mom had to drive because Dad hurt his ankle. The bite's just a scratch, a nothing nick through his sock, but he said his foot felt like it was getting numb and he was sleepy, just like they're saying on the radio. "You need a hospital, Dev," Mom said. We just gave her a look, and almost laughed. Almost. We could only go home.

On the road, people were driving like they were drunk, and the radio was babbling about how crankheads were biting people. Maybe twenty cases across Portland, and hundreds of cases across the country. I heard the word "terrorist" fifty times in thirty minutes. Somebody else said something about the flu shot. (Thank you, God, for saving me from that shot. I'm not a psychic, but I knew I shouldn't get it.) The radio was all dueling doctors, this expert talking over that expert, and nobody sure of anything. Some guy with a southern accent said that it wasn't the flu shot, blaming that yahanna mushroom diet. Bottles of the stuff had been found in the houses of lots of the biters. Yahanna was that mushroom that kills your appetite. Chubbies love it. Cheaper than tummy staples, and safe as baby aspirin. Yeah, right.

Mom's all over the theories, already appointing herself an expert: "What if it's both? What if this is only happening to people who take both?"

The I-5 was belly-to-butt all the way back up to Longview. I saw two people wrestling around on the side of the road. At least . . . I think they were just fighting. I hope.

We got home and locked the door. And the windows. Mom dressed Daddy's ankle and talked about taking him to the clinic, but after what happened in Portland, I think they're afraid to leave the house. I didn't get bitten, but I'm tired just like Dad. All I want to do is sleep. Writing this down has helped. Some. Not enough. But some.

I smell smoke outside. Someone is screaming and the air is filled with sirens. Please, God. Help me. Someone help us. I'm so scared.

Daddy says it's time to go to the basement. He says no matter what Mom thinks, he has to go to sleep.

FIVE

It was dark by the time Terry Whittaker glimpsed the rectangular blue sign marked ROUND MEADOWS. He'd nearly driven off the dirt road a dozen times. He hadn't thought about how handy streetlamps were until he realized there weren't any, not a single one, in the woods. He had cramps in his ankle and fingers from his steady pressure on the accelerator and his death grip on the steering wheel.

Jolly Molly Stoffer met them at the turnaround, her plump face bright with alarm. "Are you all right, babykins?" she said to her husband, Vern, pulling open the back door.

". . . just . . . really tired." His face sagged like a melting Mr. Potato Head.

Really tired. Total understatement. For the last hour Piranha had fought to keep Vern's eyes open. He might have even slapped Vern once.

"Wish you coulda seen a doctor. You were right near the best hospitals!" Molly scolded him, but Terry wasn't sure Vern heard her, the way his head rocked.

"No way we wanted to stay in Seattle," Piranha said. His real name was Charlie Cawthone, and his skill at coin matching and three-card monte had brought him to the attention of the Seattle juvenile justice system. Hacking his stepdad's office computer had been the frosting on the cookie. Like the rest of the Round Meadows Five, he'd been sentenced to a summer of chopping nettles and herding brats. That was bad enough, but this afternoon's chaos at Pike Place Market was just the pickle on the turd sandwich Terry currently called his life.

Molly sighed, tugging at Vern's eyelids to try to see his eyes. "Yeah, there was a ruckus down at the hospital in Portland, so maybe it's for the best. Let's get you under the light," she said. "Take a look at that head. You hit it?"

Vern yawned, a cavern. "No. Just that goddamn bite. Itches like hell."

Molly half-gasped, more shocked by his language than his condition. "Well, let's take care of you and get you to sleep. God had nothing to do with that bite."

That's for sure, Terry thought, remembering the crazed cop who had attacked Vern at the marketplace during their run to pick up fish from Vern's cousin. At least the guy had been dressed like a cop when he started chomping everyone around him. Damn.

Vern moved so unsteadily that Piranha and Terry each took an arm to lead him out of the van, but his eyes were only on Molly. "I'm sleepy, but . . ." Vern swallowed. "Not just that.

I closed my eyes, and got scared. Really, really scared, Molly. Like . . ." He ran out of words for it.

"You poor old bear," she said.

"Need help getting him inside?" Terry said. He hoped she'd say no. Terry wanted to be far away from Vern and his troubles. He wanted to start telling the story, embellishing with enough jokes to siphon some of the acid out of his veins. *McGruff the crime dog says Seattle's found a new way to take a bite out of crime!*

"No, you boys have done enough," Molly said. "Thanks, but it's all right. If I need anything, I'll let you know."

She put an arm around Vern's wide waist and led him up the half-dozen wooden steps to the weathered wood-frame main house, which they called the Palace. Their dog, Hipshot, a friendly and territorial black retriever mix, approached Vern with a feverishly wagging tail. At first. But instead of doing his happy dance and pawing Vern's thigh, Hippy whined and backed away, his tail curled between his legs.

Weird. So weird, in fact, that Terry and Piranha exchanged a look. That dog worshipped Vern. Would drink his piss out of a Dixie cup. What did Hipshot know that the rest of them didn't?

If only they'd had a clue.

The staff lounge was drab wood-plank walls except for its picture windows; the walls were decorated with huge mounted fish someone had caught, or bought, over the years. The Red Hot Chili Peppers were piping from the old CD player; not Terry's favorite group, but he'd take any music over the news. The room smelled like mildewed carpet and simmering soup. Home sweet home.

Terry never thought he'd get sick of pine trees, fresh air, and sunshine, but sometimes prison only *looked* like paradise. Round

Meadows—or as Terry liked to call it, Alcatraz North—was a tiny chunk of the six-hundred-thousand-acre Olympic wilderness area, flat land between two jagged hemlock-and-red-cedar-covered ridges near Mount Washington. It was federal land, leased to the state and rented to church and youth groups for summer camp. Nursemaiding brats at summer camp was the last way Terry wanted to spend the summer before senior year in high school. And if he hadn't used the nail gun on stepdad Marty, he wouldn't be in this jam—that and a couple of other incidents where he had given people who desperately needed a black eye or busted lip their heart's secret desire. It wasn't his fault: his fist was merely the instrument of their deliverance.

Terry had almost chosen juvie over summer camp duty, but his sister had begged him not to punish himself for what Marty had done to her. Lisa had been through enough. Between his sister's pleas and the promise of fresh air, he'd signed up. In the old days, guys went to war to avoid jail. Terry figured this wasn't much better.

The Indian Twins, Dean Kitsap and Darius Phillips, were back from whatever gentler errands they'd been assigned, sitting with their feet up on the ends of the sagging couch, as they always did. They weren't really twins, or brothers at all; actually, they were distant cousins. And Dean didn't even have to be in Round Meadows—he just hung around to amuse himself. Both Darius and Dean were Suquamish Indians, but Darius's mother had left Bainbridge Island as a teenager and married a Red Lobster crew chief over in Seattle.

One day, car-thieving Darius had gone to the trading post in Sequim to buy supplies and ran into his doppelgänger. The way they looked, everyone assumed they were brothers, so they let campers and parents believe it. Dean had hung around so much, and had such a wide cross-section of useful skills, that Vern had hired him for the summer. Their olive skin and long black hair reinforced the image they liked to project: Plains warriors trapped in the wrong century. They both loved cherry-red motorcycles: Dean's was a Honda Interceptor, Darius's a Kawasaki Ninja 250R, and the *brrrr* of the engines could be heard around the camp at the oddest places and hours. Brothers from other mothers.

Sonia Petansu was also lounging, doing a Sudoku puzzle at the wobbly pinewood table. She was the only female in their group, tallish with a sinewy body, straight black hair with a streak of white, and a fondness for shoplifting. She'd taken her cooking rotation last night, and despite her abundance of attitude, actually served a mean marinara. Tonight, Darius was making some kind of stew.

Hipshot's nails clicked on the faded linoleum as he trailed Terry into the kitchen. Terry realized he was hungry, but when he lifted the pot's lid, he clamped it down again fast. Ugh.

Piranha sank into his usual silence, grabbing a soda out of the fridge, so Terry was alone with the story and didn't feel like making jokes. "We need help putting the fish away," Terry said instead.

The freezer was an industrial-size Master-Bilt, deep enough to hide Darius's Ninja. That had been fun. After ten minutes of stacking and packing in the freezer while Hipshot shadowed them, Terry finally said, "Hope Vern's gonna be okay."

"What happened to Vern?" Sonia said, only halfway interested. That was her shtick, really. Chronic disinterest. She actually had a black sweatshirt with BLASÉ emblazoned in white letters.

So he told them. All work ceased. Even Sonia seemed impressed.

"You've gotta be *kidding* me," they kept saying. "You have *got* to be *kidding* me!"

29

"You saw a cop get nailed by a driver on Pike Street?" Darius said. He sounded far more impressed than horrified. "A real cop?"

"Yeah, after the dude chomped Vern's arm," Terry said, because Darius seemed to have missed the point. "It's all over the news. Not just in Seattle. Portland too. Something's up."

After the fish were stacked and their gloves were put away, they all trudged to the counselors' bunkhouse. Technically, Sonia had a nearby cabin to herself, but she hung out with them as late as she could get away with it. Somehow Terry didn't think Vern would be swinging by with his flashlight tonight to make sure, as he put it, nobody got any "foolish ideas."

Darius was Evel Knievel on the asphalt, but a bust in the kitchen. He seemed to think that monosodium glutamate could magically transform him into Wolfgang Puck. Piranha took a tentative sip from the wooden spoon and then scowled. "Aw, *hell,* no."

"Like you could do better," Darius said.

"I do better on a regular basis," Piranha said. "I do better asleep."

"You know it," Sonia said, and gave Piranha that sly, heavy-lidded look that made it obvious that they'd engineered a few hours of privacy. Terry wondered what Sonia would think of the calls to girls back home in SeaTac that Piranha had made on the ferry.

Terry didn't bother tasting the stew. Instead, he warmed up enough leftover pasta for everyone and broke out the playing cards. They listened to music while Piranha dealt, and they bet pennies on cards that seemed cold for everyone. Nobody got a hand worth a damn, just hammers and deuces until just about yawning time, when Darius dealt Sonia a royal flush, and she won the entire pot, about enough to buy a gallon of gas.

Sonia brayed laughter and slapped her palm on the table. Sometimes Sonia seemed kind of flat-faced and skinny, but in victory she was oddly attractive. "Thanks for the change, boys. It's been a slice," she said, and sashayed across the room while all of them watched. Except Piranha.

Terry saw her glance back at Piranha. That look always came sooner or later, but Piranha's eyes remained on the table, ignoring her message. That boy was beyond cool—he was cold. Too skinny or not, if Sonia had given Terry the are-you-coming-or-not look, Terry would have beaten her to the door.

Terry flicked on the ancient TV, bracing himself. Vern was too cheap to spring for satellite, so the best he could get was the local news on a fuzzy UHF station. Footage from the Pike Place Market, of course. The newscaster said two residents had died that afternoon, which was a surprise to Terry. He'd missed the details about who had died besides the rabid cop he'd seen hit by a car, hearing only *"officials blaming the melee on an unknown form of methamphetamine Officer Norgren and others might have ingested."*

Officer Norgren. So, the dead cop had a name. A chart came up on the screen: Two dead, forty-six wounded in Seattle. Three dead, sixty-five wounded in Portland. *"And reports continue to pour in from other major cities: in Los Angeles—"*

Piranha snapped off the TV. Terry hadn't seen the big guy sidle up beside him.

"Hey, man," Terry said, and turned the ancient set back on, anger flaring. "My sister's down there!" But by the time the channel was clear again, the newscaster had moved on to a list of instructions for anyone who had been bitten.

Piranha shrugged. "Got sick of it. L.A.'s a helluva big place, right?"

Terry turned up the volume, which gave the newscaster's

voice a sudden urgency: "*. . . extreme drowsiness. If you were bitten during the attack, you should report to a hospital immediately for treatment. Bites from human beings carry more germs than dog bites, so seek out a public health facility or police station immediately.*"

Police station. Yeah, right.

Darius Phillips tossed Hipshot a chunk of meat from the stewpot, and the dog wolfed it up. "Hear that, boy? People are dirtier than dogs. Dogs have better taste in food too."

Dean Kitsap sucked his teeth. "Vern shouldn't wait 'til morning. I wouldn't."

"That's 'cuz you're a mama's boy," Darius said.

"Least I got one," Dean said.

"One?" Darius smirked. "Your mom's big enough for two."

Terry would have split someone's lip for half the things those guys said to each other, but their words bounced off like Ping-Pong balls.

"Vern's a grown-ass man," Piranha said, grabbing the cards, since Vern was the one they were really thinking about. Piranha gave Terry's shoulder a pat, a silent apology for turning off the TV. "Blackjack. I'm dealing straight. Who's in?"

They were all in. When Piranha said "dealing straight" he could be trusted not to engage in bottom-dealing, palming, or peeking. Nobody wanted to say how nervous they were, and playing cards was easier than doing nothing. Terry hoped whatever was happening in the cities would be over in the morning, but he didn't think so.

Terry's first card was the king of hearts, followed by an ace. Blackjack.

"Look at this lucky suckhole," Darius said.

"The white devil wins again," Dean said.

"Got that right," Piranha said, throwing down his cards.

Hipshot sniffed at Darius's hand, hoping for a snack.

"What's Hippy doing here?" Piranha said. He said it mildly, but with that calm clarity Terry had come to expect from a guy who didn't waste words.

"Where should he be?" Terry said.

"Vern's," Piranha said. "He hangs out here, begs for food, then he bunks with Vern for the night. So I ask again: What's he doing here?"

Piranha's eyes rested on Terry; the question was for him alone. Only the two of them had seen Vern get bitten and, later, how Hipshot shied away from him. When no one answered, Piranha gathered up the cards.

Hipshot paced around the table before he sat. Then he stood up and whined, pacing some more. His big brown eyes seemed to be asking Terry a question.

If Terry had been a dog whisperer or some such crap, he would have said Hipshot looked scared.

Terry woke up when he thought he heard a sound. A woman's scream seemed to have followed him from the Pike Place Market. He looked at his watch. It was 3:33 in the morning. *Just a dream, man,* he decided, until he heard the scream again. Terry's heart slammed his chest.

Damn! Terry pushed himself up on one elbow, listening into the wind.

The bunkhouse was two rows of three bunk beds on either side of the room. Since there were only four of them, they had bunks to themselves. Even the Twins didn't share an upper and lower bunk. The room was thick with the slow breathing of sleep.

If Vern was sick and Molly was scared, she would come running down and wake them up. Maybe they should have taken Vern to the doctor. Terry hated the idea of navigating the forest roads in the dark again, but he would if he had to.

But the sound, whatever it had been, was gone.

Could have been a loon, or even a wolf or coyote. Wouldn't be the first time he'd been fooled by creatures who sounded human.

Terry fell into a deep and dreamless sleep.

SIX

Somoone was in the room.

Chuck "Piranha" Cawthone knew it the minute he came awake, without opening his cyes. The weight of the air was different. The temperature. *Something.*

Hipshot was whining near Piranha's bunk. The mutt almost never stayed in the bunkhouse with them, but tonight he hadn't wanted to haul his furry butt back to the Palace. And now he was whining. In the darkness behind his closed eyes, Piranha saw dancing red rosettes, bloodred, capering madly. For a minute he thought his contacts were only itching, since he'd kept both in tonight instead of taking out either the right or left one to rest his eyes. He didn't own a pair of glasses, although he was so blind that he couldn't see the E on the eye chart. But he hated feeling helpless overnight, and tonight he'd known he would want them both.

He'd felt helpless too damned often, a punching bag for the first and second "uncles" his mother installed in her bedroom after

Daddy fled his brief tenure as sperm donor. He never wanted to feel that again. Piranha didn't want to open his eyes. If he opened his eyes, whatever was wrong in the room would solidify. Right now, it was like that Schrödinger's cat paradox Mr. Fairbanks talked about in physics class. Right now, there was a bad thing in the room, but it both *was* and *was not,* just like the cat in the box was both dead and not dead. Opening the box collapsed it into one state or another. Opening his eyes would make it real. It couldn't hurt him if he didn't open his eyes.

Hipshot's whimpering sounded like it was directly underneath Piranha's bunk, and the dog's fear made sleep slide from Piranha like a sheet of oil. With full consciousness came acuity of senses. Hearing. Was anything moving in the room? No. *Wait.* A ragged whisper. Yes. And . . . a smell. A hint of rotten oranges or lemons, as if someone had spritzed a whiff of Glade into the garbage can. Piranha opened his eyes slowly and saw the shape standing there. The moonlight left Piranha more in shadow.

Vern stood there. Vern, with some kind of black stain on his face, as if he'd been licking a jam jar. In this strange dream, and Piranha *definitely* hoped this was a dream, Vern was Yogi Bear. *Hey, Boo-Boo!* Vern grinned and stepped forward, just one step, as if testing the floorboards, and the quality of the moonlight changed enough to show Piranha that that wasn't jam smearing Vern's face. What was there was too runny to be jam, and another scent blended with the citrus. Piranha's stomach cinched and twisted simultaneously, wringing his guts into knots. Hipshot suddenly barked and growled like a dog much bigger and meaner than he was. An order to get moving.

When Piranha rolled off the bunk, Vern came straight at him, all wobbly two hundred thirty plus pounds of him, but without the waddle. His usual uncoordinated lurch was purposeful and quick as Vern lunged at Piranha's bottom bunk. Piranha slid in the opposite direction with a huff of air. Piranha's *thump* as his feet hit the floor was like lightning striking the bunkhouse, electricity surging from one person to the next.

Maybe they'd all been waiting. Maybe they'd all known.

The Twins jumped up from their side of the room and saw old Vern rooting around in the lower bunk like a pig after slop. Then Vern snatched at Terry, but Terry was like a cat, could fall out of a bed sound asleep without harm, so half awake was no problem. The cabin was a yelling, screaming cacophony while Vern snarled and grabbed at them. He got a grip on Dean's bare leg and snapped at it, his face diving down toward exposed skin.

"Don't let him bite you!" Piranha screamed. Dean did a dance, shaking Vern off as the big man's belly flopped, and his eyes . . .

His eyes, caught for a moment in the moonlight, were swollen with blood and rage. Piranha hadn't been sure with the fish market cop. He'd never met that guy before, and maybe he looked like that from the time he pinned on his badge in the morning, but now the same eyes on Vern looked right evil.

In darkness, confusion reigned. They scrambled away from Vern, flinging their mattresses and chairs in his path to try to slow him down. Piranha grabbed his blanket and threw it toward their erstwhile boss, hoping it would cover his eyes long enough for them to subdue him and stay clear of his snapping teeth. The blanket was a direct hit, draping Vern's head completely and sending him into a mindless, frustrated spin. All of them cried out, summoning strength and luck, and piled on Vern to wrestle him to the ground.

Piranha kicked at the squirming figure, wishing he wasn't barefoot and his kick would stop Vern's wriggling. Darius leaped and landed on Vern with a pile-driving elbow that would have ended a steel-cage match. Vern finally fell still. The way

Darius moaned and grabbed his elbow, he might have hurt himself nearly as much as he'd hurt his boss.

They all gasped for breath, leaning on one another. Piranha had never wanted to hug other guys as much as he wanted to cling to these, but they all caught one another's eyes and backed off, spooked by the impulse to be close. What had happened with Vern was weird enough already.

Hipshot whined, shivering in the corner. *Big help you were,* Piranha thought.

But Hipshot had been a help, he realized. Hipshot had been trying to warn them about Vern since they drove up in the van.

"Did we kill him?" Darius said, breathless. "Did I . . ."

The shape under the blanket groaned, thrashing feebly.

"He's not dead," Piranha said, although his fists were ready to help Vern make the transition. "He's acting like the cop. No matter what, we do *not* want to get bitten."

"We'll shut him in the meat locker," Terry said. "Lock him in."

"He'll freeze in there!" Dcan said. "We can't do that."

"Says who?" Darius growled.

"He won't freeze in ten minutes," Terry said. "We just need time to think."

Piranha heard himself try to laugh. "Think? I think I pissed my briefs."

"Wondered what that smell was," Terry said, but his voice sounded hollow.

There was an aroma, but it was more than panicked sweat. Vern had a smell now. Like rotten oranges.

Carefully, Piranha picked up one corner of the blanket, and Terry another, and Vern's new smell floated out, impossible to miss.

Hipshot backed into a corner, whining as he watched them.

Vern lay there as if he'd curled up to sleep on the floor, eyes closed. His face was a mess, but in the dark Piranha tried to tell himself it was only chocolate syrup.

Piranha looked up, his eyes wild. "Damn! Sonia . . ."

As if her name was a conjuring, Sonia suddenly appeared in the doorway, wrapped in a terry-cloth bathrobe. In the moonlight, her skin looked chalky. Piranha took her shoulder and steered her back outside. He might never have been happier to see anyone, but there was no time for a reunion. "Stay back," he said. "We gotta handle this."

"What the . . . ?"

"Just *stay back*," Piranha said, more sharply than he'd meant to.

"Vern went crazy." Terry's voice was hushed. "Tried to bite us."

Sonia's eyes squinted with confusion as she brushed loose hair from her face. "What? You mean like on TV?"

Sonia was usually cool, but panic was rising in her face, her lips trembling. Piranha couldn't tolerate hysterical women. His mother had been hysterical when she should have been packing her bags, and he didn't want his anger at a dead woman to freak Sonia more than absolutely necessary. He forced gentleness into his voice as he curled strands of hair around her ear with his index finger. "Relax, baby," he said. "Stay back and let us handle this, a'ight?"

Sonia nodded as if his voice had suddenly hypnotized her. She stepped away.

While Sonia watched from a healthy distance, sucking on one of the cigarettes she kept stashed in her robe pocket, Piranha and the boys dragged Vern out to the meat locker, rolled him in with the salmon, and closed the door. Vern's head was still covered with the blanket, but Piranha held his breath until he heard the gears go *ca-chink*. The freezer was locked tight.

Sonia finally joined them, and they stood in a semicircle around the metallic freezer door, as if they expected it to come flying open from the inside. Their reflections stared back at them, muddy and indistinct.

"You guys were making a hell of a racket," Sonia said. "So I've got a stupid question . . ." Her voice was hard, as if a blade were buried inside.

"What?" Piranha said.

"Why didn't Jolly Molly poke her nose in?" Sonia said.

They all looked back up at the Palace. The windows were dark.

Piranha had forgotten about Molly. Maybe he'd wanted to. *Whose blood did you think it was, dummy?* They were all thinking the same thing, but wouldn't say so.

Darius checked his flashlight, turning it on and off. "Think I'll wander up there," he said, and sighed. "Maybe she's got some of those chocolate chunk cookies."

Piranha felt like he should go too, but he wasn't in a hurry to volunteer. His heart knocked against a wall of ice.

"I'm going too," Sonia said. "Love those cookies."

"Hold up," Piranha said. "Lemme get my pants on first."

"I could use some milk," Terry said.

They left Dean at the icehouse with a baseball bat, although Piranha thought it would have been smarter to bring both Dean and the bat. Silence hung like fog as they trudged the path to the main house. Sonia walked beside Piranha, her hand occasionally brushing his, but it didn't have the usual electric spark, and she barely noticed he was there.

He *wasn't* there. None of them were. The night was composed of silence, the dark house up ahead, and a waiting horror they couldn't pretend away.

SEVEN

The door stood an inch ajar, enough for Terry to see a sliver of the foyer table covered in cheerful lace. Terry had reached the door first after the others fell behind, so he knocked, staring down at the welcome mat in the beam of Darius's light. *Got Love?* it said in a flowery script, beneath two hands pressed in prayer. Terry didn't know much about praying, but he gazed at the hands and realized how much he hoped there was a God, because just about now a little God might come in handy.

He waited for a sound, any sound, but there was nothing. He knocked again.

Piranha sighed, impatient. "It's open. Why are you knocking?"

"It's the middle of the night. We can't just barge in. What if she's not dressed?"

"Screw that. What if she's not breathing?" Darius muttered.

When Terry pushed the door open, the house exhaled a hot breath of stale air. The living room smelled like cedar, old furniture, and doggy musk. So much for cookies. Terry's eye caught on the antique gold-framed wedding photo, Molly skinnier than she'd been in decades, Vern brilliant in his navy whites. Time had swollen them both, but the young man and woman in the photo still lived in their faces.

Terry took two careful steps inside, as if the floor were a thin sheet of glass. The living room was crowded with plush guest chairs, doilies, and shadows. "Mrs. Stoffer?" he called toward the darkened home. "It's Terry. We're checking on you!"

Utter silence, except for an antique clock ticking somewhere.

"Yeah," Darius whispered. "And we wanted to tell you we just beat hell out of your husband and stuck him in the freezer. Okay, 'bye."

"Stop being an ass," Sonia said. "If that's your 'thing' under pressure, don't."

"Free country . . . *Mom.*" Darius shrugged.

"Shut. The hell. Up." Piranha's growl ended the bickering.

The small square kitchen, open at two ends, stood between the living room and the bedrooms, so Terry checked the kitchen first as the others trailed him, instinctively sticking close. Terry flipped on the light, reassured by the spotless counters and sink. A plate covered in foil sat on the stove—maybe cookies after all—but nobody touched it.

Terry's heart shook his knees.

"Molly?" Sonia called toward the foyer. "Are you okay?"

The hall bathroom beyond the kitchen looked fine too. With each light that went on in the house, the more plausible it seemed that Molly was just a deep sleeper, and the blood on Vern's face had come from somewhere else.

Did they know it was blood for sure?

But the farthermost room, the bedroom, told the true story.

The bedroom was painted red. And the paint was still wet.

42

Terry had never seen a dead body before, not even at a funeral, never mind a body as ill treated as Molly Stoffer's. The hallway light was enough to see too much, and they backed out of the bedroom much faster than they had entered.

Sonia clung to the kitchen sink to puke while Terry picked up the kitchen phone and dialed 911, his hand shaking. His efforts were rewarded by a grating busy signal. He was about to dial again when he got a sharp tug from Piranha, and he realized the others were already halfway out the front door.

"Our cabin!" Darius said.

The phone in the counselors' quarters didn't bring much better luck. This time Terry got a recorded message, a woman's voice that said, "No one is available to take your call, but please leave a message." At 911? Worse, the phone cut him off before he could finish describing where they were or what had happened. Hipshot still cowered in the corner, as if he knew better than any of them the trouble they were in. Doggy instinct.

Sonia pulled a tattered phone book from beneath the counter, and they finally found the number for the sheriff's department. Busy again. Dean drifted in from Vern duty, his bat over his shoulder, gape-jawed while Darius whispered in his ear.

"This is bull . . . This can't be happening," someone was saying over and over in a quivering voice, annoying the hell out of Terry—until he realized it was him.

Darius gestured from the doorway. "Guys? You need to see this," he said.

Darius had turned the TV back on—the same TV Terry now wished they had *kept* on and stayed planted in front of like a campfire all night instead of going to bed.

The channel, thankfully, looked much clearer now. So did the overall situation.

Terry barely remembered 9/11, except for a stomach-twisting

feeling that the roof had fallen in on his world. He had never seen so many adults crying before. The news left no room for denial. There was so much footage from so many regions of the country—labeled *Atlanta, Detroit, Washington, D.C.*—that street mayhem played continuously in a video box in a corner of the screen while the president of the United States spoke to an unseen audience. The chief executive leaned against his podium, as if he hadn't slept in days.

"All of us are waking to a nation that is very different from the one we knew when we went to sleep last night," the president said, his red eyes holding the camera, barely blinking. "Nationwide, U.S. citizens are being attacked, and sometimes killed, by friends, family members, and strangers exhibiting symptoms very similar to animal rabies. But make no mistake: this is *not* an outbreak of rabies. This may be the most severe health crisis our nation has faced, and beyond any doubt the most sudden and confusing in nature. Law enforcement and health officials are so flooded with reports that they are unable to provide figures on the number of infected or the number of dead . . ."

"Oh, God," Sonia whispered. She sat on the floor in a heap, as if her legs had folded beneath her. "Holy . . ."

The muscles at the corners of the president's jaw bulged, as if he was cracking walnuts with his teeth. Terry imagined FDR might have looked that way on D-day. "If you are in a secure place . . . stay there. If you have loved ones who have been bitten . . . keep them awake as long as you can, but isolate yourself from them. Do not attempt to transport or otherwise assist anyone exhibiting symptoms of this infection."

"So what the hell are we supposed to do with Vern?" Dean asked the TV screen.

Someone off-camera handed the president a sheet of paper, which he read silently before raising his eyes again, a pall of fear hollowing his cheeks. His face reminded Terry of President George W's deer-in-the-headlights panic in a documentary he'd seen once, when W was reading to schoolchildren and looked as if he'd dropped a load in his shorts.

"I'm gonna try the sheriff again," Terry said. His mouth was so dry that it hurt to move his tongue.

As Terry turned, the president went on as if to answer him directly: "Law enforcement cannot keep pace with the emergency calls nationwide, especially in densely populated areas. Please use restraint if you must take measures to protect yourself . . . but some of you *will* be forced to take such measures, often against people you know. Wear thick clothing. Avoid exposing your skin. More drastic measures may be required. If you do not protect yourself from bites at all costs, the infection will continue to spread at this harrowing pace . . ."

Terry stopped short, suddenly realizing how Sonia's legs might have felt before she flopped to the floor. His body felt liquefied.

What was the point of picking up a phone? The president of the United States had just told him he would be wasting his time. Their Vern terror, which had seemed so deep and personal, had been reduced to a statistical blip. No one gave a damn about Vern Stoffer, his very dead wife, or a handful of juvie offenders.

Terry shuffled back to the huddle at the TV.

"Sheriff's busy tonight, huh?" Piranha said.

They watched TV until they could no longer ignore the muffled, frantic pounding from the freezer.

EIGHT

By sunrise, they had a plan. They would wait until Vern exhausted himself banging against the icehouse door. Then, once he was unconscious, they would open the freezer, mob Vern up with blankets, and hog-tie him. Once he was tied, they could feed him, give him water, and keep him alive until they heard instructions on a treatment or cure for Vern's bad case of what Darius called "Cujo."

By noon, they all realized the major flaw in their plan: Vern never stopped banging, except for a minute at a time, maybe two. Just when they started lining up with the blankets, whispering last-second instructions before their ambush, the ramming sound started again, as if Vern was running into the door headfirst.

By four, it dawned on Terry, probably all of them, that they couldn't save Vern. Even if he'd finally knocked himself out like they'd hoped, there wasn't a whisper of good news on the TV or radio. Far from it. Piranha speculated that scientists had to be gathered somewhere working overtime on a cure the way the eggheads came up with the A-bomb to drop on Japan, but the white-smock types Terry saw on TV looked like they needed a doctor themselves. Or a shrink.

Nobody was talking about fixing anybody—only surviving. The president never said it himself, but the message was obvious from spray-painted signs on people's houses and survivalist types relishing all those years of jerking off to the Second Amendment: *The infected will be shot.*

"Dude, I just shot my mom!" one wild-eyed man from Denver said to a news camera, waving his .45 in the air. His face streamed tears. *"DO YOU GET IT NOW? I shot my mom!"*

They searched the camp for weapons. For the first time, they were glad that Vern was an NRA member, with two hunting rifles and a shotgun for home defense. They found two hundred rounds for the rifles and thirty shotgun shells. Plenty of edged implements: saws, axes, knives, and a half-dozen machetes for clearing brush. Archery bows hung in rows on the wall, but the arrows were just for kids to shoot haystacks, nothing they could use. Still, they kept it all nearby, just in case.

Sonia tried the phone for hours, until she finally got through to her grandmother's house east of Centralia, where she'd figured her mother would take her sister. Sonia let out such a shriek when she finally got through that Terry woke from his nap on the sofa, convinced Vern must have clawed his way free.

Sonia was wet-eyed during the whole call. Under ordinary circumstances this might have seemed strange, because like most of them, Sonia couldn't stand her family. Her mother begged her to stay where she was. "There's nowhere safer than that camp for you," her mother said, her voice so crisp on the line that they could all hear her. "The roads are a war zone. Let it blow over! We'll be fine. Suzy wants to talk to you—"

Then the line went dead, and Sonia cried some more when she couldn't call back.

While Sonia wailed, Piranha called Terry aside. They walked on the path in the peaceful woods under a waning sun that, although it was only four o'clock, already seemed too close to the horizon. The evergreens above them were unchanged, a souvenir of yesterday.

"The Twins are thinking about hitting the road," Piranha told him quietly, checking to make sure Darius and Dean couldn't hear. The Twins were on Vern duty, and in an hour it would be Terry's turn. "I heard them talking. They might want to take off right after freezer patrol. They figger they'll be okay on their bikes. Dean wants to check on his mom and sisters. And let's be real: none of us wants to be here at night waiting around for whatever, you know?"

Terry didn't recognize what he felt at first, except that it was a blade in his gut. Not fear, which he was used to, or even anger . . . something else. Grief?

Vern's van was parked where they had left it last night. Molly's old Rabbit was parked in the driveway, but the battery had been dead since one of the brats had climbed in and left the lights on. The only other vehicle they had was Blue Beauty, the rickety navy blue school bus Vern had bought secondhand and painted with the eagle-and-rabbit Camp Round Meadows logo. Terry could drive it decently, and Piranha could grind the gears into submission, but none of the others could handle its nearly worn-out manual transmission.

"Where's the keys?" Piranha said.

"What?"

"You were the last one driving the van," Piranha said. "I

49

don't remember you giving the keys back to anybody, so where are they?"

Suddenly, Terry noticed how much taller and broader Piranha was, with a wrestler's build. Remembered Piranha's stories about kids he'd whaled on after school when they didn't know when to back off. And there was something about a "look" that Piranha had when he wanted someone to keep his mouth zipped. Although he was larger than Terry, Piranha had never tried to push him around. Perhaps that had something to do with the fact that Terry was in for assault, while Piranha was up for a long list of nonviolent mischief.

Hipshot trotted beside Piranha and sat. "Where are the keys?" the big guy asked again.

Terry patted his jeans. He was wearing his faded blues, not the black jeans he'd worn when they'd driven to Seattle. "Hell, I don't know. Maybe still in my pocket."

"Let's go look," Piranha said.

Finding the van's keys was a good idea. Terry suddenly burned with curiosity himself, and a spark of panic. He'd been assuming all day that they had *decided* to stay at the camp, but it was different if the keys were lost. Who knew where old Vern might have tucked that treasure? As they walked toward the counselors' quarters, Terry tried to ignore the increasingly sour taste in the back of his mouth.

"And when we find the keys?" Terry said. "Then what?"

He almost said *if* instead of *when*. He hoped he hadn't handed the keys to Molly after all, that they wouldn't need to search Vern's house or Molly's clothes. They'd already been back to his bedroom once in search of a gun, and Terry never wanted to see that room, or the inside of the Palace, ever again.

"Then we have options," Piranha said, and left it at that.

Terry closed his eyes in a silent prayer as he reached under his bed for the plastic Hefty bag where he stashed his dirty clothes. His throat nearly squeezed shut when his jeans didn't jingle and his two front pockets were empty . . . but he felt a lump in the back pocket.

Two keys on Vern's VFW key ring. The van had less than half a tank of gas left, if he remembered right, but it was better than nothing.

Piranha held out his hand for the keys, but Terry hesitated.

"The van belongs to everybody," Terry said.

"Damn right," Piranha said. "And everybody includes me."

"Why do you want the keys?" Terry tried to keep anger or challenge out of his voice, because things were working fine while he and Piranha were buddies, but nothing would work if they weren't.

"I'll drive down to the road, go down a couple miles, check things out. See if I can catch a cell signal." He lowered his eyes. "Call my stepdad."

"If the landlines aren't working, what makes you think your cell will? I bet all the towers are jammed."

"Gotta try," Piranha said. "Maybe I can get my e-mail, send a note, update my Facebook status. Right?" Piranha's palm lay outstretched. He seemed to be waiting patiently, but Terry saw his fingers tremble. If Piranha had to ask for the keys again, he wouldn't ask nicely. He might not ask at all.

"Then what?" Terry said.

Piranha licked his lips. His dark eyes fixed on Terry's, a clear signal that he was tolerating his last question. He spoke slowly. "Then I come back here, tell you guys what I saw, what my stepdad said, and we all decide what to do. Maybe before the Twins go. Give them something to think about. While we're still all together."

Terry considered Piranha's plan, but only for a second or two. He dropped the keys in Piranha's palm, and Piranha closed his fingers around them like a gold nugget.

They both breathed out slowly, glad they still trusted each other. Hoping trust would last.

"If I'm not back in two hours," Piranha said, "you know shit's gone south."

Terry nodded soberly. In two hours, the late summer sun would just be starting to dim, readying for a new night. A problem for Piranha was a problem for all of them.

"Get gas if you can," Terry said.

They'd been crouching by the bunk, but they both straightened and stood upright. Terry's father had once told him he would know the day he became a man in his bones, and it had nothing to do with turning eighteen. Terry suddenly missed his dad fiercely.

"Anybody you want me to call for you?" Piranha said.

Terry's mother had moved to Tucson to live with the meth cooker she'd met in rehab, but Terry had dropped his cell phone in the pool a week ago, so he didn't have her number. Terry would have gnawed off his left arm to call Lisa in L.A., but Aunt Jessie had unlisted her number, dammit. Thinking about Lisa and the footage he'd seen from Southern California made Terry's stomach turn, so he forced himself not to worry. Lisa was fine. End of story. Like Piranha had said, L.A. was a big place. In L.A., people locked their doors.

"Nah," Terry said. "I'm good."

"If Vern gets quiet, cross your *t*'s before you go in," Piranha said. "And don't let Sonia do anything stupid."

"I'll watch out for Sonia," Terry promised. "You've got two hours, man."

They bumped fists to seal the contract. Terry thought, and

not for the first time, how much better life would have been if he'd had a brother.

Well, hell. Looked like he had one now.

During the longest two hours of Terry's life, Vern never got quiet. The constant pounding on the freezer door gave him such a headache that he screamed *"Shut the hell up!"* and thumped the door with his bat. The impact hurt his elbows, and barely made a dent. Inside, Vern emitted an outraged cry and only pounded harder.

"Not very smart," Sonia said from the doorway, her arms folded. She drifted in and out of the icehouse, keeping Terry company while she cooked what she could from the pantry and fridge for dinner. Anything in the freezer would have to wait. "That door's our friend. Save the psycho for a rainy day."

A rainy day. One of Jolly Molly's favorite lines. In the Northwest, it seemed most days were rainy days.

Terry didn't have to ask Sonia if Piranha was back. He wasn't; Terry could tell by the way she was gnawing her lip, playing with the unlit clove cigarette in her fingers. She'd made Terry promise not to let her smoke another cigarette until dark, since she was afraid she would run out. She had only a pack left besides the half-pack of Djarums in her pocket.

A motorcycle's revving outside made Terry's heart race. He looked at his watch: it was eight-thirty. Piranha was five minutes late with the van. The Twins had promised to wait for him, but they were getting anxious.

After listening to the news all day, he hadn't thought the situation could get any worse, but it just had. "Dammit," he said.

Sonia shrugged. "Dean's worried. His family doesn't have a landline, and the cell towers are down."

Terry went to the doorway, handing the bat to Sonia. "Stay here with Vern. We shouldn't split up."

Sonia took the bat with a sour chuckle. "Like they'd listen. The Twins only care about the Twins."

Darius and Dean had already gassed their bikes, and both wore backpacks and leather jackets. Darius was riding in a lazy circle around Dean, stirring a thin dust cloud while Dean strapped his leather travel bag shut. Dean took off his sunglasses and straightened when he saw Terry, but Darius never acknowledged him, revving his engine.

"What the hell, man?" Terry said. "What about Vern?"

"You've seen the news." Dean shrugged. "What about him?"

"What are you taking with you? What's in the bags?" Terry said.

"Don't sweat me, Terry," Dean said. "We left plenty."

"You should probably take more."

Darius laughed from his bike. "Quit trying to stall us."

"It's almost dark," Dean said.

"Exactly!" Terry said. "Why not wait 'til tomorrow?"

"If your mom wasn't a crackhead, would you wait?" Dean said. "We already waited too long. My sisters need me."

At the word "crackhead," the world went red. Terry's legs tensed, ready to leap at one of the Twins, either of them, both of them . . . until he heard the approach of a new engine, heavier than the bike. Darius's bike fell still as he rested on one foot, and they stared toward the dirt driveway, waiting for a vehicle to appear from beyond the stand of Douglas firs. Sonia hung back, watching from the icehouse doorway, as they all shared a thought: *What if it isn't Piranha?*

But it was.

Piranha was alone in the van. Instead of driving up to them, Vern's van bumped over the scattered firewood at the edge of the driveway as Piranha swung around to park at an odd angle fifteen yards back, blocking the driveway as if to pen them in.

As they trotted up to him for a report, Piranha opened the van's side door, where he had stored a red gas can and a box of supplies, including what looked like a scarred laptop. Terry and the Twins grinned when they saw the stash, but Piranha's face had forgotten smiling. Even Sonia's full-body hug didn't bring a glimmer to his dull eyes.

"What'd you see?" Terry said.

"Nothing good," Piranha said, with a long gaze at the Twins.

"Did your phone work?" Sonia said.

Piranha shook his head, his face clouding more. "Dinner ready? I'm starving."

Like the rest of them, the Twins were dying for details of Piranha's recon mission. All talk of driving off ceased as Sonia heaped pasta on paper plates, and they waited for Piranha to start talking. The news played at its usual low volume while they heard the distant thunder at the freezer door.

Wham . . . wham . . . wham . . .

No one was guarding Vern anymore, and Terry realized it didn't matter. Guard duty had only been their attempt to have order and control, something they could do. Vern wasn't going anywhere.

One of the items in Piranha's box was a warm bottle of merlot, so they shared the wine at dinner, although there was nothing festive about it. Terry figured he would need six bottles like it before he felt anything remotely resembling a decent buzz. Instead, the wine made him so tired that he wanted to crawl under the table and pass out.

"More of a weed guy myself," Darius said, pouring his glass. "But whatever."

Other than that, the box was full of geek stuff. The laptop, wires, adapters. Terry remembered the Professor from *Gilligan's Island* building radios out of coconuts.

"Does this thing work?" Sonia said, opening the laptop.

Piranha grunted, shoveling a forkful of pasta into his mouth. "Battery's dead, but it fires up when you plug her in. Too bad we don't have Wi-Fi."

Terry pulled out a spool of phone line. "Dial-up?"

"Better than nothing," Piranha said. "Maybe we can get e-mail."

"And Facebook!" Sonia said, looking rapturous, as if maybe her friends were busy poking each other and posting YouTube videos.

"Don't suppose you found anything useful, like more ammunition?" Dean said.

Piranha shook his head, the brooding silence falling over him again.

"Where'd you get this stuff?" Terry said finally. "A yard sale?" He could have asked sooner, but he'd been afraid of the answer.

"Know that little lake house about five miles out?" Piranha said. "By the road?"

The table went silent. Nothing but Vern's *bang bang bang.*

"Friendly people, huh?" Terry said finally.

"Wouldn't know," Piranha said. "Nobody home. Windows dark all summer, same Toyota sitting in the driveway. Couldn't hot-wire it, but I got the gas." He took a sip of wine from a paper cup and sloshed it around in his mouth before swallowing.

"Don't send a boy to do a man's job." Darius had boasted that he could hot-wire any car more than ten years old. That skill might come in handy later. "But good job with the gas."

"You *broke into* their house?" Sonia said, midway between

impressed and shocked. Terry was tempted to remind her that she proudly referred to herself as the Vanisher, since she'd been such a great shoplifter.

Piranha concentrated on his wine.

"How's the road look?" Dean said.

"Toxic," Piranha said. "I only drove out a couple miles to try to get a signal, save gas. Saw smoke. I got close enough to see it was a car, but I turned the hell around when I heard the gunshots. Wasn't Cujos doing the shooting and burning. I've got news for you: the Cujos aren't the biggest problem." He turned to Dean and Darius. "You guys wanna go riding on your little toy bikes? Do what you want. But the rifle and shotguns stay here."

When no one said anything, Piranha stood up, grabbing the wine bottle by the neck. It was three-quarters empty, maybe a glass left. "You guys good?"

They all eyed the wine, but mumbled that they'd had enough. With his free hand, Piranha grabbed his box of geek supplies and headed for the desk by the TV, where there was a phone line. Considering how often the phone signal was busy, Terry didn't think he'd have much luck finding the Internet. But if anyone could, it was Piranha.

"He's right," Terry said, his voice steady, loud enough for the big guy to hear. "We've all got people we're scared about and want to help. I've got a baby sister I'm thinking about all the time, but we need to hole up here and wait it out. Right now, we're the only people we can trust. We've got enough food for weeks, if it comes to that." Months, actually, if the food in the freezer was intact, but he didn't say it. He couldn't imagine living for months in this bad dream. "When it's time to go, we'll know it. But we'll do better together than any of us would do alone."

Terry wasn't used to making speeches, but he sounded convincing, at least to his own ear. He saw a spark in Sonia's eyes. Maybe a tear.

But the Twins left the table without a word, heading to the door. When the bikes' engines fired up outside, Sonia gave Terry a *Well? DO something* look. Terry glanced toward Piranha, but he didn't look up from his stolen laptop.

Screw it. They'd tried. Why was it his problem, anyway? Terry stirred his pasta, mad at the Twins for being stupid, mad at Sonia for her expectations, mad that he felt somehow responsible.

Then the engines cut off. The Twins came back inside to sit at the table. Darius sopped up the last of his spaghetti sauce with a slice of bread from their dwindling loaf.

"Getting dark," Dean said.

Later, Terry would see that they'd parked their bikes in the shed.

Piranha worked nearly all night trying to rig an Internet connection, plagued by busy signals. The few times he got past the *beep-beep-beep,* the connection refused to take. He drew on patience he didn't know he had, numbing himself. He'd hoped the wine would drown the hot snakes writhing deep in his belly or the stitch he'd had in his side since they locked Vern in the freezer. But nothing had changed when the bottle was empty. He was still stuck in hell.

Piranha's AME church life had died with his mother, even on Christmas, since he'd told his stepfather he didn't believe in God. Piranha's excuse wasn't exactly true: he believed in God, but he was so pissed off that he'd stopped speaking to him, and he didn't see a reason to visit his house. God had lost his visiting privileges.

Piranha's anger was still there, but it felt petty now that he was stuck in hell without a plan. Piranha had been telling himself *be cool* all day, but his cool was wearing thin, especially since he'd seen the smoke and the gunshots. News footage was one thing, but he was out here alone, the only brother for miles. He didn't have a gun, not that he knew how to use one. He had a girl to protect.

And he couldn't get a damn Internet connection.

Piranha didn't like his stepfather, Ed Simmons, with his Brooks Brothers suits and pomposity. He'd *hated* Ed Simmons when he filed charges after the hacking incident—who would send his own stepkid into the jaws of the criminal justice machine? Yeah, Piranha had hacked into the computer system at Simmons's office and embarrassed him in front of his boss, maybe lost him a little corporate cred, but you call the cops? Piranha's rage flared anew. But since his older sister was married and living in Dallas, Ed Simmons was the only person who could give Piranha an answer about what to do now. *He'll never replace your father, Charlie,* his mother had told him when they got married, *but Edward Simmons will always be there for you.*

So Piranha sat at the old laptop he'd found in the office nook of the abandoned house and tried again. And again. He hoped the servers were only flooded, not blown.

At one a.m., he nearly gasped when the Gmail logo finally appeared on his screen. His mind tried to blank out on his screen name and password, but he typed with shaky fingers, careful with each letter, and his mailbox presented itself like a hallucination. A note from "Edward Simmons," the latest in a string of at least twelve from his stepfather, sat at the top of his list. The time stamp said it had been sent only thirty minutes earlier. Ed was alive! And he was the only person on the planet trying to get in touch with him, just like his mother had promised. Maybe the SOB wasn't all bad.

Piranha held his breath as he tried to open the most recent note. "Please, God, I know I haven't done right by you, but let me have this one thing . . ."

Working, the screen promised.

Except that it *wasn't* working, or didn't seem to be. For ten eternal minutes, Piranha was sure the overloaded server would boot him off and ask him to try again, severing the last bare thread of his life.

Suddenly, the note was there:

> Charles,
>
> I remember you telling me you don't have access to a computer, but I'm praying you'll see this note. I can't reach you on your cell. I'm trying to send the same note again and again.
>
> You must have heard by now, but there's a terrible national crisis, an epidemic of a kind of hysteria and insanity involving an infection from people who may try to bite you. A single bite spreads the terrible disease. I have not been bitten, and neither has Lori. I heard from her, and she and Tyrone are staying with friends in Dallas. So far, she is safe, and I pray you are too.
>
> May God protect you in the woods, far from anyone who might try to hurt you. PLEASE DO NOT TRY TO COME TO ME, because it's too dangerous and I don't know how long we'll stay here. So far, we've avoided contact with any infected, but the radio keeps warning us that we'll be asked to evacuate and go to a camp near the military bases if the situation doesn't improve.
>
> Charles, we are living through a war. Neighbor against

neighbor. I've seen things on TV, and with my own eyes, I cannot describe in words. I keep thinking of that quote by Nietzsche: "He who fights with monsters should be careful lest he become a monster." These are the days of monsters.

ONCE IT IS SAFE, I WILL COME TO YOU.

Until then, be careful. Watch everyone for abnormal behavior and red eyes, friends and strangers alike. DO NOT LET ANYONE BITE YOU. Wait for me to come for you. Above all, SURVIVE. I've lain awake many nights wondering if I did the right thing by sending you there, what your mother would have thought. I believed I saw you headed down a path of no return, and I made the hard choice, praying you would be a better man for it. I lost two brothers in prison because no one stepped in when they were young, and I didn't think I could live through that heartache again. This is the first time I'm glad you're tucked far away in wilderness. You have no idea how much weight has been lifted from my soul.

I love you, Charles. I look forward to the day when we can start again.

Dad

The note stayed frozen on Piranha's screen long after the connection died.

Dad. Not Ed. *Dad.*

Piranha was glad the others had left him, because sobs fought from his throat like flames.

Vern banged on the freezer door all night and most of the next day.

On the third morning, they woke to silence. When they finally opened the freezer, blankets readied like fishing nets, Vern was curled on the floor, silent and cold in a slick of frozen blood. His banging had pulped his face so badly that even Jolly Molly wouldn't have recognized it.

Even working together, it took two hours to dig holes deep enough to bury Vern and Molly Stoffer, two people they barely knew. They'd waited a day too long to bury Molly. At least. Her stink was a revelation. Even Hippy stayed far away.

Nobody said anything over the graves. What could they say? They were burying far more than Vern and Molly, and there were no words to describe what they had lost.

NINE

August 15

The morning after burying Vern and Molly, they woke to discover that Dean and his cherry-red Honda were gone. Darius raged about it, calling his cousin every profane name he could think of, but Terry got it: Dean hadn't wanted to risk anyone else's life. He must have rolled his bike far enough down the path to prevent them from hearing the engine.

They finally found a note on the kitchen counter, meant for Darius more than anyone else: *Have to check on my folks. Stay safe. Still Here.*

No promise to return.

The last part, *Still Here,* probably meant he was still with them in spirit, but it was a slogan they'd seen on the news. People were spray-painting it on their houses and rooftops in case rescuers came to evacuate them, or scrawling it in big letters on signs and T-shirts so no one would mistake them for a freak and shoot them while they walked on the side of the road. Caravans of pickup trucks with armed riders were patrolling some areas, spraying anything that moved with bullets. *Still Here* meant you hadn't been infected. Hadn't turned into one of Them. Wouldn't give up. Sometimes it wasn't true, of course. No declarations or signs could change what was happening out there, the bodies piling up on the roadsides. Terry had seen footage of burned-out houses, their front yards littered with dead.

They took quiet bets on whether Darius would follow his cousin, but he didn't. Darius slipped into the woods to be alone, but he left his bike in the shed. He was back by lunchtime, his eyelids swollen and his knuckles raw from hitting something. Trees? The soil? They accepted his return without comment, and ate canned ravioli.

"Dean is smart, and he's fast on that bike," Terry told him. "He'll be fine."

He was both right and wrong.

Two days later, Dean came back without a scratch or a bite. But whatever he'd seen had changed his eyes, not red like Vern's, just stripped blank. He wasn't fine.

It didn't take a psychic to know that none of them would be fine again.

Camp Round Meadows, once a prison, had transformed into the closest thing to a safe haven they could imagine. The only path to the camp was two miles of a bumpy dirt road most people would want nothing to do with. Since Vern had been preparing for fifty new campers, there was an obscene amount of food for the five of them, as long as they didn't waste it.

They avoided the freezer the first days after Vern died, but exploring paid off: the shelves were crowded with ground beef, hot dogs, bags of chicken legs, corn on the cob, Fudgesicles, and, of course, fish. Vern must not have left the door or thought about food while he was locked inside, because none of the packages had been marked or moved from their neat stacks. Terry and the others debated how sanitary the space was, whether or not the infection might have spread in the freezer, but in the end, they chose the food. Chef Boyardee's mustache was starting to wilt.

They lost their milk fast, within a week. The bread was gone before that, except for the hot dog and burger buns, which apparently were so crammed with preservatives that they could sit forever without molding. They froze buns to defrost later.

The television went to emergency broadcasting, and that devolved to frightened people talking against blank backgrounds, and from there to test patterns with intermittent static-filled footage. As television faded, Terry felt an eerie sense that they were lifting off in a balloon far from the world, floating aimlessly into the sky.

The radio was a little better, thank God. FM died fast, but AM radio kept broadcasting for a month, with signals coming in from Moscow, Idaho, and Vancouver, British Columbia. It was all the same, increasing despair and confusion. After the news stations died, most of what they could pull in was that movie guy, who called himself Reverend Wales, or "Josey" Wales, based in some place called Domino Falls down in Northern California. Preached an end-of-the-world broadcast with a new and impressive enthusiasm.

Hell, it was hard not to see his point.

As fall stretched on, they finally caught an emergency radio broadcast from a man whose voice sounded like sugarcoated panic. He congratulated anyone listening for holding out, and advised them to report to the Seattle National Guard armory.

"Power in numbers!" he preached. "We *can* rebuild, but we need your help!"

It was the first time anyone had offered a solution.

By then, the rains had started up again, night fell sooner, and all of them were long past ready for a change . . . even if they were afraid to go.

Dean suggested a Council meeting the way his ancestors had made important decisions, so they built a rousing campfire and sat in a circle around flames that painted their faces golden orange. The cons, eloquently argued by Sonia and Dean, were obvious: The Outside was a hellhole. What if they got ambushed? Rape and murder were rampant, unchecked by authorities. What if they could never find another secluded place to hide from the chaos?

Piranha and Darius were equally passionate about the pros: They couldn't hide forever. They were bound to get raided eventually, and it was better to leave before they exhausted their food. They could take the old school bus in the shed and bring enough supplies to barter and survive. *And they had to find more guns,* or they were done.

On that last point, no one could argue.

Terry suggested that they put off the final vote until morning, so they could all think it over in the quiet of the dark.

Fate decided for them: by morning, scattered reports on the radio hinted that the fledgling Seattle encampment had been overrun by freaks.

Terry tried to feel disappointment just to feel something, but he didn't feel anything. He'd always suspected the Seattle National Guard armory would be a version of Dorothy's Oz—a whole lot of hype that boiled down to doing it your own damned self. Still, he searched Vern's house until he found the keys to the Blue Beauty, the Blue Bird Vision school bus, in a kitchen drawer and started driving the big monster, warming up the engine to keep the battery alive, navigating past the trees to learn the hang of the steering. He hoped he would never need to drive the Blue Beauty if it mattered, but he figured he'd better turn the engine over every few days, just to keep it honest.

A week later, the power sputtered off. Vern's generator wasn't powerful enough to run the fridge, much less the freezer. The frozen food began to rot. That left the cans: mostly tuna, salty veggies, and SpaghettiOs.

By early December the days were short, the sky misted, and the rain was ice water. Winter was coming, and with it the possibility of being snowed in. The threat of winter finally convinced them to take another vote—to try to reach Portland, Oregon, this time, about six hours' drive south under normal conditions. The newest Oz. In Portland, the emergency broadcast promised, there was a functioning compound protected by National Guardsmen.

They didn't need a campfire Council this time. As soon as they heard about the possibilities in Portland, they knew they had no choice. No one argued against it.

They spent a day fitting the snowplow to the front of the Blue Beauty, stocked it with their remaining food, water, and gas, and planned to pull out at first light. Hipshot didn't sleep with them that night, as if he knew what was up.

At dawn, it took a while to find the pooch. He had hunkered down on the Stoffers' shallow grave behind the house, soaked and shaking. Despite their whistles, clapping, and cooing, Hipshot wouldn't budge.

"Leave him," Darius said. "Just another mouth to feed."

"No way," Sonia said. "At least he's some protection."

"Protection how?" Darius said. "Where was he when Vern jumped us?"

"Under my bed," Piranha said. "Whimpering." Sonia gave Hipshot a sour look, as if she felt betrayed. Piranha and Sonia sometimes went off alone, but he usually didn't sleep in her bunk, even without Vern to keep them apart. They had all been sharing the main bunkhouse.

"But he can sniff out freaks," Terry reminded them. "He smelled it on Vern from the minute we brought him back. Before Vern went all Cujo."

They decided to bring Hipshot whether he wanted to go or not.

But they didn't have to force him. Hippy rose unsteadily to his feet, shook the mud and rain from his shaggy black coat, and climbed slowly into the bus.

The dog's head hung as if he had failed his humans.

The Days of Monsters

Be careful when you fight monsters, lest you become one.

—FRIEDRICH NIETZSCHE

TEN

December 15

Jellyfish. *That's what they look like at first, wispy reddish tendrils floating in blackness. A few at first, but then a nest of them waft down in the dark with a reddish glow, like dawn, growing brighter as they drift like snowfall.*

They are everywhere now, like a spider's web. No, not jellyfish. Red threads.

Some of the threads fall close to her. As she watches, the threads wriggle and unite, weaving themselves to form mass, shape. Something tall stands over her. The shape looks like a glowing man, his features obscured in the reddish light.

She looks closer, trying to see him. He seems familiar.

She knows him . . . doesn't she?

The face that stares back at her isn't human.

Another nightmare.

Kendra didn't remember the dream yet, although she knew

she would soon. For now, she felt its remnants: a racing heart, damp palms and armpits. Her dreams seemed to have a faint smell, like rotting citrus, hanging just beyond the tip of her nose.

"Bad dreams again?" a sleep-roughened voice said.

When Kendra opened her eyes, Grandpa Joe was standing over her bed. Mom used to say that guardian angels watched over you while you slept, and Grandpa Joe looked like he and his shotgun might have been guarding her all night. Kendra didn't believe in guardian angels anymore, but she was glad she could believe in Grandpa Joe. His beard covered his dark chin like a coat of fresh snow.

"Could be worse," Kendra thought. Her dreams weren't as bad as her life, anyway.

Most mornings, Kendra opened her eyes to only strangeness: dark, heavy curtains; wooden planks for walls; a brownish-gray stuffed owl mounted near the window with glassy black eyes that seemed to twitch in the reflected sunset. A rough pine bed.

And that *smell* everywhere, like the smell in Mom and Dad's closet. Cedar, Grandpa Joe told her. Grandpa Joe's big hard hands had made the whole cabin of it, one board and beam at a time. For the last two months, this had been her room, but it still wasn't, really. Her Death Note DVDs and makeup case full of fruit-flavored lip gloss weren't here. Her Justin Timberlake and Kobe Bryant posters weren't on the walls. This was her bed, but it wasn't her room.

"Up and at 'em, Little Soldier," Grandpa Joe said, using the nickname Mom had never liked. Grandpa was dressed in his hickory shirt and blue jeans, the same clothes he wore every day. He leaned on his rifle like a cane, so his left knee must be hurting him like it always did in the mornings. He'd hurt it long ago, in 1967, in a place called Dak To.

"I'm going trading down to Mike's," he said. "You can come if you want, or I can leave you with the Dog-Girl. Up to you. Either way, it's time to get out of bed, sleepyhead."

Dog-Girl, the lady who lived in a house on a hill by herself fifteen minutes' walk west, was their closest neighbor. Once upon a time she'd had six pit bulls that paraded up and down her fence. In the last month that number had dropped to three. Grandpa Joe said meat was getting scarce. Hard to keep six dogs fed, even if you needed them. The dogs wagged their tails when Kendra came up to the fence because Dog-Girl had introduced her to them, but Grandpa Joe said those dogs could tear a man's arms off. *Don't you ever stick your hand in there*, Grandpa Joe always said. *Just because a dog grins don't make him friendly. Especially when he's hungry.*

"Can I have a Coke?" Kendra said, surprised to hear her own voice again, so much smaller than Grandpa Joe's. She hadn't planned to say anything today, but she wanted the Coke so bad she could almost taste the fizz. An exotic treasure.

"If Mike's got one, you'll get one. For *damn* sure." Grandpa Joe's grin widened until Kendra could see the hole where his tooth used to be: his straw hole, Grandpa Joe called it. He mussed Kendra's hair with his big palm. "Good girl, Kendra. You keep it up. I knew your tongue was in there somewhere. You start using it, or you'll forget how. Hear me? You start talking again, and I'll whip you up a lumberjack breakfast, like before."

It *would* be good to eat one of Grandpa Joe's famous belly-busters again, piled nearly to the ceiling: a bowl of fluffy eggs, a stack of pancakes, a plate full of bacon and sausage, and buttermilk biscuits made from scratch. Grandpa Joe had learned to cook in the army. But whenever Kendra thought about talking, her stomach filled up like a balloon and she thought she would puke. Some things couldn't be said out loud, and some things *shouldn't.* There was more to talking than most people thought. A whole lot more.

Kendra's eye went to the bandage on Grandpa Joe's left arm, just below his elbow, where the tip peeked out at the edge of his shirtsleeve. Grandpa Joe had said he'd hurt himself chopping wood yesterday. Kendra's heart had turned into a rock when she'd seen a spot of blood on the bandage. She hadn't seen blood in a long time. She couldn't see any blood now, but Kendra still felt worried. Mom said Grandpa Joe didn't heal as fast as other people because of his diabetes . . .

That stung. That thought of her mother . . . and then of her father . . . ripped open the scabs protecting the ugly memories. Dad. The bitten foot growing hot and swollen with infection, Dad running from the house, afraid to be with his wife and daughter because of the radio reports.

Mom, trying to pretend she wasn't worried sick about Dad. Then she'd tried to help Carolyn Stiller, their next-door neighbor, a nice old local playwright . . . and discovered that the old lady scratching at the window was infected too. But too late. Too late. Mom in shock, shoulder bandaged, knowing what was coming. All the people on the radio said that if you were bitten, it was the end. No cure, one hundred percent infection. Mom had gotten a shortwave message to Grandpa, and then tried to hold on until Grandpa could drive down and get her. Mom had locked Kendra in the basement for never-ending hours, sobbing, *"Bolt the door tight. Stay here, Kendra, and don't open the door until you hear Grandpa's 'danger word'—NO MATTER WHAT."*

She made her swear to Jesus, which was a very big deal. Kendra had been afraid to move or breathe. She'd heard other footsteps in the house, the awful sound of crashing and breaking. A single terrible scream. It could have been her mother. Or maybe it was someone else completely. She didn't know.

Followed by silence; for one hour, two, three. Then, the hardest part. The worst part. *Show me your math homework, Kendra.*

The danger word was the special, secret word she and Grandpa Joe had picked. He'd insisted on it. Grandpa Joe had made a special trip in his truck to tell them something bad could happen to them, and he had a list of reasons how and why. Mom didn't like Grandpa Joe's yelling much, but she'd listened. So Kendra and Grandpa Joe had made up a danger word nobody else knew in the world, not even Mom. And she had to wait to hear the danger word, Mom said. No matter what. She'd heard Grandpa's truck. Footsteps, and then Grandpa had said the right thing, and Kendra opened the door. Mom was nowhere in sight, and Kendra had wanted to search for her.

Grandpa had dragged Kendra from the house, kicking. Had she seen her mother one last time, peeking out between the boarded-up front windows, waving to them as Grandpa sped away? Was that a shadow, or a shadowed, lost face? She might never know. Grandpa would never talk about it. Was Mom still . . . alive? Was Dad? Were any of those blood-eyed things *alive,* really? And could she even think about it and not go insane? All she had now was Grandpa, a man she'd barely had time to know. And if anything happened to him . . . The idea made Kendra's chest seize up, stanching her breath.

She couldn't let herself think about being alone, or she might suffocate.

"That six-point we brought down will bring a good haul at Mike's. We'll trade jerky for gas. Don't like to be low on gas," Grandpa said. His foot slid a little on the braided rug as he turned to leave the room, and Kendra thought she heard him hiss with pain. "Maybe we can find that Coke for you. Whaddya say, Little Soldier?"

Kendra couldn't make any words come out of her mouth

this time, but at least she was smiling, and smiling felt good. For once, they had something to smile about. Three days ago, a buck had come to drink from the creek. Through the kitchen window, Kendra had seen something move in the brush— antlers, it turned out—and Grandpa Joe grabbed his rifle when Kendra motioned. Before the shot exploded, Kendra had seen the buck look up, and Kendra thought, *It knows.* The buck's black eyes reminded her of Dad's when he had listened to the news on the radio in the basement, hunched over the desk with a headset. Trapped.

Dad and Mom would be surprised at how good Kendra was with a rifle now. She could center punch an empty SPAM can from twenty yards. She'd played with shooting on Left 4 Dead and Call of Duty, but Grandpa Joe had taught her how to shoot for real, a little every day. Grandpa Joe had a room full of guns and ammunition—the back shed he kept locked—so they never ran low on bullets.

Kendra supposed she would have to shoot a deer one day soon. Or an elk. Or something else. The time would come, Grandpa Joe said, when she would have to squeeze that trigger whether she wanted to or not. *You may have to kill to survive, Kendra,* he said. *You're sixteen, a grown woman, so you need to be sure you can protect yourself.*

Before the Bad Times, Grandpa Joe used to ask Mom and Dad if he could teach Kendra how to hunt during summer vacation, and they'd said no. Dad didn't like Grandpa Joe much, maybe because Grandpa Joe always said what he thought, and he was Mom's father, not his. And Mom didn't go much easier on him, always telling Grandpa Joe *no,* no matter what he asked. *No,* you can't keep her longer than a couple of weeks in the summer. *No,* you can't teach her how to shoot. *No,* you can't take her hunting. Now there was no one to say *no.* No one except

76

Grandpa Joe, unless somehow Mom had survived. And somehow came for her. It was possible. Almost anything could happen, in a world like this had become. Anything . . .

The tears were coming. She had to change her thoughts, or curl up and cry.

Show me your math homework, Kendra.

By the time Kendra dressed, Grandpa was outside loading the truck, a beat-up navy blue Chevy with so many scratches it looked like it had lost a fight with a tractor. Kendra heard a thud as he dropped a large sack of wrapped deer jerky in the truck bed. Grandpa Joe had taught her how to mix up the secret jerky recipe he hadn't even given Mom: soy sauce and Worcestershire sauce, fresh garlic cloves, dried pepper, onion powder, a pinch of wasabi. He'd made sure Kendra was paying attention while strips of deer meat soaked in that tangy mess for two days, and then spent twelve hours in the slow-cook oven. Grandpa Joe had also made her watch as he cut the deer open and its guts flopped to the ground, all gray and glistening. *Watch, girl. Don't turn away. Don't be scared to look at something for what it is.*

Grandpa Joe's deer jerky was almost as good as the lumberjack breakfast, and Kendra's mouth used to water for it. Not anymore. His jerky loaded, Grandpa Joe leaned against the truck, lighting a brown cigarette. Kendra was sure that smoking wasn't a good idea for an old man who spent a half hour hacking up his lungs every morning.

"Ready?"

Kendra nodded. Her hands shook a little every time she got in the truck, so she hid them in her jacket pockets. Some wadded-up toilet paper from the safe room in Longview was still in there, a souvenir from her house. Kendra clung to the wad, squeezing her hand into a fist.

"We do this right, we'll be back in less than an hour," Grandpa Joe said. He spit, as if the cigarette had come apart in his mouth. "Forty-five minutes."

Forty-five minutes. That wasn't bad. Forty-five minutes, then they'd be back.

Kendra stared at the cabin in the rearview mirror until the trees hid it from her sight.

As usual, the road was empty. Grandpa Joe's rutted dirt road spilled onto the highway after a half mile, and they jounced past darkened, abandoned houses. Kendra saw three stray dogs trot out of the open door of a pink two-story house on the corner. They looked well fed. She'd never seen that door open before, and she wondered whose dogs they were. And what they'd been eating.

Suddenly, Kendra wished she'd stayed back at Dog-Girl's. Dog-Girl was from England and Kendra couldn't always understand her, but she liked being behind that high, strong fence. She liked Ringo and Prince Edward and Lady Di, the old lady's pit bulls. She tried not to think about Windsor and Muppet and . . . she'd forgotten the names. The ones that were gone now. Maybe Dog-Girl had given them away.

They passed tree farms, with all the trees growing the same size, identical, and Kendra enjoyed watching their trunks pass in a blur. She was glad to be away from the empty houses.

"Get me a station," Grandpa Joe said. The radio was Kendra's job. The radio hissed and squealed up and down the FM dial, so Kendra tried AM next. Grandpa Joe's truck radio wasn't good for anything. The multiband at the cabin was better. A man's voice came right away, a shout so loud it was like screaming.

"*. . . this isn't one of my damned movies, not some rancid Hol-*

lywood concoction, although they sat back and let it happen, made it happen with their filth and violence, demeaning life and extolling death . . ."

Joseph Wales, broadcasting from someplace down San Francisco way, picked up and rebroadcast by some local wildcat station. She'd liked him better when he was making movies.

"Turn that bull crap off," Grandpa Joe snapped. Kendra hurried to turn the knob, and the voice was gone. "Don't you believe a word of that, you hear me? That's b-u-double-l *bull crap.* Things are bad now, but they'll get better once we get a fix on this thing. Anything can be beat, believe you me. I ain't givin' up, and neither should you. That's givin'-up talk."

The next voices were a man and a woman who sounded so peaceful that Kendra wondered what they were smoking.

". . . mobilization at the Vancouver Barracks. That's from the commander of the Washington National Guard. So you see," the man said, *"there are orchestrated efforts. There has been progress in the effort to reclaim Portland and even more in points north. The Barracks are secure, and running survivors to the islands twice a week. Look at Rainier. Look at Astoria. In California, you have Domino Falls . . . and even Devil's Wake."*

Grandpa grunted in happy surprise, grinning. "Devil's Wake! Your dad's aunt Stella runs the library there, 'less she retired. She nabbed me a Paul Laurence Dunbar original edition, 1903. Bet Devil's Wake made out fine, an island like that."

"As long as you stay away from the large urban centers, there are dozens of pockets where people are safe and life is going on."

"Oh, yes," the woman said. *"Of course there are."*

"There's a learning curve. That's what people don't understand."

"Absolutely." The woman sounded medicated.

"Amen!" Grandpa Joe slapped his steering wheel. "Devil's

Wake! That's somewhere we could go, Kendra. If we stored enough gas . . ."

Kendra didn't like the idea of going anywhere, island or not. Why should they move, when they never heard fingers scrabbling against their windows at night and there was a trading station an easy drive away?

"Everybody keeps harping on Longview"—the man on the radio said "Longview" as if it were a normal, everyday place; Kendra's stomach tightened—*"but that's become another encouraging story. Contrary to rumors, there is a National Guard presence. There've been three airdrops of food and medicine. There's a gated community in the hills housing over four hundred. Remember safety in numbers. Any man, woman, or teenager who's willing to enlist is guaranteed safe lodging. Fences are going up, roads barricaded. We're getting this under control. That's a far cry from what we were hearing even five, six weeks ago."*

"Night and day," the cheerful woman said. Her voice quavered with joy.

Grandpa Joe reached over to rub Kendra's head. "See there?" he said. Kendra nodded, but she wasn't happy to imagine a stranger sleeping in her bed. Maybe it was another family with a teenage girl. Or twins. But probably not. Dog-Girl said the National Guard was long gone and nobody knew where to find them. *Bunch of useless bloody sods,* she'd said, the first time Kendra had heard the little round woman cuss. Actually, she hadn't even known what *sod* meant until she looked it up, then felt a certain degree of admiration. Dog-Lady's accent made cussing sound exotic.

If she was right, dogs might be roaming through her house too, looking for something to eat.

"There's talk that a Bay Area power plant is up again. It's still an unconfirmed rumor, and I'm not trying to wave some magic

wand here, but I'm just making the point, and I've tried to make it before, that life probably felt a lot like this at Hiroshima."

"Yes," the woman said.

Kendra vaguely remembered studying Hiroshima in her history class, back when she was going to school. Would there be schools again too?

"Call it apples and oranges, but put yourself in the place of an earthquake victim in Haiti. Or a Jew at Auschwitz. There had to be some days that felt exactly the way we feel when we hear these stories from Seattle and Portland, and when we've talked to the survivors..."

Just ahead, along the middle of the road, a man was walking south.

ELEVEN

Kendra sat straight up when she saw the man by the side of the road. She wadded up the tissue in her pocket so tightly that her fingernails bit into her skin. The walking man was tall and broad-shouldered, wearing a brick-red backpack. He lurched along unsteadily. From the way he bent forward, as if bracing into a wind, Kendra guessed the backpack was heavy. It was the first time in weeks she'd seen anyone walking on this road. Her neck snapped back as Grandpa Joe sped up his truck.

"Don't you worry," Grandpa Joe said. "We ain't stoppin'."

The man let out a mournful cry as they passed, waving a cardboard sign. He had a long, bushy beard, and as they passed his eyes looked wide and wild. Kendra craned her head to read the sign, which the man held high in the air. STILL HERE, the sign said. "He'll be all right," Grandpa Joe said, but Kendra didn't think so. No one was supposed to go on the roads alone, especially without a car. Maybe the man had a gun, and maybe they would need another man with a gun. Maybe the man had been trying to warn them something bad was waiting ahead. But the way he walked . . .

Kendra kept watching while the man retreated behind them. She had to stop watching when she felt her stomach knot. She'd been holding her breath without knowing it. Her face was cold and sweating, both at once. "Was that one?" Kendra whispered. She hadn't known she was going to say that either, just like when she asked for a Coke. Instead, she'd been thinking about the man's sign. *Still here.*

"Don't know," Grandpa Joe said. "It's hard to tell. That's why you never stop." They listened to the radio, neither of them speaking again for the rest of the ride.

Time was, Joseph Earl Davis III, now forever known simply as Grandpa Joe, never would have driven past anyone on the road without giving them a chance to hop into the truck bed and ride out a few miles closer to wherever they were going. Heck, couple of months back he'd picked up a group of six college-age kids and driven them to Centralia when most folks were running over strangers without even honking their horns.

But Joe hadn't liked the look of that hitcher. Something about his walk. Or maybe times were just different. Christ as his witness, if Kendra hadn't been in the car, Joe might have run that poor wanderer down where he walked. A stitch in time was worth a pound of cure. That was what it had come to in Joe Davis's mind. Drastic measures, just like the president had said in his first Apocalypse Address. The president hadn't said it plainly, but his meaning had been clear as the summer sky.

ƎЯƎH ᒫᒪITƧ, the backward letters of the man's sign said in the mirror, receding into a tiny, indistinct blur. *Yeah, I'm still here*

84

too, Joe thought. And not picking up hitchhikers was one way he intended to *stay* here, thanks a bunch for asking.

Freaks clustered in the cities, but there were plenty of them wandering through the countryside nowadays, actual packs. Thousands. Tens of thousands. Millions. He didn't know. No one really did. Joe had seen his first three months ago, coming into Longview to rescue his granddaughter. His first, his fifth, and his tenth. He'd done what he had to do to save the girl and shut the memories away where only their tiniest tendrils could sneak into his dreams. Then he'd drunk enough to make the dreams blurry. A week later, he'd seen one closer to home, not three miles beyond the gated road—not three miles from the cabin! Its face was bloated blue-gray, and flies buzzed around the open sores clotted with that dark red scabby stuff growing under their skin. The thing could barely walk, but it had smelled him, swiveling in his direction like a weather vane. Joe still dreamed about that one every night. That one had *chosen* him. Joe left the freaks alone unless one came at him—that was safest if you were by yourself.

He'd seen a poor guy shoot one down in a field, and then be slaughtered by a swarm attracted by the sound of the shot. Some of those biters could walk pretty fast. The new ones could still run, and they weren't stupid, by God. But Joe had killed that one, the pivoting one that had chosen him. He'd kill it a dozen times again if he had the chance; it was a favor to both of them. That shambling mess had been somebody's son, somebody's husband, somebody's father. People said freaks weren't really dead—they didn't climb out of graves like movie monsters—but they were as close to walking dead as Joe ever wanted to see. The red fungus was eating them from the inside out, and if they bit you, the freak stuff would start eating you too. You fell asleep, and you woke up different. The movies had that part right, anyway.

85

As for the rest, nobody knew much. Most folks who met freaks up close and personal didn't live long enough to carry tales. Whatever they were, freaks weren't just a city problem anymore. They were everybody's problem.

Can you hold on, Dad? My neighbor's knocking on the window. That's what Cass had said the last time they'd spoken, then he hadn't heard any more from his daughter for ten agonizing minutes. The next time he'd heard her voice, he'd barely recognized it, so calm it could be nothing but a mask over mortal terror. *DADDY? Don't talk, just listen. I'm so sorry. For everything. No time to say it all. They're here. You need to come and get Kendra. Use the danger word. Do you hear me, Daddy? And . . . bring guns. Shoot anyone suspicious. I mean* anyone, *Daddy.*

Daddy, she'd called him. She hadn't called him that since hell was a hatchet, and it was sure as hell a broadax now. That day, he'd woken up with alarm twisting his gut for no particular reason. That was why he'd raised Cassidy on the shortwave two hours earlier than he usually did, and she'd sounded irritated that he'd called before she was up. *My neighbor's knocking on the window.*

Joe had prayed he wouldn't find what he knew would be waiting in Longview. He'd known what might happen to Cass and Kendra as soon as Devon had freaked out. That's what they called the change: "Freaking out." Dammit, he should have dragged her out of that town right then. Then he'd found her letting the neighbors use the shortwave and drink her water like she'd been elected to the Rescue Committee. One time, she couldn't even name one of the women in her house. That was Cass for you. Acting like a naive fool, and he'd told her as much.

Still, even though he'd tried to make himself expect the worst, he couldn't, really. If he ever dwelled on that day, he might lose his mind . . . and then what would happen to Kendra? Any time Joe brought up that day, the kid's eyes whiffed out like a dead pilot light. It had taken Kendra hours to finally open that reinforced door and let him in, even though Joe had used the danger word again and again. And Kendra had spoken hardly a word since.

The Little Soldier was doing all right today. Good. She'd need to get tougher, and fast. The kid had regressed from nearly sixteen to six, just when Joe needed her to be as old as she could get. As Joe drove beyond the old tree farms, the countryside opened up on either side; fields on his left, a range of hills on his right. There'd been a cattle farm out here once, but the cattle were gone. Wasn't much else out here, and there never had been. Except for Mike's. Nowadays, Mike's was the only thing left anyone recognized.

Mike's was a gas station off Exit 46 with Porta Potties out back and a few shelves inside crammed with things people wanted: flour, canned foods, cereal, powdered milk, lanterns, flashlights, batteries, first-aid supplies, and bottled water. And gas, of course. How he kept getting this stuff, Joe had no idea. *If I told you that, you'd tell two friends, and they'd tell two friends, and pretty soon I'd be out of business, bro,* Mike had told him when Joe asked, barking a laugh at him.

Last time he'd driven out here, Joe had asked Mike why he'd stayed behind when so many others were gone. Why not move somewhere less isolated? Even then, almost a full month ago, folks had been clumping up in Longview, barricading the school, the jail, and the three-story hospital. Had to be safer, if you could buy your way in. Mike wasn't quite as old as Joe—sixty-three to Joe's seventy-one—but Joe thought he was foolhardy to keep the place open. Sure, all the stockpiling and bartering had made Mike a rich man, but was gasoline and Rice-A-Roni worth the risk?

I don't run, Joe. Guess I'm hardheaded. That was all he'd said.

Mike had always been one of his few friends around here. Now he was the only one. Joe didn't know whether to hope his friend would still be there or to pray he was gone. *Better for him to be gone,* Joe thought. One day, he and the kid would have to move on too, plain and simple. That day was coming soon, and had probably come and gone twice over.

Joe saw a glint of the aluminum fencing posted around Mike's as he came around the bend, the end of the S in the road. Although it looked more like a prison camp, Mike's was an oasis, a tiny squat store and a row of gas pumps surrounded by a wire fence a man and a half tall. The fence was electrified at night: Joe had seen at least one barbecued body to prove it, pulled off the wire but tacked on a post as warning. Everyone had walked around the corpse as if it wasn't there. With gas getting scarcer, Mike tended to trust the razor wire more, using the generator less these days.

Mike's three boys, who'd never proved to be much good at anything else, had come in handy for keeping order. They'd had two or three gunfights, Mike had said, because strangers with guns thought they could go anywhere they pleased and take anything they wanted. Today, the gate was hanging open. He'd never come to Mike's when there wasn't someone standing at the gate. All three of Mike's boys were usually there with their greasy hair and fleshy tattooed bellies bulging through their too-tight T-shirts. No one today. Something was wrong.

"Damn," Joe said aloud, before he remembered he didn't want to scare the kid. He pinched Kendra's chin between his forefinger and thumb. His granddaughter peered up at him, resigned, the expression she always wore. "Let's just sit here a minute, okay?" Little Soldier nodded. She was a good kid. Joe hoped she wouldn't have to add rape to her litany of life's horrors, but how long could he protect her?

Joe coasted the truck to a stop outside the gate. While it idled, he tried to see what he could. The pumps stood silent and still on their concrete islands, like two men with their fingers in their ears. There was a light on inside, a super-white fluorescent glow through the picture windows painted with the words "gas" and "food" in red. He could make out a few shelves from where he was parked, but he didn't see anyone inside. The air pulsed with the steady *burr* of Mike's generator, still working.

At least it didn't look like anyone had rammed or cut the gate. The chain looked intact, so it had been unlocked. If there'd been trouble here, it had come with an invitation. Nothing would have made those boys open that gate otherwise. Maybe Mike and his kids had believed all that happy-crappy radio chatter, ditched their place, and moved to Longview. The idea made Joe feel so relieved that he forgot the ache in his knee. *And leave the generator on?*

Tire-tread calligraphy in hardened mud. Mike's was a busy place. Damn greedy fool. Beside him, Joe felt the kid fidgeting in her seat, and he didn't blame her. He had half a mind to turn around and start driving back toward home. The jerky would keep. He had enough gas to last him. He'd come back when things looked right again.

But dammit, he'd promised Kendra a Coke. It would help erase a slew of memories if he could bring a grin to the kid's face today. Little Soldier's grins were a miracle. Her little pouchy cheeks were the spitting image of Cass's at her age. *Daddy,* she'd called him on the radio. *Daddy.*

Don't think about that don't think don't—Joe leaned on his horn. He let it blow five seconds before he laid off. After a few seconds, the door to the store opened, and Mike stood there leaning against the doorjamb, a big ruddy white-haired Canuck with linebacker shoulders and a pigskin-size bulge above his belt. He was wearing an apron, like he always did, as if he ran a butcher shop instead of a gas station. Mike peered out at them and waved. "Come on in!" he called out.

Joe leaned out of the window. "Where the boys at?"

"They're fine!" Mike said. Over the years, Joe had tried a dozen times to convince Mike he couldn't hear worth a damn. No sense asking after the boys again until he got closer.

The wind skittered a few leaves along the ground between the truck and the door, and Joe watched their silent dance for a few seconds, considering. "I'm gonna go do this real quick, Kendra," Joe finally said. "Stay in the truck."

The kid didn't say anything, but her eyes went dead, just like they did when he asked what had happened at the house in Longview. Joe cracked open his door. "I'll only be a minute," he said, trying to sound casual.

"D-Don't leave me. Please, Grandpa Joe? Let me c-come."

Well, I'll be damned, Joe thought. This girl was talking up a storm today. Joe sighed, mulling it over. Pros and cons either way, he supposed. He reached under the seat and pulled out his Glock 9mm. He'd never liked automatics until maybe the mid eighties, when somebody figured out how to keep them from jamming so damned often. He had a Mossberg shotgun in a rack behind the seat, but that might seem a little too hostile.

He'd give Kendra the sawed-off Remington 28-gauge. It had some kick, but the Little Soldier was used to it. He could trust Little Soldier not to fire into the ceiling. Or his back. Joe had seen to that. "How many shots?" Joe asked him, handing over the little birder. Kendra held up four fingers, like a toddler. So much for talking.

"If you're coming with me, I damn well better know you can talk if there's a reason to." Joe sounded angrier than he'd intended. "Now . . . how many shots?"

"Four!" That time, she'd nearly shouted it.

"Come on in," Mike called from the doorway. "Got hot dogs!"

That was a first. Joe hadn't seen a hot dog in months, and his mouth watered. Joe started to ask him again what the boys were up to, but Mike turned around and went inside.

"Stick close to me," Joe told Kendra. "You're my other pair of eyes. Anything looks funny, you point and speak up loud and clear. Anybody makes a move in your direction you don't like, *shoot* him right through the nose. Hear?"

Kendra nodded.

"That means *anybody.* I don't care if it's Mike or his boys or Santa Claus or Sweet Baby Jesus. You understand me?"

Kendra nodded again, although she lowered her eyes sadly. "Like Mom said."

"Damn right. Exactly like your mom said," Joe told Kendra, squeezing the kid's shoulder. For an instant, his chest burned so hot with grief that a heart attack might have seemed a mercy. The kid might have watched what happened to Cass. Cass might have turned into one of them before her eyes.

Joe thought of the pivoting, bloated freak he'd killed, the one in the plaid print dress, its red-clotted nostrils flaring as it caught his scent. His stomach clamped like a big sour fist. "Let's go. Remember what I told you," Joe said.

"Yes, sir."

He'd leave the jerky alone, for now. He'd go inside and look around for himself.

Joe's knee flared as his boot sank into soft mud just inside the gate. Crap. He was a useless old man, and he had a Bouncing Betty fifty klicks south of the DMZ to blame for it. In those happy days in Southeast Asia . . . or French Indochina . . . or just "the 'Nam," none of them had known that the *real* war was still forty years off—but coming fast—and he was going to need both knees for the real war, you dig? And he could use a real soldier at his side for this war, not a piss-pantied girl.

"Closer," Joe said, and Kendra pulled up behind him, his shadow. When Joe pushed the glass door open, the salmon-shaped door chimes jangled merrily, like old times. Mike had vanished quick, because he wasn't behind the counter. A small television set on the counter erupted with ancient, canned laughter from people who were either dead or no longer laughing.

"DOH!" Homer Simpson's voice crowed. Mike was playing his DVD.

"Mike? Where'd you go?" Joe's finger massaged his shotgun trigger as he peered behind the counter. Suddenly, there was a guffaw from the rear of the store, matching a new fit of laughter from the TV. He'd know that laugh blindfolded.

Mike was behind a broom, one of those school-custodian brooms with a wide brush, sweeping up and back, and large shards of glass clinked as he swept. Mike was laughing so hard his face and crown had turned pink. Joe saw what he was sweeping: the glass had been broken out of one of the refrigerated cases in back, which were now dark and empty. The others were still intact, plastered with Budweiser and Red Bull stickers, but the last door had broken clean off except for a few jagged pieces still standing upright, like a mountain range, close to the floor.

"Y'all had some trouble?" Joe asked.

"Nope," Mike said, still laughing. He sounded congested, but otherwise all right. Mike kept a cold six months out of the year.

"Who broke your glass?"

"The boys are fine." Suddenly, Mike laughed loudly again. "That Homer!" he said, and shook his head.

Kendra too was staring at the television set, mesmerized. From the look on her face, she could be witnessing the parting of the Red Sea. The kid must miss TV, all right.

"Got any Cokes, Mike?" Joe said.

Mike could hardly swallow back his laughter long enough to answer. He squatted down, sweeping the glass onto an orange dustpan. "We've got hot dogs! They're—" Suddenly, Mike's face changed. He dropped his broom, and it clattered to the floor as he cradled one of his hands close to his chest. *"Ow!"*

"Careful there, old-timer," Joe said. "Cut yourself?"

"Ow, ow, ow, ow, ow!" Sounded like it might be bad, Joe realized. He hoped this fool hadn't messed around and cut himself somewhere he shouldn't have. Mike sank from a squat to a sitting position, still cradling his hand. Joe couldn't see any blood yet, but he hurried toward him.

"Well, don't sit there whining over it."

"Owowowowowow." As Joe began to kneel down, Mike's shoulder heaved upward into Joe's midsection, driving the breath from him in a *woof!* and lifting him to his toes. For a moment Joe was too startled to react, the what-the-hell reaction stronger than reflex that had nearly cost him his life more than once. He was frozen by the sheer surprise of it, the impossibility that he'd been *talking* to Mike one second and—

Joe snatched clumsily at the Glock in his belt and fired at Mike's throat. Missed. The second shot hit Mike in the shoulder, but not before Joe had lost what was left of his balance and crashed backward into the broken refrigerator door. Three things happened at once: his arm snapped against the case doorway as he fell backward, knocking the gun out of his hand before he could feel it fall; a knife of broken glass carved him from below as he fell, slicing into the back of his thigh with such a sudden wave of pain that he screamed; and Mike hiked up Joe's

93

pant leg and took hold of his calf in his teeth, gnawing at him like a dog with a beef rib.

Cursing, Joe kicked away at Mike's head with the only leg that was still responding to his body's commands. Still, Mike hung on. Somehow, even inside the fog of pain from his injury, Joe felt a chunk of his calf tearing, more hot pain. He was bit, that was certain. *He was bit.* Every alarm in his head and heart rang.

Dear sweet God, he was *bit.* He'd walked right up to Mike. They could make sounds—everybody said that—but this one had been *talking,* putting words together, acting like . . . acting like . . .

With a cry of agony, Joe pulled himself forward to leverage more of his weight and kicked at Mike's head again. This time, he felt Mike's teeth withdraw. Another kick, and Joe's hiking boot sank squarely into Mike's face. Mike fell backward into the shelf of flashlights behind him.

"Kendra!" Joe screamed. The shelves blocked his sight of the spot where his granddaughter had been standing. Pain from the torn calf muscle rippled through Joe, clouding thought. The pain shot up to his neck, liquid fire. Did the freaks have venom? Was that it? Mike didn't lurch like the one on the road. He scrambled up again, untroubled by the blood spattering from his broken nose and teeth.

"I have hot dogs," Mike said.

Joe reached back for the Glock, his injured thigh flaming while Mike's face came at him, mouth gaping, crimson teeth glittering. Joe's fingers brushed the automatic, but it skittered away from him, and now Mike would bite, and bite, and then go after the Little Soldier—

Mike's nose and mouth exploded in a mist of pink tissue. The sound registered a moment later, deafening in the confined space, an explosion that sent Mike's useless body toppling to the floor. Then, Joe saw Kendra just behind him, her little sawed-off birding rifle smoking, face pinched, hands shaking.

Holy God, Kendra had done it! The kid had hit her mark. Sucking wind, Joe dug among the old soapboxes for his Glock, and when he had a firm grip on it, he tried to pull himself up. The world whirled. He tumbled back down.

"Grandpa Joe!" Kendra said, and rushed to him. The girl's grip was surprisingly strong, and Joe hugged her for support, straining to peer down at his leg. Maybe he was wrong about the bite. It was possible he was wrong.

"Let me look," Joe said, trying to keep his voice calm. He peeled back his pant leg, grimacing at the blood binding the fabric to flesh. There it was, facing him in a semicircle of oozing slits. A bite. Not a deep one. But damn well deep enough. Freak juice was already shooting all through him. Damn, damn, damn.

Night seemed to come early, because for an instant Joe Davis's fear blotted the room's light. He was *bit*. And where were Mike's three boys? Wouldn't they all come running now, like the swarm over the hill he'd seen in the field?

"We've gotta get out of here, Little Soldier," Joe said, and levered himself up to standing. Pain coiled and writhed inside him. "I mean now. Let's go."

His leg was leaking. The pain was terrible, a throb with every heartbeat. He found himself wishing he'd faint, and his terror at the thought snapped him to more alertness than he'd felt in weeks. He had to get Little Soldier to the truck. He had to keep Little Soldier safe. God only knew what would happen to a girl left on her own. If the freaks didn't get her, the survivors would.

With each step, the back of his left thigh screamed bloody murder. He was leaning so hard on Little Soldier, the kid could hardly manage the door. Joe heard the tinkling above him, and then, impossibly, they were back outside. Joe saw the truck waiting just beyond the gate. His eyes swept the perimeter. No movement. No one. Where were those boys?

"Let's go," Joe panted. He patted his pocket, and the keys were there. "Faster." Joe nearly fell three times, but each time he found the kid's weight beneath him, keeping him on his feet. Joe's heartbeat was in his ears, an ocean's roar. "Jump in. Hurry."

After the driver's door was open, Little Soldier scooted into the car like a monkey. The hard leather made Joe whimper as his thigh slid across the seat, but suddenly, it all felt easy. Slam and lock the door. Get his hand to stop shaking enough to get the key in the ignition. Fire her up. Joe lurched the truck in reverse for thirty yards before he finally turned around. His right leg was numb up to his knee—*from that bite, oh sweet Lord*—but he was still flooring the pedal somehow, keeping the truck on the road instead of ramming it into a ditch.

Joe looked in his rearview mirror. At first he couldn't see for the dust, but there they were: Mike's boys had come running in a ragged line, all of them straining as if they were in a race. Fast. They were too far back to catch up, but their fervor sent a bottomless fear through Joe's stomach.

Mike's boys looked like starving jackals stalking an antelope.

TWELVE

Kendra could barely breathe. The air in the truck felt the way it might in outer space, if you were floating alone in the universe, a distant speck, too far in the sky to see.

"Grandpa Joe?" Kendra whispered.

Grandpa Joe's face shone with sweat. He was chewing at his lip hard enough to draw blood. Grandpa Joe's fingers gripped at the wheel, and the corners of his mouth turned upward in an imitation of a smile. "It's gonna be all right," he said, but it seemed that he was talking to himself more than to her. "It'll be fine."

Kendra stared at him, assessing. He seemed all right. But Dad had seemed fine too.

She and Mom had been all right for a while, living off the refrigerator, and then the pantry after the power went out. But Mom got bit by their neighbor Carolyn Stiller and had forced Kendra to hide in the cellar. Made her promise not to open the door, even for her. No matter what. *Not until you hear the danger word.*

Kendra felt warm liquid on the seat beneath her and she gasped, thinking Grandpa Joe might be bleeding all over the seat. Instead, when she looked down, her jeans were dark and wet, almost black. It wasn't blood. She'd peed herself, like a baby. Damn. She was losing it.

"Are you sleepy?" Kendra said. Grandpa Joe shook his head, but Kendra thought he'd hesitated first.

Grandpa Joe's eyes were on the road half the time, on the rearview mirror the rest. "How long before your mom or dad got sleepy?"

Kendra remembered her mom's voice outside the door, announcing the time. *It's nine o'clock, Kendra.* Worried it was getting late. Worried she should get far away from Kendra and send for Grandpa Joe to come get her.

"A few minutes," Kendra said softly. "Five. Or ten."

Grandpa Joe went back to chewing his lip. "What happened?"

"We were . . . at the hospital."

For the first time, Kendra told Grandpa Joe about Portland General. How her father had been bitten. How they'd been lucky to get home, and heard the radio guy saying that sleepiness came just before the urge to attack, so bite victims shouldn't sleep. Dad had fought yawning for a few hours, drinking cup after cup of coffee, but he'd finally panicked after a micronap. He had fled in the middle of the night, refused to go to sleep in the house, telling them to lock their doors. He'd slept in the car. And by morning, he was foaming at the back door, trying and trying to get in, eyes bloody.

Kendra heard herself tell the story, but her voice sounded like someone else's.

"So . . . was it about . . . twelve hours?" Grandpa Joe said. He sounded hopeful.

Kendra's throat felt like a pinprick. She could barely breathe. "Something like that. I . . . guess. But . . ."

"But what?"

"It was different for . . ."

Shadows wrestled across Grandpa Joe's face. "Your mom?" His voice rumbled.

Kendra nodded.

Grandpa Joe sighed and cleared his throat, girding himself to hear the rest. "How was it different for Cass?" he whispered finally. His voice broke on her name.

Kendra glanced at the bloodied mess on her grandfather's leg before she blinked away. "The bite was worse. Like yours. She got real sleepy real fast. It took less time."

This story would be harder, she realized. She hadn't loved her mother more—she couldn't have chosen one parent over the other at gunpoint. But Dad had left them so quickly, absorbed in the surreal fog of the first day of the crisis, that he didn't seem truly gone. But she and Mom . . . They had weathered it together. Made plans together. They had listened for news of a cure, determined to find Dad and help him one day. For weeks, they had been the only part of the world that still felt right.

"I was in bed," Kendra said. "Mom poked her head in my room and said our neighbor was knocking on the window. Mrs. Stiller. Carolyn. Nice lady who wrote plays. They perform . . . *performed* them at the local theater. They even made a movie of one of her plays."

Grandpa Joe tried to smile. "Would I have seen it?"

"I think it showed on cable. Her husband was an insurance agent. Had a sailboat, and took me out on it." A pleasant, wistful memory, even though she'd been thwacked twice by a swinging boom.

A nice man. Hardworking salesman, and a good husband, until he'd knocked on the door offering a variety of Whole Life beyond Prudential's wildest dreams.

"A lot of us had a buddy system, someone to go to for food.

Or a generator. Or news. She was ours. Her husband helped put up the boards on our house. Mom said Carolyn looked upset, and I should stay in bed . . . I guess when Mom saw her out there, she . . ."

"She wasn't thinking," Grandpa Joe finished. "She forgot."

Kendra nodded.

Mom had come back shouting, clapping her hand to her left shoulder, blood oozing between her fingers. Kendra had thought she was dreaming—*willed* herself to be dreaming—but Mom had pulled her out of bed, yanking her arm and pulling her to her feet. Kendra had cried the whole way to the basement. *I'm bit, Kendra. You can't trust me anymore. Don't open this door until you hear the danger word.*

"Mom stayed outside the basement door for ten minutes, maybe. Not long. She said she"—Kendra swallowed hard, forcing the words out—"she was so sleepy she could barely . . . stand up. She was scared to be near me, so she went away. Four or five hours. Then I heard her voice again, and she was knocking on the door. I was so . . . relieved." Kendra sobbed, trying to catch her breath.

"But it wasn't her?" Grandpa Joe said gently.

Kendra's eyes went to Grandpa Joe's bleeding wound again, and her limbs shook as if she wore no clothes. Her damp jeans felt frozen. "She said, 'Where's your math homework? You were supposed to do your homework.'"

"That's how you knew," Grandpa Joe said, whispering again.

Kendra nodded. "There was no more school." Her nostrils leaked, but she didn't move to wipe her nose. "I didn't open the door."

Grandpa Joe nodded, considering the story. Struggling with it.

His hand came toward her knee, but the sudden movement made her flinch. Even after she relaxed, reminding herself it

100

was too soon, her hand rested near the door latch. With a heart-broken smile Grandpa Joe pulled his hand back.

"Good girl, Kendra." Grandpa Joe's voice wavered. "Good girl."

All this time, Joe had thought it was his imagination.

A gaggle of the freaks had been waiting for him in Cass's front yard. He'd plowed most of them down with the truck so he could get to the door. That was the easy part. As soon as he got out, the ones still standing had surged. There'd been ten of them at least; an old man, a couple of teenage boys, the rest of them women, moving quick. He'd been squeezing off rounds at anything that moved. *Daddy?*

Had he heard her voice before he'd fired? In the time since, he'd decided the voice was his imagination, because how *could* she have talked to him, said his name? He'd decided God had created her voice in his mind, a last chance to hear it to make up for the horror his Glock had made of the back of her head. *Daddy?* It had been Cass, but it hadn't been. Her blouse and mouth had been a mess, and he'd seen stringy bits of nastiness caught in her teeth, just like the other freaks. It hadn't been Cass. It hadn't been.

People said freaks could make noises. Walked and looked like us. The newer ones didn't have the red stuff showing beneath their skin, and they didn't start to lose their motor skills for a couple of days, so the new ones could run fast. He'd known that. Everybody knew that. But if freaks could talk, could recognize you . . .

Then we can't win. The thought was quiet in Joe's mind, from a place that was already accepting it.

Cass had only lasted ten minutes, Little Soldier had said. Half of them already gone, maybe more than half. Joe tried to bear down harder on the gas, and his leg felt like a wooden stump.

Still, the speedometer climbed to ninety before the truck began to shiver. He had to get Little Soldier as far as he could from Mike's boys. He had to get Little Soldier away . . .

Joe's mouth was so dry it ached.

"We're in trouble, Kendra," Joe said. He couldn't bring himself to look at her, even though he wanted to so much he was nearly blinded by tears. "You know we're in trouble."

"Yes," the girl said.

"Don't go back to the cabin," Joe said, deciding that part. "It's not safe."

"But Mom might . . ." This time, Joe did gaze over at Kendra. The girl was sitting as far from him as she could, against the door. He'd gotten so used to Kendra waiting for her parents to come that he'd sometimes felt himself waiting too.

"That was a story I told you," Joe said, cursing himself for the lie. "You know they're not coming, Kendra. You said yourself she wasn't right. You could hear it. She was out in the front yard, before I got inside. I had to shoot her, Little Soldier. I shot her between the eyes."

Kendra gazed at him wide-eyed, rage knotting her face.

That's it, Little Soldier. Get mad.

"I couldn't tell you before. But I'm telling you now for a reason . . ."

Just that quick, the road ahead of Joe fogged, doubled. He snapped his head up, aware that he had just lost a moment of time, that his consciousness had flagged.

But he was still himself. Still himself, and that made the difference. Just maybe he would stay himself and beat this damned thing.

If you could stay awake for the first few hours . . .

Then he might stay Joe for another, what? Ten days? He'd heard about someone staying awake that long, maybe longer.

102

Right now, he didn't know if he'd last the ten minutes. His eyelids felt as heavy as tombstones. *There'll be rest enough in the grave.* Wasn't that what Benjamin Franklin had said?

"Don't you close your eyes, Daddy." Cass's voice. He snapped his head around, wondering where the voice had come from. He was seeing things: Cassie sat beside him with her pink lips and ringlets of tight brown hair. For a moment he couldn't see his Little Soldier, so solid Cassie seemed. *"You always talked tough this and tough that. Da Nang and Hanoi and a dozen places I couldn't pronounce. And now the one damned time in your life that it matters, you're going to sleep?"* The accusation in her voice was crippling. *"We trusted you, and you walked right into that store and got bitten because you were laughing at* The Simpsons? *I trusted you, Daddy."*

Silence. Then: *"I* still *trust you, Daddy."*

He swerved the wheel, too late. His mind had been fogged by confusion and voices, and he missed the motorcycle lying on its side, hidden by a stalled car in the inside lane. Joe yelled "Hang on!" as the truck slewed sideways, the rear wheels going sharply right, off the edge of the road. Something bumped sharply, *cracked* under the engine. He looked over at Kendra, who was braced with her feet against the glove compartment. Her eyes were wide, mouth open, breathing quick.

"Grandpa Joe?" He turned the key, and all he heard was a click. Joe's hands were shaking, sweating. Where was he? How had he gotten here? He felt a terrible itching sensation at the base of his jaw. With sudden, blinding clarity, Grandpa Joe realized what was happening to him. And for the last time in his life, Joe felt wide awake.

"Listen to me: you have to go," Joe said.

"Where? Where will we go?"

"Not us. You."

Shock melted from Kendra's face, replaced by the bewilderment and terror of an infant left naked in a snowdrift. Kendra's lips quivered. "No, Grandpa Joe. I can't. Not alone. I can't. You can stay awake," she whispered.

"Grab that backpack behind your seat—it's got a compass, bottled water, jerky, and a flashlight. It's heavy, but you'll need it. And take your Remington. There's more ammo for it under your seat. Put the shells in the backpack. Do it now."

Kendra sobbed, reaching out to squeeze his arm. "P-please, Grandpa Joe . . ."

"Stop that damned crying!" Joe roared. Kendra yanked her hand away, sliding back toward her door again. The poor kid must think he'd already crossed over.

Joe took a deep breath. Another wave of dizziness washed over him, and his chin rocked downward. Joe's pain was easing. He felt stoned, like he was smoking some of that mind-busting Cambodian the little bicycle peddlers used to sell the troops in 'Nam. He hadn't driven far enough before killing the truck. They were still too close to Mike's boys. So much to say . . .

Joe kept his voice as even as he could. "There were only two people who could possibly love you more than me, and they couldn't fight it, not even for you. That tells me I can't either. Understand?"

Kendra nodded.

READ REVELATION, a billboard fifty yards ahead advised in red letters. Beside the billboard, the road forked into another highway. Thank Jesus.

"Get up to that road. *Run.* Hear me? Fast as you can. No matter what you hear . . . don't turn around. Don't stop. It's twenty miles to Centralia, straight south. There's National Guard there, and air drops." He was starting to struggle for words, struggling for breath. "Caravans. Tell them you want to go to Portland. That's where I'd go."

"What about that place . . . Devil's Wake? The radio said it was safe. You said I had an aunt there."

"Your daddy's aunt. But that's California, sweetheart. That's a world away." He closed his eyes, and said dreamily, "A world away."

His eyes snapped open again, and he licked his lips with the tip of his tongue, almost as if tasting them for the first time. "When you're running, stay near the roads, but keep out of sight. If anyone comes before you get to Centralia, hide. If they see you, tell 'em you'll shoot, and then *do it*. You hear me? *Do it!* And don't go to sleep, Kendra. Don't let anybody surprise you."

"Yes, sir," Kendra said in a sad voice, eager to be commanded.

Joe's leg was numb. He wouldn't have been able to keep driving anyway. Feeling in his arms was nearly gone now too.

"I love you, Grandpa Joe," he heard his granddaughter say. Or thought he did.

"Love you too, Little Soldier. You're the best granddaughter anyone ever had." *Still here. Still here.*

"Now, go. *Go.*"

Joe heard Kendra's car door open and slam. He turned his head to watch her, to make sure she was doing as she'd been told. Kendra had the backpack and her rifle as she stumbled away from the truck, running in the embankment that was alongside the road. The girl glanced back over her shoulder, saw Joe wave her on, and then disappeared into the roadside brush.

With trembling fingers, Joe opened the glove compartment, digging out his snub-nosed .38. He rested the cold metal between his lips, then eased it past his teeth. He was breathing hard, sucking at the air, and he didn't know if it was the toxin or his nerves working him. He looked for Kendra again, but at this angle couldn't see her.

Now. Do it now.

It seemed that he heard his own voice whispering in his ear. *I can win. I can win. I saved my whole goddamn squad when the gooks hit the bridge. I can beat this thing . . .*

Joe sat in the truck, feeling alternating waves of heat and cold washing through him. As long as he could stay awake . . .

Joe heard the voice of old Mrs. Reed, his sixth-grade English teacher; saw the faces of Sergeant Bob and Private Eddie Kevner, who'd been standing beside him when the Bouncing Betty blew. Then he saw Cassie in her wedding dress, giving him a secret gaze, as if to ask if it was all right before she pledged her final vows at the altar. Then in the midst of the images, some he didn't recognize. Something red, drifting through a trackless cosmos. Alive, yet inanimate. Intelligent but unaware.

He'd been with them all along, those drifting spore-strands drawn toward a blue-green planet with water and soil . . . floating through the atmosphere . . . rest . . . root . . . grow . . .

A crow's mournful caws awakened Joe, but not as much of him as had slipped into sleep. His vision was tinged red. His world, his heart, was tinged red. What remained of Joe knew that *it* was in him, awakening, using his own mind against him, dazzling him with its visions while it took control. He wanted to tear, to rend. Not killing. Not eating. Not yet. There was something more urgent, a new voice he had never heard before. *Must bite.*

Panicked, he gave his hand an urgent command: *pull the trigger.*

But he couldn't. He'd come this close and couldn't do it. Too many parts of him no longer wanted to die. The new parts of him only wanted to live. To grow. To spread. Still, Joe struggled against himself, even as he knew struggle was doomed.

Little Soldier. Must protect Little Soldier. Must . . .

Must . . .

Must bite girl.

THIRTEEN

For ten minutes Kendra had been running and sobbing, never far from stumbling, before her thoughts woke up again. Her legs and belly ached. She had to slow down because she couldn't see for her tears.

Grandpa Joe had been hunched over the steering wheel, eyes open so wide that the effort had changed the way his face looked. Kendra thought she'd never seen such a hopeless, helpless expression in her entire life. If she had been able to see Mom from the safe room, that was how she would have looked too.

She'd been stupid to think Grandpa Joe could keep her safe. He was just an old man who lived in the woods.

Kendra ran, her legs burning and throat scalding. She could see the road above her, but she ran in the embankment like Grandpa Joe had told her, out of sight. For an endless time Kendra ran, despite burning legs and scalded throat, struggling to stay true to Grandpa Joe's directions. South. Stay south. *Centralia.*

National Guard. Portland. Then she remembered the words she had heard on the radio. *Devil's Wake. California. Safe.*

By the time exhaustion claimed Kendra, the sky had darkened, and she was so tired she had lost any assurance of placing her feet without disaster. The trees, once an explosion of green, had been bleached gray and black by twilight. They were a place of trackless, unknowable danger. Every sound and shadow seemed to call to her. Trembling so badly she could hardly move, Kendra crawled past a wall of ferns into a culvert, clutching the little sawed-off Remington to her chest.

Once she sat, her sadness felt worse, like a heavy quilt over her. She sobbed so hard she could no longer sit up straight, curling herself into a ball on the soft soil. Small leaves and debris pasted themselves to the tears and mucous sliming her face. One sob sounded more like a wail, so loud it startled her.

Grandpa Joe had lied. Mom had been dead all along. He'd shot her in the head, like Old Yeller. He'd said it like it hardly mattered to him.

Kendra heard snapping twigs, and the back of her neck turned ice-cold. Footsteps. Running fast.

Kendra's sobs vanished. She sat straight up, propping her shotgun across her bent knee, aiming, finger ready on the trigger. A small black spider crawled on her wrist—one with a bloated egg sac, about to give birth to a hundred babies like in *Charlotte's Web*—but she made no move to crush it: there had been enough death. Kendra sat primed, trying to silence her clotted nose by breathing through her mouth.

Waiting.

Maybe it was that hitchhiker with the sign, she thought. But it didn't matter who it was. *Hide.* That was what Grandpa Joe had said.

The footsteps slowed, although they were so close that Kendra guessed her pursuer couldn't be more than a few feet away. No longer running, as if he knew where Kendra was. As if he'd been close behind her all along, and now that he'd found her, he wasn't in a hurry anymore.

"I have a gun! I'll shoot!" Kendra called out, and this voice was very different from the one she'd used to ask Grandpa Joe for a Coke. Not a little girl's voice. It was a voice that meant what it said.

Silence. The movement had stopped.

That was when Grandpa Joe said the danger word. The word he'd used at the cellar door to let her know she was safe.

Kendra's finger loosened against the trigger. Her limbs gave way, and her body began to shake. The woods melted away, and she remembered wearing this same jacket in the safe room, waiting. Waiting for Grandpa Joe.

There had never been a gunshot from Grandpa Joe's truck. Kendra had expected to hear the gunshot as soon as she ran off, dreading it. Grandpa Joe always did what needed to be done. Kendra should have heard a gunshot.

"Go back!" Kendra said. Although her voice was not so sure this time, she cocked the Remington's handgrip, just like she'd been taught.

Kendra waited. She'd tried not to hope—and then hoped fervently—that her scare had worked. The instant Kendra's hope reached its peak, a shadow moved against the ferns above her, closer.

Grandpa Joe's watery voice spoke again. Their danger word. The word that was their secret, that meant safety, and hope.

"Breakfast," said Grandpa Joe. *"Breakfast."*

FOURTEEN

Kendra ran until her legs hurt and the shambling thing that had once been her grandfather was far behind her. He'd been running faster than she'd ever seen him move, as if the pain in his joints was gone or irrelevant, but there was still little chance he could outrun her. Kendra ran until her chest flamed, until she could barely take another step without the shakes, then hid in a stand of trees until darkness fell. Hadn't Grandpa Joe once said he thought one had *smelled* him? She prayed he was wrong.

She shivered through the night, unable to sleep. Soon after sunrise she ate a handful of the precious jerky and began to walk south along the I-5, the sawed-off Remington crooked in her arm. The road never left her sight, but she tried to provide herself cover when she could, listening for the sound of car engines that didn't come, at first.

She had a vague plan to try to reach Portland. Even Longview might have help, if only she knew where to look. Hadn't the radio said something about the Heights in the hills? That would be the rich kids' houses, built by the original mill owners lording it over the mill workers, who lived down near the river. And now it was the last stronghold in Freak Central? Great.

Abandoned cars dotted Interstate 5, their doors left yawning open. Most of them in the middle of the lane, not even pulled to the side. One car, a small green Honda Civic, was upside down, its windshield shattered. Kendra found suitcases or duffel bags in some of the cars, but scavenged no food except a strawberry Zone bar. She ate half and folded the rest neatly in its silver package, stuffed deep into her pocket. Later, the protein bar and a little jerky would be her dinner. A feast.

Twice, cars passed her on the road, but she heard them coming from far away. She remembered what her grandfather had said, and hid until they had passed. Freaks weren't the only ones on a killing spree. Human beings were hunters or hunted now, with few in between. Besides, would she trust the motives of anyone who wanted to give a teenage girl a ride? Yeah, right. A ride into a *very* special episode of *Criminal Minds.* Dog-Girl had warned her that young girls were being trafficked Outside, which meant anywhere that wasn't hidden away. Now that she was stuck Outside, mistakes weren't a luxury.

As night began to fall, she took a chance and headed through an overgrown cabbage patch toward a farmhouse. The two-story wood-frame colonial seemed abandoned despite the shiny pickup truck tucked into the carport, but she couldn't be sure. Nothing was sure anymore. The door was unlocked, partly ajar, as if the owners were entertaining guests. *Yeah, guests who just dropped in for dinner.*

"Hello?" she said in a helium-squeak of a voice. It might be safer to sound like a little girl than a sixteen-year-old. People weren't afraid of little girls, and they tried to protect them, not hurt them. At least, that was the way it used to be.

No one answered. Kendra ventured inside, locking the door behind her. She also checked the windows, which were all unbroken and had working locks. Good. After a stop in the bathroom, which was full of bowls with fragrant potpourri and soap that smelled like medicine, Kendra entered the kitchen with an empty bladder and a clean face and hands. Feeling clean was a gift. She even washed the jeans she'd soiled.

The kitchen was food paradise, as if someone had prepared for her. Cans were stacked on the counter: franks and beans, peas, SpaghettiOs! Armed with a can opener, *Fools make feasts, and wise men eat them,* as Grandpa Joe use to say.

Kendra was feeling wise.

After she'd eaten, she realized how tired she was. The *Itis,* Grandpa Joe had always called his drowsiness after a big meal. Could she find a bed too?

Upstairs, looking for a bedroom, Kendra detected an acrid, oily stench wafting from beneath the nearest closed doorway. She was tempted to open the door and see for herself, but saw an ant trail, little black specks coming and going under the door. Kendra backed away. Her imagination was more than enough.

She went back downstairs. Once on the couch she pulled her journal out of her backpack and wrote down everything she could think about the previous day. *Today, Grandpa Joe drove to Mike's to sell deer jerky,* she began. As she wrote, it felt like she was telling a story about someone else, not a terrible thing that had happened to her. Kendra didn't cry, or couldn't, as she wrote.

Writing helped, emptying out her head. Kendra fell deeply asleep, her pen still in her hand.

December 16

In the morning Kendra searched the house, discovering canned peaches and evaporated milk in the pantry. A little water pressure remained, which made her wonder if somewhere, perhaps, someone was trying to put the world back together.

She wished she could stay at the house and claim it. It was so tempting! But staying would mean cleaning up the body, or bodies, and the house was too close to the interstate. If the occupants hadn't died in a freak attack or suicide pact, they'd likely been overrun by the pirates. In some ways, the pirates were worse than the freaks. There was no such thing as rest, no such thing as safety. Grandpa Joe had said to get to Portland.

So Kendra carried what she could and slipped out through the back door, extra careful as she passed the windows. Kendra tried to make sure that no one . . . either human or freak . . . shambling through the fields or passing on the dirt road could glimpse her. In the back of the house, she finally found something that justified her shaky faith in the world: an aged Schwinn three-speed bicycle. When she first saw the bicycle's black paint, she thought her imagination had created it. But it was still there after she blinked.

Giddy with glee, she checked the tires. A bit squidgy, but five minutes' searching found a compact hand pump, and two minutes of pumping made the tires taut as drums. She climbed aboard. The brakes and handling were decent, not great, but now she could hope to make better time, perhaps reach Centralia by nightfall. Kendra packed her backpack with food—

saltines and nuts, not heavy cans, thank you very much. She also found an empty Gatorade bottle and filled it with the water dribbling from the faucet.

As an afterthought, she found a fleece jacket in the coat closet and tied it around her waist. She might need another jacket. At the very least, the jacket would give her something to trade. Even if she'd had cash, it was meaningless now. Trade was everything. She had learned that from Grandpa Joe.

Pain stabbed her chest when she thought of Grandpa Joe and his cabin, but she tried to turn her pain to strength the way Mom and Dad had always said. She could almost hear all three of them urging her on: *Keep going, Kendra. Don't stop.* So Kendra went back on the road. She kept her Remington balanced across the handlebars, which made it hard to steer, but it was better than leaving her protection behind.

Traveling south by bike, she took access roads paralleling I-5, keeping her eyes peeled for rocks that could blow her tires. And people. Finally, she saw others: always at a distance, as eager to avoid her as she was to avoid them. At times, pumping the pedals, it felt as if she were totally alone in the world. Even more, it sometimes seemed that she was standing still, the rest of the world moving around her. The bike was a little rusty, so she couldn't really make fast time, but she was grateful not to be walking.

For the first time in a long time, Kendra Brookings felt just a little bit in charge of her life.

She had just passed the big white WELCOME TO CENTRALIA poster when she noticed a pale smoke plume boiling up from the woods to her left. Distantly, she heard gunshots. A sixty-second pause. Then more shots.

Her heart thumping at her chest, Kendra walked her bike

down off the road and biked west until she found a road traveling parallel to the I-5. Then she took that route south until the smoke, and the shooting, were behind her. So much for stopping in Centralia.

Damn, damn, damn . . .

Centralia no longer called to her. The southern road beckoned.

The Schwinn was a blessing. She was able to make excellent time, three or four times faster than she could possibly have traveled by foot. By the second night, a highway sign told her that she was within twenty-five miles of Longview. Her thighs and calves ached, and she pulled off the road to another house. Similar to last night's shelter, this one was two stories high, and it looked deserted. But this house had no cars parked outside. And the door, this time, was locked. She knocked.

"Pizza!" she called.

She broke a kitchen window and climbed inside. As in the previous house, the power was dead. But unlike the previous house, she found a hand-cranked radio. Kendra spent fifteen minutes spinning the little handle and then tested the dial: mostly static, mixed in with a few scattered bursts of words, as if they were coming from far away, only available because of shifts in the clouds.

The kitchen wasn't as well stocked, but she found tuna and stale crackers, which was, in Dog-Girl parlance, a "bleedin' feast."

Remembering the stench and the ant trail from the last house, Kendra decided not to go upstairs. Besides, trying to sleep in the former occupants' beds would have felt like a violation. The sofa was soft leather, which was more than fine.

As Kendra was settling down for the night, she heard a noise from upstairs. Kendra grabbed her rifle and climbed up the steps, one at a time, more frightened than she had been since Grandpa Joe got bit, but somehow beyond her own emotions. *Above* them.

She wasn't alone in the house! She should have checked upstairs first. *ALWAYS check upstairs first!* said a voice in her head. Grandpa Joe's blessed voice.

A solid *thump-crash,* too big for a cat. A child? Bigger? Kendra's heart raced.

She found her feet mounting the stairs, and to her surprise, she realized she had a battle plan: she would stay here, on the narrow part of the stairs, and shoot at them as they came at her from the front. Hopefully not from the rear.

When she got to the top, she froze. A rail-thin man in grimy sweats stood around the corner pointing a small black pistol at her. For a moment, all she saw was the gun's tiny black muzzle, expecting it to breathe fire.

"You just made a mistake, missy," the man said, his voice unsteady. "You leave that gun and get on out of here. We would have let you be, you just gone on in the morning. But now I have to be sure you won't double back. Kill us in our sleep."

His hand was shaking slightly. In the near dark, Kendra wondered if the gun was loaded, or even real at all. She could see the guy's wife cowering behind him, her blond hair an unkempt nest. And behind her, an identically blond boy about six or seven. "Please," Kendra begged. "I was going to leave. Just let me keep my rifle."

"Drop it," the man said, and extended the pistol a few inches. Behind him, the little boy pressed more tightly against his mother.

Kendra lowered the sawed-off rifle to the ground and backed

117

down the stairs. Rage welled in her, appearing as tears. "Is it loaded, Sam?" she heard the woman say. She sounded like a kid on Christmas morning.

Kendra forgot her rage right away. The man could have hurt her, but he hadn't. She could have lost her backpack and bike too.

All in all, she realized, she'd had a pretty good day.

The sun was setting by the time she reached Longview. Amid the steep, pitiless shadows, Longview was burning. Had burned. Was dead. From the freeway she and her parents had traveled so often, she could see the shell of the McDonald's, and on the other side, a burned-out Taco Bell. The ruins of the mall. Rows of scorched, shattered houses and a blackened concrete pad where gas tanks had exploded. *Must have been quite a bang,* she thought.

What had happened to her mother's body? Was Devon Brookings, or what remained of him, still alive? Was her father wandering in the ruins of Longview, biting others? Looking for her somehow?

Kendra pulled off the freeway, waiting until a faded red pickup truck with three armed men sitting in the bed in down coats and sunglasses pulled past on the road. Who were they? How could she tell the kind of people they might be? They went about some business in the shopping center and then pulled away an hour later, whooping. One of the men fired a shot into the air.

Idjit, Kendra thought in Grandpa Joe's voice. *If you can't make bullets, don't waste shots.* Then he'd laugh. *Same goes for whiskey.* Somehow, she figured these clowns were more into drinking than reloading.

Kendra glided her bike over to the side and looked east, west, and north. Anyone watching? No. A few scraps of paper blowing across the parking lot. A dozen deserted cars were scattered across the lot in disarray, like toys awaiting the return of a giant rug rat. Kendra searched the cars one by one, keeping her expectations in check, and the fourth was unlocked. She opened it and looked inside with her heart pounding in her throat. It was a Toyota Corolla, looked to be about twenty years old. She searched around and then under the car—

And found a little black magnetic key box tucked beneath the car. Holding her breath, she took the keys out and slipped it into the ignition. Turned it with a click. Then a grinding sound, and the engine turned over. *Oh God! Oh God!* It was half exclamation, half grateful prayer. She panted, feeling a deep excitement she could barely remember experiencing. Closed the car door. Opened it again. Put the rear seat back and wedged the bicycle onto the seat. Kendra shucked the backpack, tossed it beside the bike, then climbed into the driver's seat and pulled the car out of the lot.

She had a car! A car was a rolling palace. A four-wheeled fortress. She hadn't known how to drive when she'd first gone to Grandpa Joe's, hadn't even had a learner's permit because she'd been in no rush to grow up, but Grandpa Joe had made her practice with the truck. Despite a sickening wave of sadness and nostalgia, Kendra heard a strange giggling sound that almost made her turn to look over her shoulder . . . until she realized it was only her.

Kendra took a long look at the flickering lights from lanterns that made the Heights twinkle like an enchanted forest shimmering above a graveyard. She saw houses intact up on the ridge of hills overlooking the flatlands. Kendra had no idea what kind of politics had evolved. Was the city council still in charge? Was there still a mayor? She imagined that power still resided in the

Heights, the hillside homes overlooking the mill. Who lived there now? Were they her old neighbors and teachers, or had strangers taken over the town? Maybe she could find shelter there.

No. She had never been invited to parties up in the Heights, never for a drive in the too-shiny Beemers and Lexuses their parents had bought them for sweet sixteens. And the idea of placing her life in their hands now made her flesh crawl. She had more than half a tank of gas, enough to get to Portland. She would keep driving.

Frontage roads. That was the thing to do. She would evade the ghosts of whatever towns remained between here and Vancouver. From there, to Portland, and hopefully, that National Guard armory.

If not that, something else. With her new sense of confidence and wheels grinding across the road, she felt as if she could do anything.

Thankfully, Longview's streets weren't stacked with cars and bodies. Kendra drove past the industrial districts, those smokestacks that no longer belched white, the waterway now clogged with logs that, in saner days, would have gone to the Weyerhaeuser mill to build houses and make cardboard boxes. Nothing moved. Interstate 5 stayed mostly clear too. Until she'd driven twelve miles down.

There, just as the skies were growing dark, Kendra's headlights showcased an overturned truck that looked like an oil tanker blocking the road. Kendra's heart danced with images of gas for life, until she realized it was a milk truck.

Don't get greedy, girl.

She slowed and decided the embankment was gentle enough

to steer around the truck, amazed at how easily she'd adapted to the challenge. Time was, she would have panicked at the blocked road, but she wasn't the same person she'd been yesterday. Or even an hour ago. Kendra pulled off, steering toward the dirt on the driver's side, her only clear passage.

Her tires had just left the asphalt when a man stepped out of the shadows. Kendra's eyes focused on him sharply, showing her every detail in her car's harsh light. He was a big man, with dirty, pale, densely freckled skin. A wild beard speckled white and black, with flecks of yellow trapped inside. When he grinned, his teeth looked like he'd scribbled on them with yellow crayon. He'd been living outside. His hands were behind his back as if she'd interrupted him while he was pacing, deep in thought.

Or maybe, just maybe, he was a freak.

Kendra remembered Grandpa Joe's warning never to stop for hitchhikers, and she and the stranger had nothing to talk about. Without hesitating, she pressed her foot harder on the accelerator to make him think she would run him over rather than stop—and maybe she would. She didn't know yet.

That was when he whipped up his shotgun. From four feet away, the barrel loomed as huge and dark as a railroad tunnel. He'd fire if she accelerated, and was too close to miss. Heart thundering, Kendra rolled to a stop. She felt her pulse drumming as her hands grasped the steering wheel, her heartbeat shaking her body.

Take your damned chances and drive over him! Kendra's mind screamed.

But she didn't. Instead, with her trembling hands raised high, she got out of the car. She hoped she wouldn't lose more than the bicycle. Maybe he wouldn't see her backpack.

"Heard the car from a mile off," the man said. "Don't see too

121

many cars no more. And a pretty girl really ought not be out by herself. Get out—and bring your stuff. Everybody's got stuff."

Kendra's legs barely obeyed her. She didn't like the way he'd called her *pretty*. She wished she looked dirtier too. But maybe he wouldn't hurt her if she did what he told her to do. After she shrugged on her backpack, he gestured her over sideways, toward the ditch.

That was when she saw the freak.

The infected man had come down from the I-5, almost directly in line with the car, as if he were purposely concealing himself. A narrow man in a piss-stained business suit, still wearing a tie askew. It walked like most freaks, as if suffering a slow-motion seizure. This was an older one, his face scabbed red. Grandpa Joe said the older, slower ones were slowly starving to death and would do a lot more than take a single bite.

Kendra moved around, backing away, so that the man with the gun was between her and the freak. Had bad luck turned to good luck so soon? The pirate's attention was on her, so she just needed to keep his eyes occupied for another few seconds . . .

She summoned a warm-up exercise from a long-forgotten acting class. Kendra shimmied her hips slightly, as if she were about to do a private dance. She saw the way the pirate's eyes widened, lips peeling back in a grin, exposing those nasty teeth again.

"*That's* more like it, girl," he said, his breathing heavy. "Show me the goods."

Kendra slowly leaned over to rest her backpack on the ground, her eyes on the man with the gun. His eyes roamed over her, and he licked his lips as if she were a steak.

Over his shoulder, Kendra saw that the freak had halved the distance between them, within five yards, close enough for her to see how its eyes were foamed crimson with fungus. Which of them horrified her more?

The pirate still held the shotgun with one hand, but he tugged on his jeans to unsnap them with the other.

That's it, you sick bastard. Keep your eyes on me.

But he must have heard something—or, more likely, *smelled* something. He wheeled around just in time to meet the freak face-to-face. Too late to run, barely time to scream. The pirate managed to get off a single shot before the freak grabbed him, and it went so wild that Kendra ducked. But not before she saw the freak's teeth tear into his exposed neck.

Kendra ran, and as she did she saw that there were two more freaks . . . one staggering in from the west and one running from the north. The runner was dressed like a fry cook, his apron tattered and bloodstained, his eyes filled with red veins. A fast one! The older freak was a woman, thin now, but her clothes were so loose that Kendra guessed that she had once been plus-size. Skin hung in diseased folds on her face, and her eyes were clotted red. They were driving Kendra. Funneling her toward a kill zone.

They travel in packs. They lay traps. Even as she ran, Kendra struggled to comprehend.

No time to jump into the car or grab her backpack. No time to do anything but flee. She climbed up the side of the road, toward the rising bank of the I-5, the freak below her now, trying to claw toward her. She heard a shot and a scream from behind her. The scream went on so long that its gurgling echo scarcely seemed human.

Kendra's world went gray, nearly white, as the fast freak's hand clamped on her ankle, dragged her back down the incline a few feet while she kicked, expecting to feel the teeth pierce her skin at any moment. Kendra screamed like an animal. At last, a kick made contact. The freak lost its death grip and rolled away. Kendra clambered up to the road and ran.

She ran so wildly that she nearly lost her balance, flailing her arms as she crossed the I-5's eight lanes to disappear down the other side—the steeper side she hadn't been willing to chance with the car. Panting hard, she ventured a peek.

The thing appeared atop the far embankment and lurched like a drunk, trying to figure out which way she'd gone, and could not. It lost focus and staggered north.

Sobbing, Kendra curled into a ball behind a pine tree. She had lost everything. One piece at a time her fragile world had been dismantled, the pieces ripped from her hands. She had lost her backpack, her bicycle, her rifle, the car. Her mother. Her father. Her grandpa. Everything and everyone. How had she been deluded enough to feel anything remotely resembling joy just yesterday?

She'd been a fool to dream of living.

Might as well just stay here, curled up in the dark. Wait to die.

Then . . . she heard the engine. Just a groan at first, something that might almost have been mistaken for wind in the trees. Then a blue truck appeared on the I-5 . . . no, a bus. Some kind of school bus, a wedge-shaped snowplow mounted on the front.

The bus slowed, pulled off along the road the way she had, its lights suddenly so bright that she could only see its hazy outline. Kendra hadn't moved, was pinioned directly in its headlights.

Kendra felt no fear. No curiosity. In fact, nothing at all. Exhaustion and terror had congealed into a kind of quiet courage. She only held up one arm to shield her eyes from the bright light.

The bus stopped with a tremendous squeal of brakes and a smell of burned rubber. The door opened, and she was able to look in past the stairwell to the driver's seat. The bus driver was just a boy, only a year or two older than she was.

He wasn't dirty. He didn't have a gun. He had an angel's face with dark, curly hair and bright eyes. Behind him, she saw others on the bus: a pale girl with long black hair with a single streak of white. A narrow face, cradling a rifle in her sinewy arms. One guy standing next to her, tall, thick-chested, darker than Kendra, a toothpick in the corner of his mouth, and his lips curled in a lazy smile. A dog stood at the top of the stairwell, some kind of Lab mix, eyeing her suspiciously.

The driver's eyes were wide, intelligent, and kind. So kind.

They were, *he* was, the most beautiful sight Kendra had ever seen.

He smiled at her. "Need a ride?"

FIFTEEN

Terry had to shake his head. The girl standing outside the Blue Beauty's accordion door gazing up at them with wonder-filled eyes looked like a trapped rabbit. He hadn't opened the door for a stranger since they'd left the campground—been tempted plenty, but always thought better of it. This time, he couldn't resist. This girl was someone's sister, or daughter. If he couldn't reach Lisa, at least he might be able to help this girl.

The arrival of the Twins' motorcycles behind them made her jump backward as if she'd changed her mind and decided to run. The Twins circled back around after doing their usual wide sweep. The girl only gaped as their shoulder-length hair flagged out like Apaches on mustangs instead of four-stroke engines.

"You bit?" Darius called to her. When the girl didn't answer, Darius looked at Terry. "She looks bit."

"Could be," Dean said. He nodded at the girl. "Gotta ask you to strip."

"Only way to be sure." Darius grinned.

Sonia pushed up from behind Terry on the bus. "You guys suck. Leave her alone. Poor thing's in shock."

"Or she's bit," Darius muttered, his leer gone, a serious scowl in its place.

The girl looked at Sonia, mouth working without producing words.

"Does it speak?" Sonia asked. "*Parlez-vous* talk-talk?"

The girl nodded.

Darius wagged his head. *"Once I met a pretty little freak,"* he sang tunelessly. *"Stole my heart and bit me in my sleep . . ."* He revved his bike loudly, and the girl nearly jumped out of her socks.

"Shut up," Sonia said, more forcefully. "Think of what she's been through."

"Join the club," Dean said.

The girl with the cocoa skin folded her arms across her chest, hiding herself. "I can talk," she said, in a tiny voice. "But some of *them* can too. Like a regular conversation, almost. It fools you and then . . . it's too late. There's one just up the road, walking north. But I'm not bitten." She paused, as if trying to remember words. "My name is Kendra."

Terry had heard the cop in Seattle speaking but hadn't come across other talking freaks. Vern hadn't said a word, and neither had the gaggle they'd run into near Centralia. Or run *over*, to be more accurate; the snowplow was coated with dried blood. Terry liked the girl already. She was smart, or she never would have survived so long on her own. He would lose sleep if he left her behind. It would be kinder to shoot her.

Terry glanced at Sonia and knew she was thinking the same thing. Piranha's face was harder to read, but he might have a soft spot for her. It's not like there were that many "colored kids" wandering around the Pacific Northwest, as Mom would say. With Piranha on his side, he'd have three votes even if the Twins were against it.

Terry gave Piranha a look that said *Well?*

Piranha shrugged. "Another mouth. But I guess I'm cool if she passes the sniff test."

The girl squirmed uncomfortably, her arms folded across her chest.

"You want a ride?" Terry asked her.

The girl studied their faces one by one, lingering on the Twins. Darius winked at her. Slowly, the girl nodded.

"Time for the test," Darius said.

Dean whistled and Hipshot bounded out of the bus. He ran straight for Kendra, circling her, sniffing with furious deliberation. At first, his tail curled firmly between his legs, and Terry's heart caught. He hadn't thought about what they would have to do if it turned out she was infected!

Then Hippy's tail wagged.

When the girl extended her hand, Hippy licked it.

"Well, all right," Darius said. "Clean, fresh meat to feed the freaks."

"You are *such* a jerk," Sonia said.

The girl by the side of the road seemed to relax, realizing that the Twins weren't as menacing as they seemed.

"They've got to catch me first," she said, staring at Darius with steel in her eyes.

They all laughed.

"That's right, girl," Sonia said. "Tell him to kiss your ass. That's what I do."

"Where I come from, princess," Darius said to Sonia, "that's called an invitation."

"Lay off," Piranha said in his end-of-the-conversation voice. He didn't like the Twins flirting with Sonia, even in fun, and they flirted more each day. Even Terry found himself staring at Sonia sometimes, seeing in her angular features a softness he hadn't noticed before Freak Day. It would be good to have more than one girl in the bus. Might lighten the tension.

Terry took a step toward the girl, gestured with his head. "Come on, Kendra," he said with his best smile. "Hippy can smell a freak a mile away, so you're officially sterile. Welcome to our dysfunctional family."

The bus barely made it past the overturned truck Kendra had warned them about and the Twins had confirmed after their recon. They saw no sign of the pirate Kendra had mentioned, but a dead freak in a business suit confirmed her story. Kendra said the pirate had been badly bitten, so he'd probably fled in panic . . . or fallen asleep nearby. If sleeping, he wouldn't wake up before a couple of hours, but none of them wanted to linger.

They all climbed out of the bus except for Terry and Kendra, who didn't want to leave the safety of her seat. Piranha drove her little Toyota out of the way, and Terry inched past the truck without overturning, although there was a nasty scraping sound against the undercarriage. Ugh. Terry tried not to think about it, but the bus hadn't been in great shape before their road trip, and survival prospects weren't improving.

The Toyota was a find, with more than half a tank's worth of gas. Too bad it wasn't an SUV, but all gas was good gas. It didn't make sense to add another vehicle to their caravan, but Terry hoped they wouldn't wish they'd kept the car.

"Let's move!" Terry said once the bus was clear. Darius and Dean chained their bikes to a rack on the back of the bus, and they continued their journey south.

Once they were back on the road, Dean hunched over the

seat behind him. "We're pretty clear for the next five miles," he said. "But there's a messed-up accident after that."

"Messed up how?" Terry asked.

"Messed up in the usual way everything is messed up. More time. More hassle."

The Blue Beauty's wheel vibrated under his hands. The alignment was off, and if the whole world hadn't gone to hell, he might have found a truck repair place and put her up on the rack. But that wasn't possible anymore, and all he could hope for was that Blue Beauty would get them somewhere safe before laying down life's weary burden.

Kendra stayed far in the back, near the supplies, giving them all mistrustful glances as she clung to the seat in front of her as if she were on a roller coaster.

Based on the Twins' report, Terry drove three miles, creeping along at twenty miles an hour, weaving through the dead cars, and then found a turnout far enough off the road that they couldn't be seen easily from the interstate.

Time to camp.

No one prodded her, but Kendra finally emerged from the back of the bus after they'd been parked for about a half hour. Terry's first impression had been correct: she was quite pretty, with huge dark eyes, even though they were filled with all the terrible things she had seen.

Darius stood guard while the others ate.

"It's hot dogs tonight, before they turn," Terry said.

"Sounds delicious." Sonia made a face. Then she winked at Kendra, trying to make her smile. Didn't work, but Kendra looked less likely to bolt at the first sneeze. Kendra was staring at them as if she was sure one of them had been bitten. How many people had she lost, and how? How much had the talking freaks fooled her? Terry wanted to ask her more, but decided to

131

let her recover from her brush with the pirate. They would have time to talk on the road. He hoped so, anyway.

Kendra finally sat on a stone, knees up to her chest, arms around her knees, gazing into the fire. "So," Terry said, "where are you headed?" A safe subject.

"Hot dog?" Sonia asked, putting a paper plate and a swollen, sizzling dog before her. They had enough paper and plastic for a landfill.

The girl took one bite, looked as if she was about to cry, and then took another. "Portland," she said. Then took another bite and reconsidered. "Maybe Southern California, if I can get that far."

Terry felt a pang. He'd suggested driving to L.A. in his secret wish to find his sister, but the group had responded by vetoing him. None of the radio rumors about L.A. were good, and since he didn't have a clue where Lisa was, he had to admit it would be a foolish plan. But maybe Kendra knew something.

"What's down in SoCal?" Terry said.

"Devil's Wake."

"Devil's what?" Dean asked.

"Devil's Wake," Piranha said. "One of the California Channel Islands. Might as well be Mars. Why so far, girl?"

"Supposed to be a colony," Kendra said. "Safe. I have an aunt there. My grandfather said if I could make it there, she'd be sure they took me in." She said "grandfather" as if the word hurt. A story for later, perhaps.

But a colony on an island and a ticket in? Terry's heart jumped, and Sonia hitched her eyebrow with an *I've heard worse ideas* expression. They'd all agreed that Vancouver Barracks was their destination, that the promise of guns and ammo outweighed any other plans, since any other plans would require more guns and ammo. During all of the hours he'd spent driving the Blue Beauty, lines blurring together on the interstate, he hadn't asked himself: *And then what?* None of them had.

"Well, Southern California is a long way," Terry said, keeping his voice neutral. "Tomorrow we'll make it to the Barracks, if we get lucky. And I feel lucky."

Whether or not he wanted to admit it, their original plan had seemed like a fantasy. Now that they were so close, Terry didn't think he would be able to sleep. He was sick of being afraid, and with more guns they could leave fear behind.

"Where's the Barracks?" Kendra said.

"Vancouver. Near Portland."

Kendra's eyes dropped to her food. "Portland wasn't lucky for me," she said. "I was there . . . when it started."

Piranha slapped off crumbs of his stale hot dog bun. "I make my own luck."

"Where do you guys sleep?" Kendra said. She shivered again, perhaps wary of his answer.

"On the bus," Terry said. "The seats are pretty wide, if you hang your feet off the side. The back is jammed up with food, but it's not too bad. And we close the door."

"I . . ." Kendra's eyes flew back and forth between them, helpless. She was willing to ride with strangers, but apparently not ready to close her eyes among them.

Sonia gripped her shoulder. "They look rough, but they're gentlemen. If they aren't, I'll kick their nuts up into their throats. You're safe."

Sonia's reassurance softened Kendra's face again. "I'd like that," Kendra said. "I'd like a little of that luck too."

Kendra seemed so young, so lost, that for a moment Terry was horrified at the new responsibility he'd just accepted. If he had driven past her, none of them might have objected, not even

Sonia. They had driven past so many people already. They'd looked like people, anyway.

He had stopped. *He* had decided to pick her up.

Terry surprised himself by leaning forward to kiss Kendra's forehead, the way he would have kissed Lisa's if he could. Her skin was cool and smooth beneath his lips. "I'm your luck, lady," Terry said, and the others groaned and rolled their eyes. Darius threw his paper plate at Terry Frisbee-style and bopped him on the forehead.

For the first time, Kendra smiled.

SIXTEEN

December 17

Kendra awakened slowly, hearing snoring. Her dreams had been . . . almost peaceful, but her waking body stiffened. Where was she?

No bed. Rows of narrow windows above her. *The bus,* she reassured herself, nearly breathless. She was on a bus.

The dawn was creeping west toward Idaho; darkness and night ruled. Once her surprise at her new surroundings passed— and the inevitable wave of sadness when she remembered why she wasn't at Grandpa Joe's cabin, or back in Longview—the peaceful feeling came back, stronger than before. What right did she have to feel peace?

She didn't know these people. Grandpa Joe had loved her like only family could, willing to kill or die to make sure she was safe. Strangers wouldn't do that.

Yet . . .

She hadn't seen other kids since the outbreak shut down her school, and now she and a bunch of kids were all on their way somewhere. They were taking action, not just hiding in the woods with the Dog-Lady, waiting for the world to shift back to normal while she ate Doggy Chow chili. *Won't you come over and wait with me, dear? And have a nice bowl of Rover while we listen to the shortwave?*

The kids' dog, whose name was Hipshot, lay on his side in the center aisle, almost inviting someone to step on him. The mutt slept with his head very near her dangling hand. As soon as Hipshot had accepted Kendra, the others had too. She owed him. Darius and Dean were curled up on seats opposite each other in the third row; she didn't trust them yet, and didn't think she would, no matter what Sonia said. Behind them, Piranha and Sonia were curled up together against a stack of boxes that filled the back of the Blue Beauty. Both asleep, snoring softly.

Sonia wasn't stupid, Kendra mused cynically; she'd landed her insurance policy. Kendra almost felt envious, wishing she'd found Piranha first. He looked strong, sounded smart. *But what would you have to do to keep him?* Kendra thought. She was a virgin, and she'd never known the secret to rocking a guy's world. Good for Sonia, then.

Kendra's eyes stopped on Terry. She could just see him from where she lay curled on his seat, just make out his tousled hair. He had a way of looking at her that got on her nerves, some combination of pity and amusement, but her irritation was a revelation. At least it was a feeling, and she hadn't allowed herself feelings since everything had gone wrong in Longview a lifetime ago.

She felt . . . hopeful.

I think I'm okay for now, Grandpa Joe. She tried not to see the terrible stranger with the red, hungry eyes. Instead, she imagined Grandpa Joe standing over his stove, scrambling a pan of eggs. *Breakfast.*

Kendra's heart stuttered, then peace came again. She rolled over and went back to sleep.

The next time Kendra opened her eyes, the morning was upon them, as Dad used to say. Daylight filtered hazily through the evergreens, giving the site Terry had chosen a dreamlike luster. Three abandoned cars were parked in the spaces, one empty sixteen-wheeler with a Foster Farms logo emblazoned on the side, parked sideways across several spaces. She tried not to imagine the driver slewing into the rest stop with something hanging on to the driver's side door from the outside.

An unexpected scent made Kendra sit bolt upright. Bacon? Eggs? It was almost as if visualizing Grandpa Joe could bring him back to life, just as Mom and Dad had claimed.

A face appeared in the bus's stairwell, the big bright-eyed brother they called Piranha. He reminded Kendra of her uncle Willie, only without the raucous laughter. She didn't let herself wonder where Willie was. "Wake up, Little Miss Thang," he said, his smile wide. "Powdered eggs, canned bacon, Kool-Aid. Let the wild rumpus begin."

Kendra's back was as stiff as a plank, but Piranha's enthusiasm was contagious. She checked her bundle of belongings and tucked them away under her seat. Everyone else was already off the bus. Her new companions had let her sleep in.

Kendra's mouth tasted like she'd gargled with pond scum, and she had an almost overwhelming urge to comb her hair before anyone else saw her. She figured that if she could survive what she'd been through, a morning of disarray wouldn't kill her. Without a toothbrush, maybe her breath would be bad enough to drive the freaks and pirates away.

Outside, the others were busy with breakfast. Darius, or perhaps Dean (she couldn't tell the difference between them yet), walked the outer edge of the circle, holding a rifle. He would walk a bit, then pause, rest perhaps, and then continue walking, scanning slowly left and right. He never really stopped looking out for anyone, or anything. Once, distantly, she heard the burr of a gasoline engine. Other than that, nothing. The quiet was eerie. Surreal.

"Where is everyone?" Kendra said.

"A lot are dead, I figure," Piranha said, as if it were a casual conversation about unimportant things. "Lots of the ones left went to camps. Must be some little towns, places the locals know about that are easier to fortify. They aren't gonna wave flags for us, that's for damned sure. They're keeping their profile way low."

One of the Twins laughed. Kendra noticed a pale vertical line through his right eyebrow; soon she would learn that his name was Darius, and the scar was a souvenir from a skateboarding accident. "I can see it, right?" He waved a shirt above his head. " 'Hey, here we are! Come take a bite or kill us to steal our crap.' "

Still laughing, he shoveled eggs into his mouth.

Sonia handed Kendra her plate. Sonia's goth black hair was brushed into a ponytail, and her mouth didn't reek, so she was grooming herself somehow. Kendra made a note to get a girl-friend's guide later.

"Here," Sonia said. "It's rotten, but there's plenty of it."

"Plenty and good are the same to me," Kendra said, and Sonia pounded her fist.

Kendra took the plate and sat, not knowing whether to sit

farther away from them or closer, not knowing what the rules were, desperate not to violate one unwittingly. She avoided all eye contact with Piranha so she wouldn't give Sonia even an imaginary reason to get jealous. What if one wrong move got her voted off the bus?

The eggs were lumpy, with a few coarse nuggets where the water hadn't soaked into the dehydrated powder before heating. The consistency of bad oatmeal, perhaps, but the taste was glorious. Kendra hadn't known how hungry she was until she realized she was scooping the food into her mouth from the plate. The bacon was even better, even though it wasn't bacon at all, but strips of fried SPAM. She decided that SPAM was her all-time favorite meat, that if pigs knew how delicious they were, they'd all turn cannibal. Having an armed guard nearby made the meal go down more smoothly.

"More, please?"

"Coming up," Terry said. He was having fun playing cook, dishing out scoops of steaming eggs while Sonia sliced and fried the SPAM over the other half of the fire. Kendra realized they hadn't merely found a barbecue pit; they'd dug the hole, filled it with wood, built their campfire. "How long have you been doing this?" she asked.

"Few months," Terry said. "All summer we were teaching kids how to survive in the woods. Came in handy."

"What happened at the camp?" she said.

They all exchanged looks, and Kendra almost told them to forget the question.

But Terry sighed. "Real nice couple ran the camp, Vern and Molly Stoffer . . ."

They told their stories, and listened to hers. About Portland General. And her parents. Grandpa Joe was too fresh, but she told a little about him too. The others mentioned family mem-

139

bers they hadn't heard from, or didn't know how to reach. Everyone had a story, except the Twins.

Then none of them felt like talking anymore.

Kendra nearly jumped when Sonia unexpectedly gave her a hug. "You poor thing," she said. "Can't believe you were out there by yourself."

"It's not just me," Kendra said, not wanting them to think she felt sorry for herself. "Something bad happened to everybody." Sonia's hug lingered, and Kendra wanted to pull away before she started crying. But she didn't.

"Once you're on our bus, you're not just 'everybody,'" Sonia said.

Kendra noticed Terry staring at them, almost as if he wanted to hug her too.

But cuddle time was over.

"Freak," Darius called in a low, calm voice from the parking lot.

Kendra wasn't sure she'd heard him right, until the others instantly dropped their plates, came to attention, and formed a circle around her. Their circle shifted to a horseshoe as they all scanned the parking lot, assessing the danger.

A single freak limped toward them. Grandpa had listened to every rumor or radio report, studying freak evolution like a zoologist. As a result, she knew that freaks started out fast—the runners, the most dangerous kind—but slowed down as days and weeks passed. This one might have been a couple of months old, lurching like a gauze-wrapped mummy. Its clothes were a shambles, but once upon a time they might have been overalls and a white checkered shirt. His head was big, and it looked as if birds had pecked on his right ear, now hanging halfway down his cheek. One eye socket was empty, but the other glared brightly.

140

"Coming straight for us," Darius said.

"Mine," Dean said, and leveled his rifle.

He was an excellent shot. The freak's head snapped back, and its feet went out from under him it as if it had slipped on ice. Brains sprayed around its head in a brownish-red nimbus. It kicked its feet a few times, and then was still. The Twins high-fived each other, cackling as if he'd bull's-eyed at the county fair.

"Let's not celebrate yet," Piranha said.

Terry agreed, dousing out the fire with a waiting bucket. "Where there's one . . ."

". . . there's a gaggle," Sonia finished. Despite her tough-girl act, Kendra noticed that Sonia never seemed to stray far from Piranha's shadow.

"What now?" Kendra said, her heart racing. She expected to see an army of freaks come charging from the woods.

Terry spread a road map on the ground, tracing it with his finger. "Let's see . . . We're here, twenty miles north of Vancouver. And we're heading . . . here. On Northwest Eleventh Avenue."

"How do we get there?" Darius said. Kendra realized that even when the Twins talked, they never stopped scanning their surroundings. Sonia and Piranha were gathering supplies to cart back into the bus. They all knew their jobs.

"Down the Five to what looks like the Columbia River," Terry said. "We'll cross into Oregon. I hope. Then another . . . I don't know. Five miles? And from there to maybe Southwest Alder Street."

A loud squeal and squawk from the bus startled Kendra. Someone fiddling with the radio, she realized. *Keep it calm, girl. They've got it handled.*

"Anything?" Terry called to the bus.

"Still static, mostly," Sonia said. "That crazy preacher. Not much else."

"Looks clear," Piranha said in a basso voice, and the group laughed with an inside joke Kendra didn't understand. Terry explained that Piranha liked to imitate Vin Diesel from the movie *Pitch Black*; Diesel had said everything "looked clear" right before all hell broke loose. The explanation didn't help Kendra feel like laughing.

"The rest of breakfast is to go," Terry said.

"No thanks," Kendra said. "I just lost my appetite."

"Hey, don't miss my chef's special," Terry said, grinning as he folded up his map. "Scrambled brains. With lead on the side."

More laughter. The Twins high-fived again.

Kendra felt herself trying to smile, but she fought it. How could she smile when her knees still felt weak from the sight of the shambling freak?

"You need serious help," Kendra told Terry.

Terry started to climb into the bus, then turned and looked at her over his shoulder. "That's the same thing my shrink said," he told her, sounding shocked. Then he winked.

The wink did it. Kendra smiled at Terry after all.

But she didn't smile for long. As the twins were unhooking their bikes, they heard the distant sound of a motorcycle engine with a bad muffler.

Everyone crowded the bus windows, watching the driveway from the interstate.

The engine grew closer and closer . . . and then faded away. Relief passed among them.

In five minutes, they were on the road.

SEVENTEEN

Cold December rain droplets spattered against the windshield, fogging their vision. They passed farmland, a dairy perhaps, and fields filled with weeds and dead crops. Nowhere was there a human being to be seen, although occasionally a freak listed in a field, like a drunk leaning into a high wind. Not moving, perhaps conserving energy. When they drove past, occasionally the things turned to watch.

Darius and Dean rode their motorcycles around and around the bus, scanning for trouble but also amusing themselves by weaving between stalled cars, making Kendra's heart jump every time they nearly collided. After a particularly harrowing near miss, they reached across the road to slap gloved palms.

Kendra sat near the front of the bus, near Terry, and she noticed that the gas tank was alarmingly low: a quarter of a tank! How had they traveled from upstate without any working gas stations? Memories of the gas pumps at Mike's made her shiver.

They had only been on the road fifteen minutes when Terry stopped at a clutch of abandoned cars blocking the lanes. The Twins had beaten them, circling the knot of cars. They waved to Terry. Kendra hoped that meant there were no freaks. And no pirates. The big bus squealed as it lurched to stillness, almost in protest. For a moment, no one moved or spoke.

"Gas 'n' go," Terry finally said. "Road also needs clearing. Careful, everybody. Let's not hang out here all day." The guy who'd joked about scrambled brains was gone.

Instructions given, Terry opened the bus doors.

Outside, Terry cradled the shotgun as the Twins examined the cars. Piranha stepped down too, revolver tight in his grip. Sonia carried the rifle. Kendra felt small and useless beside her outside the bus, as good as naked.

While Kendra watched, the others pried open gas tanks, hoses ready to siphon into red gas cans. Half the cars had stopped because they had run out of gas—the other half, who knew?

Two cars looked as if they had simply smacked together, and Kendra approached them slowly. The driver's side of the white Toyota was splashed with dried blood crawling with flies.

But the cars were empty.

What had happened here? Had one or both drivers been infected?

"Keys!" Darius called, and tried to start the engine of an SUV blocking their passage. A grinding protest, followed by clicks. "Battery's dead," he said.

"Can you get the brake off?" Piranha said.

"Yeah, but we flip," Darius said. "Heads, you push. Tails, I steer."

Kendra felt the mood easing now that they were in the road and hadn't been ambushed. Not yet, anyway. But Kendra kept

144

her eyes on the tree line, watching for anything that stirred. More than once, she was fooled by wind massaging the leaves.

At least one of them was always holding a gun on watch while the others pushed cars off the road. Kendra gathered enough nerve to open the door of a black PT Cruiser and look inside; the car reminded her of a miniature hearse.

Inside, she found children's clothes, a little red shirt, and blue striped pants. A sippy cup with a red conical cap, festooned with tiny tooth marks. "What happened here?" she asked again, aloud this time. Had Junior been bitten at the mall by a weird kid, and maybe fallen asleep in the backseat before they could get him to the doctor? Had he clawed his way out of his safety seat and attacked Mommy as she chatted on the cell phone, or Daddy as he drove? Was the family still wandering the roadway together?

Kendra wished she couldn't imagine those final horrific moments, but she could.

Kendra was thankful that there were no bodies.

But there was plenty of gas. By the time the siphoning was done, Terry said he would have enough to fill the hundred-gallon tank.

"What happens if you can't find fuel?" Kendra asked Terry while she watched him fit the gas can's nozzle into the huge tank. She was close enough to smell the morning's perspiration from his neck, not an unpleasant smell, considering.

"Then the party's over," Terry said. "We're on foot. It'll happen one day."

Kendra cringed at the thought.

They had to stop three more times to clear the road, and once made good use of the snowplow's blade when a Buick had no gas and the brakes were locked. The big black car groaned, its tires smearing dark skid marks across the asphalt.

"Let's hit the Barracks!" Terry said once they were back on the bus.

Kendra rediscovered her notebook. Everything in life moved so quickly, she was afraid she would misplace all the details. If she survived, she might one day make sense of it all—or at least have something to leave behind.

I made some new friends, she wrote. *We have a plan.*

Writing it down made it feel real.

EIGHTEEN

Kendra's Notebook

Today, we drove through a street so bare that no cars were in sight. Not trashed—empty. No garbage or burned cars. No bodies.

But we saw one person standing at the fork in the road.

She was a little girl, maybe twelve years old, standing with her arms at her side, almost like a soldier at attention. She had blond hair in pigtails, and she was wearing a dress she might have worn to a sixth-grade dance.

She didn't look right, standing alone in the road like that.

Look, there's a freak, somebody said.

Bets started flying about whether she'd be fast or slow, or if the bus could beat her in a race. On the bus, they laugh about everything, especially when they're nervous. But I didn't think she was a freak. I thought she could have been someone like me who needed rescuing.

And I was right. Sort of.

As the bus slowed, we saw the bite.

Before the freaks came, I would have thought she'd been bitten on the cheek and jaw by a pit bull like the Dog-Lady's. But we all knew she hadn't been bitten by a dog. And she hadn't changed yet, because her face looked like a regular little girl's except for her bite.

Was she in shock? Was she waiting for someone to stop?

By the time the bus drove past her, everyone was huddled at the windows, watching her. She never moved or looked anywhere except straight ahead. Had I looked the same way to them when they first saw me?

This time, Terry kept driving. Darius made a lame joke about an Amber alert, but no one laughed—not even Darius. Everybody got quiet.

I jumped when I heard the crack *of a gunshot echoing against the empty buildings, but I shouldn't have been surprised. Dean was leaning out of a rear window with a rifle. After one shot, Dean took his seat again. Darius patted his shoulder. Then Sonia. Then Piranha.*

Dean's eyes reminded me of the girl in the road.

The bad feeling didn't seize Kendra until after the I-5 split just above a town called Salmon Creek, and the bus took the right-hand fork. The sensation was like waking from a dream . . . or slipping back into a nightmare. Kendra remembered these roads from her trip in to the hospital . . . when? How long ago had that been? It seemed like years, and yet the journey was as familiar as yesterday.

This is not a good idea, she thought.

All Grandpa Joe had drummed into her head was how she should keep far away from the cities. Now it seemed like a miracle that their bus had been able to travel as far as it had without meeting an impassable barrier or an overwhelming attack. With every creeping mile, Kendra's belly contracted into a tighter knot.

Vancouver, Washington, was at first a residential stretch and then a downtown district, all broken windows and deserted buildings. She hoped so, anyway. She vaguely remembered hearing about an orderly evacuation of Vancouver, back when she and Mom had monitored the radio together. Once or twice she thought she saw a face pressing against a glass window, watching them, perhaps wondering who it was who still drove, however slowly, along these haunted roads. They left the freeway at Exit 1D, wound past stalled cars onto Fourth Plain, then turned left onto a narrow street called Neals, lined with abandoned cars and broken windows.

The closer they drove to the Barracks, the more Kendra felt the temperature rising in the bus, the heat of combined adrenaline. Kendra caught herself holding her breath as she stared out the window, waiting.

The streets were now so narrow and twisty, they seemed to have been designed to thwart terrorists driving trucks loaded with fertilizer bombs. Expansive green lawns had gone shaggy, covered with trash and a few sprawled corpses. Nothing alive and human could be seen amid the cluster of beige and pale gray bungalows and two-story barracks buildings. A freak or two could be glimpsed in the wavering distance. One of them turned toward the bus and took a step or two in their direction before the Blue Beauty wove out of sight. One of the Twins zipped past them on his motorcycle, pulling into a graveled road walled by portable cyclone fence. There was lots of that fencing, a ragged maze. Someone had attempted to set up aisles or sections, perhaps for different categories of refugees.

The grass was high and wild, without the telltale footprints that might have indicated frequent visitors.

The bus was quiet. What had they expected? Cheering throngs? Laughing children? Whatever they had expected, this wasn't it.

149

The bus pulled up behind the Twins, along a graveled path into a trash-strewn parking lot. There were four cars, a blue Chevy pickup, and an RV, all deserted. A brownish-red smear marred the pickup's passenger door.

The Blue Beauty sighed to a stop.

It looked as if they had stumbled onto an aged liberal arts campus, perhaps the day after homecoming, headaches and hangovers keeping the coeds tucked in their beds.

Directly to their left was a two-story barracks building, the windows shattered like those in Vancouver. The Twins' bikes were already parked. Dean had pulled his jacket up to cover his nose and mouth. Neither of the Twins waved the all-clear sign. Instead, Darius only exaggerated a hell-if-I-know shrug.

"Really helpful, thanks," Terry muttered, his face grimmer than Kendra had seen. Angry. If he'd looked that way when they first met, she might have been afraid of him.

As soon as the bus's door opened, the smell hit them. The air was heavy with a garbage-pail scent. Rotting meat.

"Stay close," Terry said. "Nobody get lost, in case we haul out in a hurry."

"You *will* be left behind," Piranha said, mostly to himself, although Terry was sure he was talking to the new girl, Kendra. Piranha had confided to him that he wasn't willing to risk himself for a stranger—even a *sister,* as he'd called Kendra. *Last in, first out,* the big guy had said. Terry had hoped to avoid that test, but they might be facing it now.

He'd tried to be realistic. Without radio broadcasts, he hadn't expected the Barracks to provide soldiers or protection. But it already looked and smelled a hell of a lot worse than he'd expected.

150

"You ready?" Piranha's eyes were tight and scared, just like his own.

Terry nodded, although he wasn't ready. This might be their worst day in a long time. Hell, it might be their *last*.

Ravens concealed behind abandoned cars and Porta Potties burst into the air only a few yards from where he parked the bus. They circled, then settled back down. Dozens of huge, overfed black birds began pecking as if someone had scattered handfuls of seed or bread crumbs. But the stench told Terry a different story. Hipshot scratched at the ground and whined.

Human bodies in various stages of decomposition lay everywhere—on the main building's steps, in the parking lot, crumpled in the grass. One of his teachers had taught them about Jonestown back in the 1970s, and the sight reminded Terry of that mass suicide in Guyana.

But he couldn't stare at the bodies long. Hipshot barked sharply, and Terry's head whipped up.

The barefoot man in olive drab military fatigues fooled Terry for half a second, speeding his heart with hope . . . until Terry noticed his odd limp. This was a *slow* freak, thank God. He was thirty yards back, close to the shadow of the headquarters, but a runner would have been on them already.

"Limper," Terry said in a low voice, just as Sonia chambered a round into her shotgun.

"I've got this one," Sonia said in a low, flat voice, and let fly with the Mossberg. The report was loud and vicious, but she missed. A few shots dimpled the ravaged face, but most spattered into the beige building behind him, scattering flecks of wood and paint. The freak ignored the shot and continued toward them.

"Damn, girl," Piranha said. "That all you got?"

Sonia snorted, and reshouldered the shotgun.

"Don't jerk the trigger," Piranha said. "Squeeze. Aim for center of mass."

"Why?" Kendra asked, huddling close. "I thought it had to be head shots."

When Piranha didn't answer, Terry spoke low to Kendra's ear. "Those are harder. Sonia needs the target practice."

Another shot. The freak spun around, staggered, went down to one knee, then came on again, only a dozen or so paces from Darius, who was watching with great interest, idling his engine. Sonia's next shot burst its head like a rotten watermelon. It dropped, quivered, and then was still.

Darius applauded sardonically. "Nice, but help the environment and conserve rounds next time! Swap you," he said. He buckled a sheathed machete to his belt and exchanged his rifle for her shotgun. "We is goin' indoors, and the Mossberg is the *perfect* home defense weapon."

"This ain't home," Dean said.

"Not to *us,* maybe."

He hopped off the bike. "Yoo-hoo! Trick or treat!"

The nearest building's exit doors were chipped, its glass broken like that of so many windows. Still, Terry propped the door open with a large stone so they could get out fast. An escape route. Terry glanced at Darius, who nodded. He'd stay outside as a lookout. Hipshot thrust his nose inside, made a deep growling sound, but took a couple of halting steps.

"Hello! Anyone here?" Terry stuck his head through the open doorway. For some reason it smelled better inside than outside. "Let's go."

The halls within were cluttered with trash, flyers, and chunks of colored cardboard. Terry picked up one of the flyers, which said: *Eyes open!!! The disease transmits through blood and possibly other body fluids!!! If you are bitten or scratched, immediately seek medical assistance!!!*

Piranha leaned the tip of his machete against the wall and read over Terry's shoulder. "Yeah, as if there was a vaccine. Can you imagine the morons who turned themselves in? 'Hey, is this where ya'll go for the vitamins?'" His backwoods twang even goosed a snicker out of Kendra. Damn. He'd thought that well had run dry.

"Yeah, good luck with that," Terry said.

Kendra stopped and stared up at a poster of an attractive but severe-looking black woman in gray-white camos saying *"Military OneSource is an excellent pool of information for our soldiers and families. Use it—I did!"*

She had no idea what a "Military OneSource" might be, but wondered if it had, on Freak Day, actually turned out to be an excellent source of information for this woman's family. She sure hoped so.

Dean was ignoring them, watching Hipshot nosing about the paper- and glass-strewn floor.

"Wonder what the hell happened here," Dean said. He flipped his hair out of his eyes with his left hand, keeping his rifle close with the other.

"That smell again," Sonia said, wrinkling her nose. "Not close by. But . . ."

"Yeah, try that morgue in the parking lot," Piranha said.

Sonia shook her head. "Not behind us. Ahead of us."

Terry caught the sour odor then. There were definitely more corpses nearby. "Kendra . . . stay close."

Kendra nodded, walking practically hip to hip. She wouldn't wander off, and she'd sworn she knew how to handle her .38. Time would tell.

Hipshot led the way, sniffing as he went. The tile beneath their feet was dark brown, the doors lining the halls marked with papers reading HAVE YOU SIGNED UP FOR FOOTBALL? And bonuses still available for overseas duty. And the buddy system: sign together, serve together. It was all so strange. If not for the deserted, trash-strewn halls, this might have been any ordinary day.

"Hold up." Piranha raised his hand. Hipshot had stopped, cocking his narrow head sideways. "I heard something."

"Close?" Terry said.

"Not sure."

The late afternoon's sunlight washed through the halls, giving them a wan, faded impression, almost like a watercolor. They walked slowly, pausing while one or another checked each door, and Hippy waited for them, whining softly. They didn't want any surprises from behind. One of the doors was locked. The rest were offices with overturned chairs and desks, papers in disarray.

Someone had moved out in one hell of a rush. Together, they climbed a narrow flight of badly painted stairs. At the first landing more patriotic posters were plastered on the wall. One called the Army Reserve *"The Essential Provider for Training and Support Operations, Engaged Worldwide with Ready Units and Soldiers."*

Yeah, well . . . Army Strong or not, they hadn't been ready for *this*.

Just at the top of the stairs, Sonia stopped, pointed at the tile. "Here," she said, pointing at the floor. "Blood."

Dean shone his Eveready down at an umber smear.

"More of it over here," Dean said. He pointed out bullet holes in an erratic pattern across a door with a broken lock. "Bad juju, man."

"No one here. Judging by the Porta Potties, the fences, there used to be."

As Piranha checked another door, Terry noticed that Kendra stepped back, raised her pistol as if someone had taught her how to use it properly. Good. There was definitely something sexy about a chick who could watch your back.

Piranha whistled, and then he and Dean crossed the threshold, disappearing into the room. Silence for a couple of seconds, then Dean said, "Empty."

They backed out, guns still at the ready, and continued down the hall, checking doors as they went.

The hall ended in an L-turn, and they headed to the left and through a door. Another office, this one strewn with papers, the walls cluttered with posters, photographs of dozens of fine young men standing in groups, perhaps preparing for deployment to Okinawa, West Germany, Iraq. The black-and-white images were dated back to 1943, color photos beginning in the mid-fifties. World War II? Korea?

"Antenna," Piranha said. He pointed the machete at a white-door brick two-bedroom across the way. Beside it stood a hundred-foot red radio tower.

The white door had been crushed in. Windows broken. Crows rustled in the entrance.

"This is starting to get just a little depressing," the big guy said.

"Stay frosty," Terry said. He remembered the line from *Aliens*.

"Stop," Dean said. "I think I heard something."

It was just a rustling at first, but that faint crackling-leaf sound was followed by something louder, more definite. Footsteps. Slightly heavy and disconnected, as if something about the walker's balance was a little off. Steady and slow.

"That's . . . not good," Sonia whispered.

The office was connected by a simple door to another room farther on, as if a suite of offices was laid out parallel to the hallway. By mutual, silent agreement, none of them wanted to

155

go out in that hall. Hipshot's floppy ears were plastered back against his head. His eyes burned, but he made no sound, save for his nails clicking against the tile floor. Then, not even that.

The windows to the inner halls were frosted, only shadows of greater and lesser depth visible to them. At first, the dimming light from the distant outer windows was faint but unbroken. Then, a shape appeared in the glass. Tall, probably male, shuffling forward a halting step at a time. It stopped, perhaps turned. He couldn't quite tell. If the freak had turned in their direction, it would be looking directly through the frosted glass.

None of them moved, not even Hipshot. The freak said something. They couldn't make it out the first time, but then it repeated itself.

"Coffee, black," it said. And then again, *"Coffee, black."*

Then it continued its shuffling way down the hall. Terry was just noticing himself exhale when a smaller shadow darkened the glass. Just the top of a head this time. If the rest of the body was to proportion, then that might have been a child. Following its father?

Two sets of clumsy footsteps, one heavy and one light, continued down the hall, and then were gone.

Kendra spoke first, softly. "Can we be sure those were what we think they were?"

"You want to yodel and find out?" Piranha was holding his machete so tight that his knuckles had paled.

"There's nothing here," Dean said. "Let's get out."

"Good idea," Terry said. "Through the door."

They continued through the linked offices, stepping around overturned chairs and desks, on into the next room, where the honey-rot odor of decomposition smacked them in the face.

Once, not too long before, it had been a woman's body. Now

156

it was just a mannequin-shaped bag of rotting meat. She had been blond, thin, and wearing a down-filled blue jacket. The white filling was now scattered, torn free, and matted with blood. Bite-size chunks had been wrenched from her cheeks and throat. What had once been her nose was now just a gaping maw in the middle of her face, blue eyes gazing out at them with a dull incuriosity beyond the need for questions and answers.

It had taken more than a few friendly nibbles to reduce a woman to this condition. Parts of her were simply *gone,* sundered by hands and teeth. Intestines, dried and fly-blown, extruded from a gash in her middle like fat, floppy shoelaces.

She was pushed up against the wall, as if she had died trying to escape, and her killers hadn't even bothered dragging her into the middle of the floor before they began to feed.

"I thought they just took bites," Kendra said.

"The fast ones," Dean said, his voice like wind blowing across a cold, wet hole. "The slow ones seem to have a heartier appetite."

Terry kept expecting the dead woman's eyes to follow them as they left. But no, they remained fixed as they crossed the room and exited. And would remain so until they were eaten or dried and sunk deep into the ravaged skull.

It took less than a minute to find the rear fire escape, and, climbing down, they found themselves in a grassy acre dotted with thin trees and ringed by low drab buildings. Sonia's nose wrinkled. No bodies in sight, but . . .

"Whatever I was smelling," she said, "it's closer."

She was right. Terry pinched his nose. His brain urged him to run back the way he'd come. A whining Hipshot now bringing up the rear, they circled the building and picked up Darius, who despite his best efforts to seem blasé was happy to see them.

"What now?" Darius said. "Still looking for weapons? Place looks stripped."

"Over there," Terry said, and pointed at a pair of beige bungalows. Rectangles on the sides might have been garage doors, except there were no driveways leading to them.

"Doors still look locked. Maybe we'll get lucky."

They passed through a gate in the hurricane fencing and crossed the grass walking in a rough circle, scanning in all directions, and Dean was the first to reach the nearest bungalow. Terry had been wrong about the lock: it was broken, and the inside, wide enough to park three limos, was a mess of torn boxes and gnawed wrappers. Nothing useful here.

But the second building had heavy, reinforced doors, and the locks and chains to match. Dean put his crowbar in and twisted, grunting and straining. When he couldn't break it, Piranha helped him. But although they groaned until they were breathless, the thumb-thick links held strong.

Terry paced, watching. The weapons had to be in there. *Had* to be.

Piranha broke his attention. "Ah . . . I think we're a little far from Blue Beauty. Maybe bring her a little closer?"

Was thirty yards too far? Well, yeah, if a freak flock descended.

"Think I should drive the bus around?" Terry said.

Dean and Piranha scanned the grass, which was broken by the trees and fences. The crowbar dropped with a clang on the concrete lip of the storage bunker, and Piranha leaned against the door to catch his breath.

"I think that might be the smartest thing you've said today."

The steering wheel twisted in Terry's hands as the Blue Beauty hit the fence. The snowplow sheared the lock and chain, and chunks of segmented metal pole went flying. Through the bug-spattered windshield he watched his group cheer. They seemed happy to have something to cheer about.

"Good girl!" he said, and patted the wheel. "That's it. Good girl."

But his euphoria dimmed when the bus sputtered, threatening to choke, before the engine sounded right again. Terry had heard that sound once before. Maybe it was just a warning: *You better treat me right.*

Coaxing quietly, Terry turned the Blue Beauty around and brought it to a stop. Then he stopped, opened the doors, and hopped out, grinning. "World's biggest lock pick," he said.

While Terry inspected the bus for damage, Dean swung his crowbar in a looping arc and approached the nearest bungalow. The double doors of an attached garage or storage unit were locked and chained. "Heavy," Dean said. "But the weak point will be where they screwed in the latch. I'm puttin' my money . . . *here*."

He wedged the crowbar between the latch plate and the wooden door and leaned his weight on the bar. It took three tries before the screws groaned in protest and began shredding the surrounding wood. Another two pulls and the lock and chain disintegrated.

Piranha entered first, his flashlight splashing around in the darkened chamber. He let out a long, low whistle. "Oh, baby!"

"Guns?" Terry asked hopefully, scrambling behind him.

"Nope, but almost as good."

The vault was piled with boxes, about half of them labeled MRE. Terry chafed from his disappointment about the guns, but could barely believe his eyes.

"MRE?" Kendra said. "What's that?"

"Meals Rejected by Everybody," Piranha said. "Actual translation: decent chow. I had a cousin in the service, and he used to get 'em all the time and they last, like, longer than herpes. He was on the Ways and Means Committee: that means he always found a way. Let's cart 'em to the bus."

"Let's keep our eyes open for the guns first," Terry said. The storage unit was crammed to the top with boxes, as if it had been packed tight—except for a space good for maybe three boxes on the right aisle. Maybe someone had been shopping.

"Pipe dream, man," Piranha said quietly. "Do I really have to say it?"

Terry's jaw tightened as if he were trying to crack a walnut with his teeth. "We're a long way from done here."

The aisles between stacks of boxes were just wide enough for a heavy-duty hand truck, a working specimen of which they found leaning against the back wall.

"Let's check out the other unit," Terry said. He grabbed the crowbar, and jogged over.

The third bungalow was only twenty feet away, but Terry felt exposed, with a strong sense that they were being watched.

The third storage unit was locked but not chained, and Terry should have known something then. The door was fastened with a compact Abus combination lock. The latch was scratched and bent, as if the lock and latch had been worked quickly and sloppily, many times. Terry set the pry bar, and after a few grunts the Abus clattered to the ground.

"Damn," Terry said, plugging his nose as the door opened. "'Bout this time I wish I'd skipped breakfast."

As the door opened the stench rolled out at them like a wave of acrid smoke. Sonia was the only one who hadn't jumped back, staring at what she had probably known all along.

Piranha looked like he was about to throw up but managed to choke it back. He turned sideways, grabbing the door by one hand.

The air was clotted with flies, the storage unit crammed with human bodies. The ground swarmed with ants and little black beetles. The syrupy decomposition stench clung to their skin and clothes like a living thing. Dozens of rotting corpses, well over a hundred. Just as in the MRE unit, they were stacked with excessive neatness, in rows.

A second, more careful look caused Terry to adjust his initial impression. True, the first layers, in the back of the storage unit, seemed to have been carefully arranged. But the upper levels and those farther to the front told another story. These were more carelessly stacked, almost discarded. As if the person or persons responsible had begun soberly and carefully and become progressively drunken. Or deranged.

"But . . ." Sonia was motionless by the door, body and mind frozen in place. Hipshot took one sniff and backed off. Damned pooch had more sense than any of them.

"We saw the blood," Terry said. "And the damage. What did we think?"

"Same shit," Dean muttered, and wrapped a kerchief around his face, trying a quick knot behind his head.

"Same as what?" Terry asked.

Dean glared at him. "Nothing," he said. Terry would have bet skin Dean was lying when he said that, but wasn't sure exactly what he was lying about.

"Breathe through your mouth," Darius said. "It's better."

"Right," Piranha said. "We choose between smelling it and chewing it."

Dean slipped on gloves that matched Darius's and ventured a few feet into the tomb to drag one of the bodies out into the light. It was a civilian, a blue-skinned, balding man who'd looked like a fiftyish Arby's manager before someone had ripped out his throat, as well as pieces of arm and a fist-size chunk of belly.

Kendra looked at her feet, and Terry followed her gaze. They were standing on some kind of sand. Of course! It was the same sort of absorbent material used in auto shops to soak up oil, but this time for blood. Terry noticed trails where bodies had been dragged over the grass, shoved into the darkness before the doors closed.

"One thing we know," Terry said. "The freaks didn't put 'em in here."

"Not unless they're evolving," Piranha said. If he was joking, he didn't seem amused.

The corpse Dean had dragged out was clad in a Portland State University sweatshirt, now tie-dyed with blood.

In a flash, Terry knew what had happened. The epidemic had ravaged Portland. Survivors and refugees had gathered here, believing they'd found a haven. *Kind of like us,* Terry thought, swallowing hard.

Something had gone wrong, and sanctuary had devolved to slaughter. How many shrieking refugees had transformed into freaks? How many corpses were there? This storage area held more than a hundred, easy, and there were dozens of bungalows and houses in the Vancouver Barracks complex, and each might conceal a similar cache. What kind of man had stayed here after the fall, stacking up those bodies so carefully? Someone had to be healthy and strong to do all of this work . . .

"Took more than one to do this," Piranha said, reading Terry's mind.

Hipshot was barking, louder and louder now. And in between the sharp canine sounds they heard the first moans.

NINETEEN

The sound seemed to be coming from everywhere, and nowhere. Outside. Floating across the grass, between the trees.

Terry's mind raced. He hadn't met freaks who made a lot of sound, but he knew they made familiar noises and even *talked,* especially the fresh ones. The fast ones. Piranha's absurd words seized his mind: *Unless they're evolving.* But there was no way. They got slower and hungrier and died. Didn't they? They sure as hell didn't stack their kill in lockers.

But they did hunt in packs.

"Ah . . ." Kendra said, nudging. "Time to go."

"Can't leave all these MREs," Piranha said.

Terry also couldn't imagine leaving without more guns and ammo, although he didn't say so. His mind mapped out a plan as they moved toward the light, away from a bungalow wall where they could be herded with nowhere to run. "Okay . . . best shots—"

"That's us," Dean said, and raised his rifle to his shoulder.

"Let's just *go*," Kendra said, nearly whining.

Piranha leaned close. "You. Shut. Up." She seemed to pale in his shadow, as if she knew he would abandon her if it would make the tiniest smidgen of difference to his own survival.

Terry wished Piranha would go easier on her, but even Sonia was too busy checking her weapon to worry about Kendra's hurt feelings. "Take the defensive perimeter," Terry told the Twins. "Get 'em from a distance, if you can."

"Easier to say," Dean said. "They've gotta be close enough for head shots."

Terry's mind soaked up the scenario, spitting him ideas. "Take the fast ones, let the slow ones get closer before you shoot. I'll move the Beauty up close enough to load the boxes, but we can't obscure the view."

"Anything else, Daddy?" Darius said.

"Yeah," Terry said. "Don't get us killed."

Kendra trotted behind him like a puppy, practically clinging to his shirt. The plan set, he finally turned to look at her. "You stay with me," he said.

Kendra looked like she wanted to hug him.

Terry and Piranha were the strongest, so they hauled boxes out of the storage garage. Armed with two rifles and a shotgun, Darius, Dean, and Sonia faced east and west and south, with the bungalow itself protecting the north. Kendra used a dolly to wheel the boxes to the bus, where Piranha had opened up the side luggage compartment. Together, they slung the boxes in, then new boxes atop the old.

The approaching moans sounded hungry. Almost . . . angry. Definitely getting louder. Where the hell were they hiding?

"Freaks!" Darius screamed, and Terry looked up as the first of them approached from the direction of the radio antenna, moving fast. A lone runner, swiftly followed by two more. Shit.

"How many?" Terry said.

"Enough."

Darius dropped to one knee, steadied himself, and aimed at the oncoming horrors. He fired. The first one down was barefoot, wearing overalls and nothing else. Darius's first shot took him directly in the center of the head, and his feet went out from underneath him like a roller skater running into a tree branch.

Piranha froze beside Terry, watching the approach.

Two . . . five . . . and now a dozen runners, with something else behind them . . . a small army of shuffling ghouls, some barely able to move, but all of them starving for flesh. Sonia standing, Dean kneeling. Firing, breathing, firing, breathing. Slow and steady, just like they'd practiced at Round Meadows.

The first wave of freaks reached the fence. At first they were stymied, then spread like oil on water, swiftly finding the gap Blue Beauty had plowed in the line. The howling horde ran and staggered on. Most were bare-handed, but some carried branches, wooden slats, metal pipes. They didn't wield these implements with anything like grace or skill, seemed almost to tote them from some dim memory of a previous tool-using incarnation.

The gunfire sounded like a war. If they didn't find ammunition, they'd be breathing fumes by the time they left here.

"Too many," Piranha said. "We gotta go, man. Maybe we'll come back."

"Keep loading," Terry said. "If Dean or Sonia need help, they'll say so."

Piranha gave him a hard look: *Are you out of your mind?* But he trusted Terry enough to keep loading. Kendra ran out two loads on the dolly while Piranha slung them into the undercarriage. The smell of rotting flesh was temporarily masked by the stench of gunfire.

Suddenly, Kendra went to stone. She stared at the oncoming army, eyes wide and arms wrapped around her waist.

"I said *keep moving*!" Terry roared at her. "Don't look."

He knew why she was staring, why her mind might be breaking. Terry had tried to be ready for a sight like this, but he realized there was no way to get ready.

The fastest freaks were also the smallest. The most newly made.

Children.

If Kendra blurred her eyes a bit—and she didn't know how they weren't already blurred with tears—she could imagine that the children running toward them were playing some kind of game. They weren't close enough to reveal the red-rimmed eyes or the blood-crusted teeth. The howls could have been a Halloween pantomime, merely some ghoulish playtime.

But what Kendra *felt* was as shocking as what she saw. She didn't care if they had once been children. God help her, she wanted to see them fall, bleed. Die. The thought of those small hands clutching at her, the cupid mouths seeking kisses . . .

Every time an infected child stumbled and flew face-first into the asphalt, her heart sang.

Get them, she thought, and this time tears burned her cheeks. *Kill them all.*

As if a prayer were being answered in the thunder of gunfire, the smaller ones fell until all of the fast ones were down, leaving the surging tide rolling over them.

Kendra was shaking, all the more for realizing that the others were getting a kind of charge too, far different from the primal, visceral fear that swamped her. Adrenaline baked off Terry in waves of heat, the corners of his mouth turned up in a Reaper's

166

smile almost as frightening as the creatures shuffling toward them. How could he feel anything other than horror?

She resolved to riddle him that when they had time. *If* they had time.

The luggage compartment was crammed now. Whatever they had expended in the week since leaving the Olympic forest area had been more than replenished.

"Let's move!" Piranha said. "We can't waste ammo trying to get 'em all."

Hipshot barked agreement and jumped up into the stairwell, back into the bus.

Terry cursed with a cry of frustration. "There's ammo here somewhere!"

"We don't know that, and we don't have time to search," Piranha said. "Will you move? That damned dog has more sense than you."

The *bang! bang! bang!* of the rifles was more a series of body blows than merely a series of sounds.

A female freak was only fifty feet away, moving slowly but steadily, as if impervious to bullets. Her dress was riddled with bright red holes, but no head shot yet.

Nothing about this situation felt right. Why the hell hadn't they fled as soon as they realized the freaks were coming? That question led to a queasy revelation: something dangerous was playing out between Terry and Piranha. The bigger man grabbed Terry's shoulders and Terry shoved him away.

The nearest freak finally went down, but there was a wave behind him, at least a hundred creatures lurching and moaning like a haunted wind through a forest of skeletal trees. "We have got to *go,* man!" Piranha said.

Kendra realized she hadn't seen anyone else drive the bus. Was Terry the only one who knew how?

"There's a bunch of other buildings!" Terry said, arguing with Piranha as if he couldn't see death marching their way.

"Probably full of corpses—you wanna join 'em?"

Sonia let out a yell that was more like a shriek. "They're getting closer. And there's more fast ones!"

Terry and Piranha were nearly wrestling, suddenly, a sight nearly as horrifying as the freaks. "Man, don't make me knock you the hell out!" Piranha said, fist curling.

Terry's face was suddenly bright red, and Kendra saw tears in his eyes.

"There has to be more here!" Terry said. "We came all this way! *All this way! There has to be more than this!*" He screamed the last words, drowning out the gunfire.

Kendra had been right to want to leave. Even Piranha saw it now. Piranha still made Kendra nervous, but she suddenly grabbed Terry's arm, pulling hard, hoping he would look at her. He did.

For the first time, Kendra really *saw* Terry. She didn't know his last name, like he didn't know hers, but she suddenly *knew* him. This standoff wasn't about finding supplies. Terry had masked his terror, compressing it behind a steely resolve. And now that the dream had died, there was a part of him that was just like she had been before they had driven up in the Blue Beauty. He was ready to give up, but not by curling up the way she had; he wanted to die like a fighter, in a blaze of glory. And his friends, even Piranha, trusted him so much that they risked dying at his side.

But she wouldn't. Not today.

"Maybe you're ready to die, but I'm not," Kendra said. "You don't think I know how hope hurts? My own *grandfather* tried to kill me! My parents are dead, or worse than dead." She fought to keep her voice strong, almost lost it, then pushed through the emotion. "But this isn't the only place left. If we stay here, we'll all die. Let's go while we still can."

Her words exhausted her. Kendra fell against Terry, clutching at him, mostly to keep standing upright. Terry pulled away from her. Then he didn't. She felt his arm wrap around her, holding on too.

When she looked up at his face, he was blinking like the people on the newscasts back in the early days, when no one understood anything anymore and no one could explain.

"We're pulling out!" Piranha said. Darius and Dean fell back to the bus, popping off final, head-shattering shots as they did. Their bikes were a world away, in the parking lot. Sonia and Kendra piled into the Blue Beauty behind them, then Piranha, and Terry last, with a final longing look at the warehouse. She felt his pain. The other lockers might have been filled with death. Or with food. Or ammunition. They would never know.

Terry took the wheel and turned the Blue Beauty around, too slowly for Kendra's taste, in a circle large enough that the first of the new freaks had reached it by the time they were headed back toward the fence.

With terrifying animal ferocity, men, women, and children hurled themselves at the bus, scrabbled toward the windows, mindless of the risk to their bodies. An older, rotting freak stared face-to-face with Kendra at her window, eyes so encrusted with a red rot that she didn't know how it could see.

Terry yanked the wheel sharply to the right, grinding the engine. Something splattered against the windshield, followed by a jarring thump against the bumper that caught Kendra by surprise. She looked back, and Sonia was gagging. Hipshot was standing on the seat, looking out at the carnage as if even a dog could be appalled by the sight of so much bizarre death.

Terry picked up speed, careening back toward the broken fence that would lead to the parking lot, the waiting bikes, and the freedom and life of the open road.

"Wait!" Darius screamed.

They all swiveled their heads around, trying to see what could be more important than outrunning a horde of freaks.

Two new freaks in olive drab and boots were running out of the rear door of the main building, the building they had explored and abandoned. The smaller one wore a backpack. Both carried rifles over their heads, pumping them up and down frantically, almost as if to catch Terry's attention. Shouting toward the bus. Strange behavior for freaks . . .

Kendra's heart caught in her throat when she realized the newcomers were . . . *National Guard!*

"Human!" Sonia screamed before Kendra could make a sound.

"They waited too long!" Piranha said. "Keep driving. Get the bikes."

"Can't leave 'em," Terry said.

Terry steered with such a wild turn that Kendra nearly fell out of her seat.

As they watched the soldiers, the smaller one stumbled, and the larger helped him up. Before Terry could wheel the bus back around, slewing in an S-turn, the freaks were on the larger soldier while he hacked and clubbed at them with the rifle. The smaller one stumbled toward the bus, nearly losing his balance, never dropping his rifle.

Terry opened the doors with a pneumatic hiss. When Kendra gazed back at the bigger soldier, the freaks had engulfed him like sharks swarming a sailor. *But they're busy with him instead of us,* Kendra thought, not wanting to.

The Twins fired out of the bus through slitted windows.

Kendra watched Piranha and Sonia drag the smaller soldier into the bus. The doors closed.

The bus roared out of the courtyard, bouncing over the broken fence.

The smaller soldier was sobbing: "Mickey! Mickey!"

The soldier was a woman.

TWENTY

No one spoke for at least five miles while the soldier sobbed, a keening cry that Kendra remembered too well—the sound of losing everyone. Everything. The soldier had been fortunate to find Terry and the Blue Beauty, but she didn't know it yet. How could she?

Armed only with machetes, Darius and Dean had recovered their bikes and roared off ahead of the Beauty, heading south. The roads were clear for a while, as if to give her a peaceful passage.

They all needed peace. Kendra's bones vibrated with the memory of the freaks chasing them down at the armory. She had never seen so many in one place, never imagined that anyone could survive being swarmed by them. In her mind, she still heard the battering against the bus, like a rain of fist-size hailstones. She didn't realize she was shaking until it stopped, her limbs magically falling still.

She thought about her notebook, but there were some things writing couldn't help.

Kendra gravitated to the seat directly behind Terry, where she sometimes saw his stonelike profile and watched his concentration in the curved mirror above them as he drove.

The soldier held tightly to her rifle near the back, in the seat Kendra had chosen at first. Her finger hovered close to the trigger, eyeing them all so suspiciously that none of them dared get too close. Kendra hoped she wouldn't start shooting in a fog of grief and rage. The soldier was brown-skinned, with a slight Asian caste to her face, as if she had Mayan blood. Her hair was cut quite short, and it occurred to Kendra that in other circumstances the girl would have been thought beautiful. A gold-on-green eagle insignia graced the right shoulder of her khaki shirt.

Her tear-smeared face was anything but beautiful now. Like the rest of them, she was far too young. No older than twenty-one, eyes already red-rimmed with grief. Piranha was studying the woman from where he sat across from her, his brow furrowed while Sonia stroked his cheek. Piranha had put his machete aside and had his finger on his trigger too.

By the time the clear stretch ended, the soldier was drying her eyes with the heels of her hands, as if trying to push her tears back. The Blue Beauty had slowed to about five miles an hour, weaving between cars, pushing a Harley-Davidson out of the way. There was a body trapped beneath the motorcycle, but Kendra barely noticed it. Crows flew up, squawking with indignation. Hipshot's bark fogged a cracked window as the birds circled and landed again behind them, undisturbed.

"It was Mickey's idea," the soldier finally said.

"What was Mickey's idea?" Piranha said.

"Joining you," she said bitterly. The girl had the trace of a Hispanic accent. She refused to look any of them in the eye.

174

There was a defiant tilt to her face, a strength to her jaw that fit the uniform. But then there was something else, hiding deeper within, something very feminine held almost at arm's length, as if softness were a snare. "We were safe, hiding in Admin."

"You were in there when we were?" Piranha asked, skeptically.

"We heard you tromping around, yeah," she said, a spark of malice in her voice. "Surprised we didn't hear you screaming and dying too."

Silence, for a few moments. No one asked the obvious question: *Why didn't you talk to us?*

"Then Mickey says, 'We should go with them. Let's be with people.'"

"We could have used some help," Piranha said, not sounding sympathetic. "Why didn't you come out sooner?"

The soldier laughed, a short, ugly sound. "That's what Mickey wanted. We didn't know who you were. What you wanted. I said we were doing fine, we didn't need you. We had food, shelter, weapons. Everything we needed, and we gave up all of it, *all* of it, because Mickey wanted to be with people." She bit off the last words, spit them out. Then a hint of something ineffably sad peeked through the cracks in her armor. "No. Mickey wanted *me* to be with people. So we grabbed as much ammunition as we could and ran out."

Piranha opened her khaki backpack, his eyes opening wide as he hauled out a rectangular box. "Nine millimeter," he said. "Jackpot."

"So . . ." Sonia said gently, "you were the ones who stacked up the bodies."

The soldier didn't answer, but she didn't have to. The bus fell into silence again.

Had Mickey been like a brother to her? A soul mate? Kendra wondered, but didn't ask.

Terry drove down the Five, toward a dead Portland. Gray tongues of smoke wafted across the city. They crossed a bridge high above a neighborhood, and below someone had spelled out a sign with white rocks on one of the rooftops: *help us.*

Piranha had craned over to stare down as well. "Don't even think about it," he said to Terry. Piranha caught Kendra's gaze but looked away. The big guy hadn't wanted to stop for her, and he hadn't wanted to stop for the soldier either.

Terry nodded, not changing his course. In the mirror, his eyes didn't blink.

They had no idea if there was even anything or anyone alive down there anymore, and they'd weathered enough risks for a day.

The bridges were clotted with stalled cars. The snowplow growled as it ground them out of the way.

Then, a stretch of blessedly clear road.

Kendra looked out of the window as they drove past an overgrown forest of freeway landscaping. Something poked out of a clump of grass beside the road. Kendra recognized human bones, gleaming and white, draped by a mass that might have been shredded clothing. Had there been more than one mass? A larger and smaller mass? A mother and child?

Kendra remembered her dad talking about the discovery of Lucy, the oldest hominid remains, in Tanzania. Lucy's bones had been found beside another, smaller, body. Anthropologists had been ecstatic to find such complete specimens. They theorized Lucy had been clinging to her child's hand when a volcano erupted, burying them both in ash. Had the excited anthropologists given any thought to the raw terror engulfing Lucy and her offspring as the boiling cloud approached?

Kendra had to look away from the shapeless mass at the side of the road as the bus crept along. Would anyone be left to find them when they were gone?

"We didn't know it was just a bunch of kids," the soldier said to her reflection in her window, asking herself for forgiveness. "We were safe, and now Mickey's dead."

She paused, batting away a stray tear. "Please, God, let Mickey be dead."

When memories threatened to overrun Terry, he focused on the lanes, the obstacles, the dashboard radio, the Twins on their solemnly lined-up motorcycles, rolling along as if leading a funeral procession. The road silenced the day's ringing in his head.

There were fewer cars on the I-5 south of Portland. Maybe a long-gone sign had diverted traffic elsewhere. Maybe someone had dragged cars off the road, salvaging them for parts or gas. No way to know.

The clear lanes were both good and bad: progress was faster, but when it was time to get gas, they would have to open twenty different cars to get enough to fill their tanks. Near the cities, fewer cars were likely to have gas. So Terry and his merry band weren't the only ones playing gas 'n' go. And where there were people, there would be predators.

"What's your name?" Sonia asked the soldier.

"Cortez," she said quietly. "Corporal Ursalina Cortez, National Guard Hundred and Fourth."

Her voice was so flat, she might have been ready to follow with her serial number.

Terry didn't know Kendra's surname, he realized, but it felt silly to ask such a basic question after what they'd been through. Piranha came up behind Terry. It was almost dark now, and they had just reached a sign that said EUGENE, OREGON.

"Whatchu think, man?" Piranha said.

Terry was glad Piranha hadn't come with any touchy-feely *How they hangin', dog?* He didn't want to be reminded of how he'd lost his cool at the armory. He'd almost gotten them killed. Amazing that Piranha still trusted him.

"I think we got no radio. Nothing local. Just the guy down in the Bay." He'd been searching the radio for three hours, and only "Reverend Wales" kept coming up. "You know this guy?"

The radio crackled. *"—and even if the world is falling apart at the seams. Even if there is nothing left, know that the powers that really created the world, peopled the world, the truth that I was barely able to tell in my movies, can still watch over us, help us. Guide us. If you are willing to trust, there is safety. If you can reach Domino Falls in Mill Valley, California, there is safety—"*

"Oh yeah. The movie guy," Piranha said. "That's the best we've got?"

"Best we've got," Terry said.

According to Sonia, Wales had made a name for himself back in the seventies with a movie called *Space Threads* that Terry only knew about because it had become a cult hit like *Rocky Horror Picture Show,* with a hugely hyped remake in the 1990s. There had also been a short-lived TV and comic book series. Terry had known super geeks at school who went to Threadie conventions and watched the movies like a religion. He'd cozied up to a Threadie girl a couple of years back, and sat through the original and remake back-to-back in the hopes of getting laid. No luck. All he'd gotten for his sacrifice was a little clumsy tongue and a play-by-play on a 2009 science fiction convention in the Seattle-Tacoma area called SeaTac ThreadieCon. No thanks.

According to Sonia (who apparently had a minor reputation as a Con Goddess back in the days such things existed), Wales had made a buttload of money and had bought a big spread north of San Francisco, town called Domino Falls. Apparently, he had survived Freak Day as well.

It figured a Hollywood hack had jumped on the radio. Anyone with a generator and an antenna could be a bandit radio king. Too bad most of them were crackpots, from what Terry had heard: end-of-the-world rants or alleged "government" bulletins, although nobody could prove there was any real government at all.

Safety seemed to rest in small, dispersed, defensible communities. But every time they heard of one functioning, it wasn't long before a frantic radio reported that one asshole had concealed a bitten brother or daughter, leading to the inevitable frightened, garbled reports, gunfire, screams . . . and then silence.

"I've been hearing the guy since Vern's," Terry told Piranha. "Their little nut-town has survived for months. Threadville, whatever he calls it. People are rebroadcasting his stuff. Hell, I think they're growing."

Piranha hung his head, sighing. "Threadies?" Piranha said. "I don't know, man. But I'll tell you what: I'm tired. We can drive around in Blue Beauty and keep siphoning gas off dead folks, but we're going to run out of luck, you know?"

Terry nodded. They had almost run out of luck a few hours ago.

"You wanna' do a Council?" Terry said. His voice was hoarse with the realization of how badly he'd let his friends down.

If not for Kendra . . . where would they be now?

"Yeah," Piranha said. "But first let's camp and break out those MREs."

The bus crept on in fits and starts, hugging the edge of the road for nearly a mile and pushing yet another car out of the way, but within an hour, and before the sun touched the western horizon, the Twins puttered back with news of a defensible camping spot up ahead.

Their chosen shelter was the blackened hulk of a burned-out gas station. The sign on the pole promised fresh coffee and gas for $3.30 a gallon, but the storage tanks had exploded, leaving twisted metal husks instead of pumps. The main minimart was shattered and looted, but a small white outlying building was still intact.

The outlier must have been a combination home and office connected to the gas station, a small cottage. Deserted now. No bodies. No stench. Terry wondered where the owners had gone, grateful they hadn't left evidence of their nightmare behind. The main area was like a studio apartment: a two-burner kitchenette, dinette set for four, a sofa, recliner, and dead TV. The fridge and shelves were empty, but who cared? The fireplace worked and a pile of wood waited. Heat and light. Home sweet home.

Kendra was more alert now, seemed to be tracking better, carried her pistol at the ready. Good. Terry liked that. She wasn't as frail and vulnerable as he had feared. And strangely, because she seemed stronger, he was more careful to keep her in his peripheral vision the way Piranha watched out for Sonia.

If Kendra was going to be around for a while, well, that changed things.

Ursalina, on the other hand, worried him. With such a challenging drive, he'd hardly had a moment to wonder about her until they camped. She came inside with them but moved to the farthest corner, taking the recliner, her legs under her, still clinging to her gun like she expected them all to go Cujo on her. She was dressed like a soldier, but the girl was unraveling. Maybe it wasn't fair, but she wasn't what he had hoped for in a soldier, jumping at loud noises. If she collapsed into herself the way he had at the Barracks, they might all pay the price.

He'd nearly died back there. Kendra had pulled him out of a hole he hadn't even realized he'd fallen into. Somehow, most of Terry's thoughts came back to Kendra.

He found himself watching Kendra's fingers, her mouth. Her lips. Enjoying the sound of her voice. For the first time, he noticed the little line on the corner of her mouth, angling up into her cheek, a faint scar of some kind. Had she gotten it on her bike? Climbing a tree?

How old was the girl? Maybe sixteen? She might have been nine when she got the scar, and he found himself wondering what kind of kid she had been.

Damn! He didn't want to wonder about her like that. He loved Piranha like a brother, but he had a *real* half brother in Phoenix who was probably shuffling and moaning by now, and he couldn't afford to care about Donovan either. Or his waste of a mother. He cared more about Lisa, but he knew she was lost to him, at least for now. If he could live with that, he could keep his mind off Kendra.

Except that he couldn't. And he couldn't help noticing that the Twins were noticing her too, even if Kendra seemed oblivious to all of them. Sonia had volunteered for first watch, so Kendra had been designated cook on their first night with the MREs. All she needed was a quick lesson from Piranha on how to use the self-heating pouches—pour water inside a chemical packet, slip the entrée inside the heated bag, and the food was hot right away. Soldiers always groused about chow, but it smelled pretty damned good, and at least there was variety.

They opened their packets, announcing their bounty like Christmas gifts: Scalloped potatoes with ham. Chicken with black beans and rice. Beef stew. Cheese tortellini. They argued over packets of military-grade M&M's and oatmeal cookies.

Terry took a bite of a cracker, but it tasted like a wood chip. He wasn't hungry. Ursalina wasn't eating either.

Piranha sat beside Terry on the sofa and spoke in a low voice, almost whispering. "Ursalina's a hottie, huh? What a waste."

"What do you care?" Terry said. "You're with Sonia. Besides, she's torn up over losing that guy Mickey."

Piranha squinted. "You're shittin' me, right?" He snorted and slapped Terry's shoulder. "You didn't get a good look?"

"What are you talking about, man?"

"'Mickey' was probably short for Michelle. They were two chicks holed up in there."

Terry felt spun. He could only clearly remember corpses and a tangle of freak limbs from the armory, but he was sure he'd seen a man waving his rifle. "No way."

"Ask the Twins. They saw it too. And they're praying she goes both ways."

Terry glanced back at the Twins at the table, who were staring in Ursalina's direction with laser eyes. Full of longing.

Terry could only shake his head. "Never crossed my mind," he said. "All I see is a chick really trashed over what happened today. Man, woman, whatever—Mickey was the glue holding Corporal Cortez together."

"True, true," Piranha said. They fell silent.

This time, Terry felt eyes on him, so he looked over his shoulder. Kendra's kitchenette was close enough to eavesdrop. She gazed at him for three seconds before dropping her eyes, her pretty lips curled in a smile.

After Piranha went outside to join Sonia on watch and Ursalina returned to the bus, Kendra sat next to Terry on the couch, staring at the useless TV screen across the room. No one bothered turning the knob. No electricity, no point. But a stash of candles she'd discovered beneath the kitchen sink gave the little room decent light. She definitely wouldn't sleep on the bus tonight, she decided.

Kendra realized she felt awkward with Terry. In some ways, they had nothing to talk about; in other ways, everything.

"I wonder . . ." Kendra said. "If we had power, would we find a channel?"

"Don't think television signals go as far," Terry said. "Is anybody out there broadcasting?" He sighed, shrugging. "Who the hell knows."

"We're gonna try this Threadville place?" Kendra said. She'd overheard Terry and Piranha talking on the bus.

"We'll take a vote in the morning, I guess."

At least Northern California was closer to Devil's Wake. Kendra knew she was only one vote, and hers probably counted less than anyone's except maybe Ursalina's, but she wanted to go where Grandpa Joe had suggested. An island was safest. Could she make Terry an ally? She'd seen something on his face when she mentioned Devil's Wake.

"If you could make a wish, go anywhere," she began, "where would you go? I mean . . . Is there anyone you want to find?" Kendra said.

Terry sighed sharply. She was sure he would stand up to cut

off their conversation, but he finally said, "In a perfect world? L.A. My sister Lisa's there."

Kendra wanted to go to Southern California too! But after what they'd seen in Vancouver, the idea of L.A. iced her bones.

But she tried to sound hopeful. "Well, if you know where she was . . ."

"I don't," Terry said. "She was with an aunt who turned out to be as big a druggie as our mom, so she ended up in foster care. Because of me."

"Because of you?" Kendra said. Terry had peeled up the edges of something hard, something terrible, and for some reason he wanted to tell her.

Terry took a bite of his beef stew, swallowed it like a rock. "My dad died in a car crash when I was ten. He was awesome, the only good decision my mom ever made. My stepdad, well, he did some stuff to my little sister I made him regret. She told me about it, and I redecorated his ass with a nail gun. Just wish I'd killed him. At least he got arrested too, and he died in a prison fight, so that part worked out. Any more questions?"

Six months ago, it might have been the worst story Kendra had ever heard about another kid. Grandpa Joe had always complained that her parents had protected her too much, hiding life's sharp corners. Kendra realized, for the millionth time, how absurdly lucky she'd been. She'd glided through her comfortable days with no idea.

"They arrested *you*?" she said.

" 'We can't take the law in our own hands,' " Terry said, mimicking a female judge. "But that worked out too. She sent me to a wilderness camp to work off my anger, and we were all there on Freak Day. That's how we survived."

"So you're all . . . ?"

Terry grinned for the first time in hours. "Badasses. You bet. Assault, confidence games, and cybercrime." He pointed at Piranha. "Shoplifting"—Sonia. "Grand theft auto"— Darius. "All except Dean—he's just hanging out with his cousin."

Kendra was surprised. If she had had to guess which of the two cousins had taken the rougher road, she would have picked Dean. Darius had an annoying sense of humor, but at least he had a spark of life. Dean seemed . . . emptied.

Maybe Dean had been more like her, completely unprepared.

"Now it's my turn," Terry said. Unexpectedly, he took Kendra's hand. His calluses startled her, like a rough glove. He spread out her fingers to pretend to study her palm, and she felt a jittery spark. "Let's see . . . Only child."

"How'd you know that?"

Terry only smiled, ignoring her question. He had a dimple that suddenly looked alarmingly attractive. Her hand seemed to squirm beneath his fingers. "Mom and Dad were always there for you . . . Never beat you . . . No drugs or alcohol for them, except wine at dinner . . . You pretty much got straight A's . . . Private school . . ."

"Not after sixth grade," she corrected him, eager to move past her parents. His vivid portrait of her family nostalgia stabbed her heart.

"The worst thing that had ever happened to you before the freaks? Maybe your grandmother died. Or your pet kitty."

Kendra's heart was pounding in a whole new way. She slipped her hand away from Terry's, suddenly nervous that her tingling palm would get sweaty. "I never had a pet. I lost two grandmothers when I was twelve, six months apart. That sucked."

But not like it had hurt to lose Grandpa Joe. The stabbing came again.

"Let's not talk about that stuff anymore," Kendra said in a soft voice.

"Fine by me." Had there been a note of triumph in Terry's voice? *You mess with mine, I'll mess with yours?* Then Terry sighed, playfulness gone. "You mentioned a place before . . . an island you heard about?"

The room seemed to brighten. "Devil's Wake. My grandfather always monitored his shortwave, and he'd heard it was safe. They're selective, but he said my aunt could get us in." She blurted it out, eager. In truth, Grandpa Joe hadn't promised her that Aunt What's-Her-Face could get anyone else in. But why not?

Terry chuckled grimly. "Devil's Wake? Where'd it get *that* name?"

"No idea."

After a pause, Terry went on, his voice solemn. "But to be honest, Threadville sounds like a bunch of weirdos to me. We're headed south anyway. If we hear any good news on the radio about Devil's Wake . . . if the island's for real . . . who knows?"

Kendra smiled. *Maybe* sounded a hell of a lot better than *no.*

"Really?" she said in a small voice. "You think the others would agree?"

"In case you didn't notice," Terry said, sighing, "it's not like we have a whole lot of places left to go."

Then he got up and walked outside. Kendra was immediately sorry for prying so much. Had she pushed him away?

For the first time since her rescue, Kendra was alone. The solitude in the little cabin sat on her chest like a dead horse. Images of infected children running toward her flashed across her mind's eye. The red-crusted eyes at the bus window, staring at her somehow. She was almost sure she could hear gunshots.

Kendra's breathing accelerated, racing with her pulse. Why couldn't she catch a good breath and hold it? The back of her neck seemed to burn with ice.

Dad wasn't here to tell her to exhale slowly from her diaphragm, and Mom wasn't here to be Mom.

Yes, *alone*. It wasn't natural, being alone. That was what Ursalina and Mickey couldn't live with, why they'd given up everything to chase a bus full of strangers. That was why Kendra had trusted Terry and the blue bus instead of running away. That was why Lucy had never let go of her little one's hand so many aeons ago even though it had meant slowing down and being buried in the ash.

The tears were starting. Every orifice felt plugged, burning her. Suffocating her.

Kendra tried to swallow back the sob in her throat, afraid it would be a scream.

She froze when she heard Terry shout from outside. Hipshot barked wildly. Kendra closed her eyes to brace herself, her finger ready on her pistol's trigger, ready for the end of the world.

"Snow!" Terry yelled. "Hey, it's snowing!"

When Kendra shuffled to the front door, she stared up with a child's wonder at the fresh, delicate white flakes floating from the sky, dancing in the strobelike flashlight beams. The snow fell fast, in glittery clumps, as if making up for lost time.

The Twins were whooping, already fashioning small, powdery snowballs they collected from the ground. Terry joined them, the boys yelling and laughing, flicking snow at one another, trying to shove ice into one another's clothes while Hipshot barked and ran in circles among them, his tail wagging merrily as if they were all at Christmas camp.

Where were Piranha and Sonia? Then Kendra saw them: they were slightly off to the side, near the crater left by the explosion at the gas pumps, holding each other. Kissing. She'd never seen them kiss like that—the way her parents used to kiss, never caring who was watching, ignoring Kendra's *Ewwwwws* before she understood what a gift they were giving her. Seeing Piranha and Sonia filled her with unspeakable peace.

Love *could* survive, even if it was only one night at a time.

Ursalina's ghostly face was framed in the bus window, her palm pressed against the unbroken pane of glass as she stared out at them, watching her new world unfold; laughter, love, sparkle, and moonlight. And just maybe, one day, healing.

Kendra wished she were an artist instead of a writer. She wanted to capture it.

It might have been the most beautiful night of her life.

TWENTY-ONE

December 18

A shallow heap of snow resisted Terry as he opened the door. He gave an extra nudge. Cold air woke up his pores. In all directions an endless mantle of white dappled with a few fir branches and corners of buildings. *A new world,* Terry thought.

He just hoped the road was navigable.

No one was waiting outside. Dean and Darius walked behind him, always wired. The cold had finally driven Ursalina inside with the rest of them overnight, and Piranha and Sonia had traded their shift from the warmth of the inside windows.

"Lookie here," Darius said, pointing. "We had company."

Out at the edge of the road, a few yards from the door, they found a large cluster of human footprints and herringbone motorcycle tracks in the snow. Not good.

Piranha bounded from behind them. "No way! I didn't see anybody."

Maybe Piranha or Sonia had fallen asleep at the window, or maybe it had been too dark to see outside. Terry had learned long ago not to waste time and energy trying to assign blame, unless a situation could be fixed. Piranha and Sonia often ended up on night watch because Terry, Darius, and Dean spent so much time driving, but usually watchers got long naps during the day on the bus. No one had a nap yesterday.

Piranha glared at Hipshot, who was sniffing at the footprints. "Great job—as usual," Piranha said, chucking a snowball at the dog. Snow puffed across Hippy's coat. He yelped, then shook it off, tongue lolling happily. "Dog stew for dinner."

Hippy whimpered as if he'd understood him. Hell, maybe he had.

"Quit it," Sonia said.

"Anyone hear engines last night?" Terry said. "There's bike tracks."

Everyone's heads wagged. Kendra and Ursalina emerged from the cabin last, both looking like sleepwalkers. But Kendra's eyes were brighter, more alive.

"Knew I should've stayed on the bus," Ursalina said, and for the first time she seemed genuinely engaged. She carried her rifle at port arms. "Eyes open, people."

They followed Ursalina's lead, bringing out their weapons. They fanned out a few feet from one another, scanning the area around the bus and cabin. Dean peeked around the corner nearest the woods sniper-style, hiding except for a dart of his head, his rifle resting against his shoulder. Ursalina crept toward the trees.

"Sneaky SOBs," Darius said, studying the trail. He pointed near the bus, where the snow was crisscrossed with wide swaths of a wiping pattern. "Tried to cover their trail with a branch or something."

"Snow was falling pretty hard 'til after midnight," Piranha said. "One, two, even. They must've come after that, or the snow would've covered it all." He stamped his foot, frustrated. "*Damn.* How'd I miss them?"

"Let's deal with it now," Terry said.

How many had come? It was hard to tell from the footsteps, but there had been more than one or two. Maybe as many as five or six—grown men, by the size of their feet. At least one of them in boots. These hadn't been freaks. Pirates could have burned them out, finishing the job someone had started before the bus arrived.

"They didn't want us to know they were here, that's for sure," Terry said. "Walked their bikes up, walked them out. Tried to hide the tracks and footprints."

"And they would have gotten away with it too," Darius said, "if not for us meddling kids." No one smiled at his Scooby-Doo riff. "Plus, they didn't factor in the deadly tracking skills of an actual Suquamish Indian."

"Yeah. That, and sunlight," Piranha said. In the sun, the fresh coat of snow sparkled like miniature diamonds, making the footprints obvious from a distance. "Don't get carried away, Squanto."

"Let's see, bro," Darius said. "My great-great-grandfather was busy killing white people. What was yours doing?"

Ursalina let out a frustrated huff of air, disgusted with them already. "Hope nobody messed with the bus, or we're screwed."

The bus! The Blue Beauty was their lifeline.

Through the frosty windows, Terry could see the boxes still piled in the rear, but they spent the next five minutes examining their vehicle from top to bottom. No slit tires, no hidden GPS tracker, no lurking ninjas. Terry didn't think the intruders had broken any windows or tried to open the door. Maybe they hadn't wanted to risk the noise.

Sonia whistled them over to the rear luggage compartment. "Was this lock nicked yesterday?"

"Crap," Terry said, and crouched to look more carefully. Hair-thin scrapes covered the lock. Someone's attempt to force it open? Or maybe the locks had been scratched at the armory, during the mad dash to load the boxes while they raced to beat the freak army. He wished he knew for sure.

Terry flipped out his keys and opened the compartment's lock. Everything inside seemed fine, except that some of the stacks had fallen in the bumpy ride.

But everything wasn't fine. Someone—a *group* of someones— had caught them sleeping last night, lurked around, decided not to say hello, but had tried to erase signs of their presence. The scratches might mean nothing, or they might be more evidence that they had used up the day's ration of luck. And they weren't even on the road yet.

After a more thorough check of the surrounding woods and a search for likely hiding places, they spent twenty minutes slipping the snow chains onto the tires.

Afterward, Terry walked out into the middle of I-5, looking both ways. Snow over asphalt. He didn't see any tracks in either direction, which was comforting in one way, but troubling in another—where were they? Hiding in the woods?

Slowly, Terry let himself relax into the whitewashed morning. In another world, at another time, the snowplows would have been busy. Once upon a time the I-5 had been one of the world's busiest stretches of freeway; early commuter traffic would have heated and plowed the road by itself. How long had it been since this stretch of road had seemed so pure, so pristine? Probably never. Had this grand interstate once been a wagon road? Back in the nineteenth or early twentieth centuries? Horses? Footpaths? Had Lewis and Clark come this way, led by Sacajawea?

Everything was so quiet now, so pure. Beautiful. Whatever values humanity had added to the world, Terry suspected that beauty wasn't among them.

He heard footsteps crunching in the show behind him, and hoped it was Kendra.

"What now?"

Not Kendra. Dean. Terry had learned that the easiest way to tell the Twins apart was by their voices. Dean's was a focused whisper, no energy to waste on volume. Not since his visit home. He still hadn't talked about it, not once. Terry hoped he'd told Darius, at least.

"You guys good with the snow?" Terry said.

"On the bikes? Hell, no. Not a good idea."

"Maybe we could find some more chains." The tiny convenience store portion of the gas station had been raided of food items and gas cans, but there might be some road gear left in the rubble if they looked.

"I've never seen chains for bikes. Too unstable."

"Our visitors had bikes," Terry said.

"Yeah, and they probably ditched the road first chance they got after the snow started," Darius said. "Unless they were crazy. That's why there're no tracks here."

Terry sighed. No bikes meant more weight strapped to the bus. No scouts. Slower progress. Another long day.

"Then we better move," Terry said. "I want to make it across the Siskiyou Pass tonight, before the snow gets worse."

His father had driven his family through the Siskiyous once, back when he had a real family. He'd been eight or nine, and he and Lisa had shrieked on the winding road like they were on an amusement park ride. He could almost hear Lisa's phantom echo. Nothing about that ride would be amusing now, especially with so much snow.

"A hundred miles," Dean said. "We haven't been making that kind of time."

"I want to try. I want out of Oregon. I feel like we've out-stayed our welcome."

Dean shrugged. "No argument there."

Terry turned to see the others, who were streaming out of the cabin after finishing breakfast. And now they were seven. After yesterday's meltdown, Terry felt more responsible for them all—even Ursalina, because her hope in them had cost her.

They were supposed to have a Council vote, he remembered. But it was getting late, and clouds drifting east meant more snow. They'd save the vote for the bus.

"Load up!" Terry called. "We're heading back to Cali."

As the bus chugged and rattled down the road at seven a.m., everyone voted to go to Threadville—even Kendra knew she couldn't offer an alternative, so they all agreed.

Except Ursalina. She was the sole "nay" vote.

"You're fools," Ursalina said. "You know how many stories I've heard from people who followed a radio signal? Those places are freak magnets. Or traps."

The radio signal brightened, as if to make their argument for them: *". . . remember the days of civilized society? When people had jobs and children went to school? It's NOT a fantasy. It's NOT a dream. Everyday Americans, hardworking, scared people like you, are seeing the threads that bind us, the threads that can rebuild us . . ."*

Ursalina clicked her teeth. "Yeah, right."

194

"Somebody's gonna figure it out," Terry said. "Maybe he's done it."

"*Estúpido,*" Ursalina said. "It's a miracle you guys survived a week."

"Just let us know, and we can drop you off anytime," Piranha said with a polite smile. Kendra understood why Piranha was sick of Ursalina's voice of gloom and doom; it was hard enough to believe in something without the constant nattering.

Ursalina suddenly stood up, and everyone tensed. She had her pistol, as she always did, as she lurched to Piranha's seat and stood over him.

"What the . . ." Terry muttered. Kendra saw his eyes go to his bus mirror. She hoped he wouldn't drive them off the road.

"Easy, *mamí,*" Piranha said.

"Ursalina—sit," Sonia said, as if addressing Hipshot. Sonia was reaching for her belt; she might shoot Ursalina faster than Piranha would.

Kendra clung to the seat in front of her, wondering if she would need to duck. Thankfully, Ursalina kept her pistol down, her arm at her side. She leaned over Piranha, her face close enough to kiss him. Piranha's jaw pinched. At close range, her pistol was less useful than his right cross.

"That's okay, bro," Ursalina said, voice so low and heavy with pain and anger that she barely sounded human. "I'll ride this bus as far as it goes, *gracias*. And then when you guys die, one by one—and believe me, you will—I'll catch the next ride. Don't get used to your happy little *familia,* 'cuz guess what? That ain't the way it works. It won't matter where you go. It always ends the same."

Kendra's eyes filled with tears, and her knees shook the way they had when she'd sat beside Grandpa Joe in his truck, waiting for him to turn. Ursalina had clawed into her mind to voice her own deepest belief, the one she'd buried. It was stupid to hope. She knew it too, deep down. Maybe they all did.

When Ursalina went back to her seat in the rear, a dead silence hung over them.

Only the radio played. The voice sounded like happy lies.

Soon, the bus had to slow to push a VW van out of the way. Next, a Ford truck.

The truck was the worst. Something still moved inside the cab, something that had once been human. It thrashed feebly inside the car, moaning and pressing its palms against the windows. The glass was cracked, as if it had battered its head against the glass until it was almost broken, but it had done so much damage to itself that it was unable to continue.

When Terry pushed their snowplow against it and pushed it off an incline, Kendra was able to see the face more clearly. Once, the thing had been a woman. Its nose was smashed, exposing sinus cavities foamed red with fungus. The face was a savage parody of human physiognomy. Certainly it felt nothing, *knew* nothing except the urge to bite. Did it realize it was about to tumble off the edge of the world?

Kendra was sure it didn't, but still felt something cold and terrible. This wasn't some dead thing clawed from the grave, like in a movie. It was still *alive*. Was now, or had, until recently, been a fellow human being. If some miracle occurred, some marvelous cure, it . . . *she* . . . might have even been saved.

All of them might be saved.

Kendra watched as the truck reached the guardrail, glancing between the truck and Terry's face in the mirror. Terry was completely focused, biting his bottom lip. He needed only to push the car to the side, but he went on, nudging it toward the guardrail. Tires squealed, sliding against the slippery snow. The truck slammed against the rail. The wheels of the bus spun, and the guardrail bent, split, and the truck tumbled over, down into the gorge. Gone.

They all craned to watch as the truck disappeared. It slid, tumbled, and groaned out of sight with a final crack of twisting steel and fractured glass.

Then, silence.

Hipshot whined. The pooch had rested his chin on her seat, and she tangled her fingers in the long hair at the ruff of his neck.

"I know," Kendra whispered. "I know."

She remembered her notebook and decided to test a few words. It took a long time for words to come, and when they did, they were few.

We're on our way to Threadville, she wrote. *And if that doesn't work, maybe Devil's Wake. We're trying to believe in something, but some of us believe more than others. I don't know what I believe yet, or if believing matters. Maybe there are no schools, no safety, no such thing as family anymore. All I know is that I want to survive. Every morning when I open my eyes and feel my heart beating and oxygen in my lungs, I know I can believe in that.*

TWENTY-TWO

For ten minutes after Ursalina returned to her seat, Sonia's fingers were shaking with the memory of how close she had come to shooting her first human being. Shooting freaks was nothing—they were target practice, and she was doing them a favor—but a fever had gripped her when the new girl leaned over Piranha.

With the freaks, the adrenaline that pumped through her was driven by fear; this time, she'd felt only simple rage. How *dare* Ursalina! After all they'd done for her, all they'd risked for her, who did she think she was?

For one moment of blind anger, it hadn't mattered to Sonia if the girl's gun was up or down, if she planned to hurt Piranha or not. Only one thought had blotted her mind, like the snow driving against her window: *Get the hell away from him, bitch.*

Sonia had never felt anything like it, and it scared her to her bones.

The snow was falling hard now, as if nature had saved the last of the sunshine for the flatlands and now that they were ascending into the Siskiyou Mountains, it was time for cold fury. Snow-dusted evergreens stood around them like a Christmas display. They had driven into what felt like a blizzard. Terry had the heavy-duty windshield wipers blitzing at full power, and he crawled at no faster than ten miles per hour. The rattling chains on the bus's wheels sounded like Blue Beauty was trying to break free.

Sonia thought of the truck Terry had knocked off the ravine and felt dizzy.

She had told herself that she wouldn't go to Piranha's seat—she didn't want to seem like an insecure high schooler staking her territory—but she quickly scooted across the aisle to sit with him. She pressed against his meaty arm, which radiated its familiar heat. Safety.

Was she imagining the daggers of Ursalina's eyes on the back of her neck? The desire to hurt the woman coursed through Sonia again. When she whipped her head around, she found the soldier staring out of her window.

"You're shivering," Piranha said. He didn't call her *baby* or *boo* the way he did when they were in the dark together, but he hadn't pulled away. And he sounded concerned in a way he usually didn't when the others were watching. He grabbed the old camp blanket draped across the seat in front of him and wrapped it around her. "Better?"

She nodded, although it was his arm and the sound of his voice that made her better, not the ratty old blanket.

"It's like a meat locker in here," she said. And it was true. She'd been so unnerved by how much she wanted to shoot Ursalina that she hadn't noticed how the temperature had dropped since the snow started falling, turning the sky gray. Despite the need to save gas, Terry had turned on the heater full blast, drying her throat, but the heat wasn't doing its job.

"Don't trip," Piranha said, and she knew he wasn't talking about the cold. He'd seen how she turned her head, knew where she'd been looking. He took her hand beneath the blanket, squeezed. "We've got bigger issues."

"The snow?"

"The snow. The ice. The world. We're gonna make a mistake." He leaned closer, lowering his voice. "Like last night. I fell asleep."

"Me too," she confessed.

He shrugged. "So there it is. And somebody's watching us."

The radio railed with static, but suddenly the voice broke through: *"How have we done it? Simple, folks: Checkpoints. A security force. Former law enforcement, former military. Some of the finest minds in Northern California have come here to weave the threads that can hold us together . . ."* Static swallowed the voice again.

How dare Ursalina try to jinx them, claiming that they would die one by one.

Bitch.

She'd known the day was jinxed since she woke up and realized she'd dozed off for at least two or three hours, and the sky outside the window where she was supposed to be keeping watch was swollen with daylight. She'd known again when she was brushing her hair in a hurry, wishing she had time to wash the greasy stink out of it, and she noticed her stud earring was gone. The earring was no big deal, cheap fake gold she'd swiped from Walmart, but it had been her only surviving pair.

She'd lost an earring the day she got arrested too.

Sonia Petansu had always felt the urge to take pretty things, even things she didn't need. She wasn't a psycho or anything— it had been a game, something to do, a kind of magic trick she performed for her own entertainment. *Now you see it, now you don't.* She'd felt a real charge keeping an eye peeled for the lame, clueless security guards—maybe the kind of charge her mother felt when she had snuck around sending texts and making quiet phone calls to her accountant friend who did way more than her taxes. Or the other "friends" her father pretended not to notice. Sonia had been swiping from stores since she was thirteen, and she never would have been caught if she'd listened to her instincts the day she couldn't find her matching hoop earring, the real gold ones her mother had given her for her seventeenth birthday, more a bribe than a gift.

The humiliation of being seen, detained, *arrested,* used to seem like the world's worst nightmare. And the look on her father's face! That memory soured her stomach even now. All she'd worried about before was her parents divorcing because That Bitch couldn't stop chasing men.

But Sonia's sentence to Camp Round Meadows had kept her alive, and she'd met Piranha. She'd given up on the idea that her mother was supposed to be a saint, or her father should have been stronger, or anything should have been different.

At Camp Round Meadows, her heart had leaped when the phone stopped ringing and her mother picked up the line. All the voices had come to her at once, fighting to talk to her, breathless with relief and worry. That call seemed like years ago now, but Sonia could remember every detail, hear every voice.

Sonia? Sweetheart . . . are you all right?

Dad had told her that everything was coming apart, that police were shooting biters and looters in the streets, and he'd borrow his brother's truck to come for her as soon as everything calmed down. Sonia couldn't have been sure, but he sounded like he was crying. *You need to pull one of your magic acts and stay safe for us,* David Petansu had said.

Sonia had studied magic long before she started stealing,

learning about sleight of hand, boxes with spring-loaded trap-doors, and how to split people's attention. She'd learned from watching her father that there was a limit to how many things a person could keep track of at one time, because he'd long since lost track of her mother. People's eyes followed an object moving rapidly without noticing what seemed to be standing still. They watched bright colors instead of black and white, noticed noise instead of quiet. If you said *one, two, three . . . five* most people would think *four,* and the instant they did that, they weren't paying attention to what was going on around them.

And somebody was playing them, just like her mother had played her father, like Sonia had played her school friends with her magic tricks and the rent-a-cops with her stealing. Last night's visitors had hidden their tracks, but not all of them. Why not? To make them nervous? To send them on their way, swiftly, through the falling snow?

She hoped she was wrong, but she'd lost her earring, and that was bad news.

Sonia leaned against Piranha's shoulder, comforted by his heat. They'd made a deal, back when this had all started, nothing formalized, nothing ever spoken aloud. But he had wanted her, and she'd only let him have her once all summer . . . until Freak Day. Then she had let him come to her whenever he wanted to, *wanted* him to come to her, the promise kept silent: *You take care of me. Give me what I need, and I'll give you what you want.*

It was much more than that now, even if neither of them gave it a name.

And Sonia suddenly felt a clutch of deep shame over her anger at Ursalina, how she'd wanted to yank out her gun and pull the trigger, how her vision had gone red. She'd never thought Ursalina would try to hurt Piranha or that Piranha couldn't take care of himself—she just hadn't liked the way Ursalina was standing over him, her face moving close. Like she thought she could take him away.

Ursalina was pissed off, that was all. How couldn't she be? Sonia couldn't imagine losing Piranha the way Ursalina had lost Mickey. Those two had had a deal in place too, even if not quite as cold-blooded as Sonia and Piranha's.

Ursalina might be right about Threadville, but she was wrong about them and their chances. She was wrong to believe they couldn't last. She would see how wrong.

As if Sonia had called her name aloud, Ursalina's hoarse voice spoke up from the back, raised loudly enough to be heard over the windshield wipers and clanking chains.

"Sorry about what I said before," Ursalina said. "It's not your fault we decided to join you. We made a choice. And you're sure as hell doing better than most."

That was all she said, and nobody answered with anything profound, just mumbles about how it was all right, how everybody was having a hard time. Piranha reached back to bump her fist, and the bus went quiet again. The snow was still blowing like the sky had lost its roof, the air was frigid, and the clouds were thick and dark.

But the day was less gray, brighter.

Magic.

TWENTY-THREE

On either side of the Blue Beauty, fresh-fallen snow had transformed trees and bushes into crystalline topiary. The stalled cars had thinned a bit but still blocked the road here and there, challenging their snowplow without slowing Terry below his steady crawl. But the snow battering the rooftop and windows rapidly filled the shrinking puddles of dark asphalt, his only hint of the road. In some patches, the I-5 was only a memory, the space between the trees or ravines. And ice was hiding in the road's cold shadows.

Terry downshifted, showing mercy to the engine as the incline sharpened. From time to time Blue Beauty's tires slid backward a foot or so before finding new traction.

This was the worst driving day yet. And the day wasn't over, with the terror of dark on its way. This day was giving steady clues that it might be the worst since Freak Day, even including yesterday. Including Vern.

Terry's stomach was still a sour knot. This leg of the I-5 had the sharpest grade of any stretch of the freeway, at the highest altitude, or so a sign he'd just passed proclaimed. The next sign echoed its warning, dangling in the wind: ATTACH SNOW CHAINS WHEN THIS SIGN IS FLASHING.

Well, the sign wasn't flashing, but their chains were damned well in place.

The snow was flurrying harder, and they were still driving deeper into it, but maybe they could get across the border before he lost sight of the quilted patches of road. Gusts scattered the snow like a leaf blower.

Should he turn around? The question nagged him every five minutes. Every two minutes, maybe. *Great idea, Terry, let's drive downhill on the ice and see how that goes.* With the ice lurking in the snowdrifts, downhill driving might be suicide. Might be more sliding than any kind of guided locomotion. Besides, if the snow kept up, they would be stuck on the wrong side of California.

Darius and Dean crouched behind Terry in the seat closest to the door, alert. Terry was glad for their sharp eyes because one pair wasn't enough. He couldn't remember the last time he'd been so sleepy. Last night, he'd had more than six hours of sleep without waking—a luxury vacation. But maybe he'd given his body the wrong idea, because it wanted more sack time. He was still exhausted from the armory, and the heater's warmth tugged at his eyelids.

Now here he was in the driver's seat, battling a demon in white.

The others had learned Blue Beauty's basics in case of an emergency—and Ursalina might be able to handle her, once she screwed her head back on—but no one else could drive in these conditions. And Kendra had never practiced with the Beauty, even if she was old enough for her license. Kendra . . .

A quick, sharp nudge to his back made Terry's eyes fly open. Shit! His windshield showed him nothing but snowy sky. He gave the steering wheel a quick correction left, a bit sharper than he usually took his curves, but not enough to make the bus slide as it righted itself around the bend. His windshield's panorama switched from sky to a wall of gray-brown rock face. Back on the road.

In the mirror, six sets of eyes stared at him, wondering if they were only imagining that he had nearly driven them off a cliff. Everyone jounced to the right, holding the seats in front of them.

Dean reached over to fiddle with the radio, and a squeal of static shot through Terry's ear—the intended effect. Terry felt more alert than he had all day. Everything was in sharper focus.

"Know what I'm thinking?" Terry said to the Twins. Very quietly. Kendra was sure to overhear from her seat behind him, but the others might not, between the heater and the windshield wipers.

"That you're a dumb-ass?" Darius said.

"I'm thinking that we can always vote to turn around, spend the night in Ashland."

"Oregon's headed into winter, not spring," Piranha said. "This ain't gettin' better. I think we should charge while the charging's good."

Darius nudged Dean. "What about you?"

"It's three o'clock," he said. "Three hours before the temperature really starts dropping. I think we can make it across the summit by then. That's what I'm thinking."

Terry exhaled a muted sigh. "So . . . here's our choices: we turn around . . ."

"Next choice," Dean said.

"We pull over," Sonia said.

"And wait for Triple-A?" Darius said. "My name's Phillips, not Sitting Duck."

"He's right," Dean said. "We'll get snowed in."

Terry nodded. "We keep going. Frankly, I think the snow is letting up. This isn't a real deep freeze, just a little warning."

Terry glanced at Kendra in the mirror and saw her wide, nervous eyes on him.

"We're not snowbound as long as we're moving," Dean said.

"Yeah, and we better git," Darius said. "We're only about"— he consulted his map—"five miles from the California border."

Five miles. That didn't sound so far, unless the snow got worse. But it would be downhill on the California side, once they were over the mountains.

"Let's get across the pass, get down below the snow line, find a camp before dark," Dean said quietly.

Piranha's voice suddenly came loudly from the back. "Anything the rest of us need to know about?"

"Just talking about the snow," Terry called back, trying to sound casual.

Piranha's stare was ice. "You okay, T? Need somebody else on the wheel?"

Trick question. No one else could handle Blue Beauty's gearshift or wonky steering, especially on a road like this. It was a rhetorical question. Terry knew he had no right to feel irritated, but he did. "I've got it."

Piranha's eyes, in the mirror, didn't blink as he stared Terry down. Terry got the message: *I'm watching you, bro.*

"Nobody knows her like I do, Piranha," Terry said.

Piranha blinked and looked away, toward his window. Letting it go, for a time.

Terry remembered to breathe. He might have been holding his breath since Kendra first woke him from his micronap, the terrible moment he'd seen an expanse of gray sky through his windshield and thought they were flying already.

He was wide awake now. Sometimes he could even see the road.

"Ice—dead ahead," Darius said.

The black patch in the shade to the right had fooled Terry, imitating asphalt. Terry steered left oh-so-gently, and only one of the rear tires gave a tentative slide before finding a grip on its chains. If he'd oversteered or braked suddenly, he could have ice-skated right into the barrier. Blue Beauty knew his thoughts. No panic, no second-guessing. Just left, right, faster, slower, or tussling with the stick to shift up and down, back and forth, their secret language.

Kendra squeezed Terry's elbow, maybe encouragement, but he pulled away from her. No distractions unless it was an emergency; anything else was dangerous. Kendra got the message, leaning all the way back in her seat. Clinging to the guardrail.

Miles ground past one aching inch at a time. Terry's muscles were locked in granite, on alert for quick reactions, corrections. But the flurries slowed as he drove south—not much, but enough to notice, and the road became less a puzzle. The California border was practically in sight.

Just when Terry thought he'd made it, Hipshot began barking.

The pooch wasn't a casual barker. He didn't yip when he was happy or hungry. He had a bladder and bowels of steel, and more patience in his front paw than the rest of them combined. So Hipshot's clipped, purposeful bark made Terry jump with surprise.

"Shhhh, it's okay," Kendra said, rubbing the black fur at the nape of Hippy's neck.

"Let him talk," Dean said sharply. "We need to hear it."

Terry downshifted, and the bus coughed into a lower gear. The upward grade slowed the Blue Beauty to a crawl; she moaned to complain. Terry whispered her promises of how she could rest soon, how he would treat her better tomorrow. As the bus ground along the snowy road, Hippy's barking grew louder.

Anxiety nibbled at the wall of resolve Terry had been building all day.

"Freaks?" Terry said. Freaks were the quickest way to set Hippy off. Terry fought the urge to look away from the road, toward the woods opening up on the driver's side, bordering the ravine. Terry thought he saw something move behind the trees—a blur, yet distinctly dark. And fast. Too fast to be a freak.

The others rushed to post themselves at windows, gazing outside into the woods on the driver's side. The steering wheel tugged against him.

"No sudden weight shifts!" Terry said.

"Don't flip the bus 'cause your mutt wants to pee," Ursalina said.

No one bothered explaining it to her.

"It's not freaks," Dean said.

The certainty in his voice made Terry see what his eyes had been hiding from him. Fifty yards ahead, a giant lump of snow lay in the road. Tires were visible underneath. Terry made out a bus underneath, probably a tour vehicle.

The stalled, darkened bus was like a mirror into their future.

The motor coach sprawled directly across his lanes, with a Ford station wagon nosing it in an inverted check mark. The vehicles might have been there all day, or longer. Had they been a two-vehicle caravan before one driver lost control? Darius clicked his tongue against his back teeth, and he and Dean

210

sprouted guns. Hipshot stopped barking to growl low in his throat.

No chance to cross to the northbound lanes—they had forked in another direction, out of his view. His only passage was the two blocked lanes ahead.

"We're gonna have to stop," Terry said.

Terry sought out Ursalina in his mirror, and he was glad to see her eyes clear and narrowed. A fighter. Good. They might need one.

"We need to move the car," Terry said. "Someone might need to steer. To disengage the brakes off that bus. Driver braked. I would have braked—even if everything was going to hell inside. To keep from sliding."

"I'd put on the brake if I was setting a trap, too," Dean said.

"And if I was a freak, I'd be hanging close to the bus," Ursalina said. "If they slept there, they'd stay there. Especially if it was a proven hunting ground." She sounded confident.

"Is that gospel? I mean, did the army figure that out about freaks, or are you guessing?"

"Little of both," she said.

Hipshot growled and barked again. The roadblock could be a trap, or infested with freaks. Or both.

"It's a good trap," Terry said. "Ground down here is slippery, and they might be dug in." He raised his voice. "Volunteers to check out the bus and get us moving?"

Ursalina raised her hand. And Piranha. And Sonia.

"Easy peasy," Sonia said. "Let's do this."

"Cover us," Piranha said, his eyes cutting into Darius.

Darius stroked his rifle's long barrel. No witty comeback this time.

Terry was surprised Ursalina wanted to volunteer. He would

have preferred to keep her behind as a sniper like Darius and Dean, but she knew her skills better than he did.

Ursalina huddled with Piranha and Sonia at the front of the bus. "No mistakes," Ursalina said. "In and out."

"Agreed. No treasure-hunting, even for gas," Piranha said. "No time."

The three of them examined one another's weapons, bumped fists.

"If you get swarmed, don't be a hero," Terry said. "Get back to the bus."

Everything important had been said. They all knew the rest. A swarm could make this the end of their ride. Pirates would be just as bad. Worse. Bullets killed at a distance. Several angles on the situation cast a bad light. The delay was a mistake waiting to happen.

Ursalina, Piranha, and Sonia were bundled in their warmest jackets and sweatshirts, but they would be cold. Cold muscles were slow muscles.

Terry almost told them not to go. Ashland was looking better all the time.

Hipshot growled again as Ursalina opened the bus door.

TWENTY-FOUR

The wind hit Piranha like flecks of frozen sandpaper. His eyes, which were already dry, stung in the snow.

But dry snow made him less likely to lose his footing in a spray of slush. He was wearing a heavy pea jacket liberated from Vern Stoffer's closet. He was glad the man had been a hunter. Piranha stepped down from the bus well onto the pavement and paused, listening while he shielded his face. On the crest of the Siskiyou Mountains, the wind bit through his jacket like a freak gnawing at his flesh.

"Ow," Sonia said.

"Ow is right," Ursalina said. "Let's finish and get back on the bus." Ursalina's gaze was everywhere, and nowhere. Roving constantly, fixing for a moment on a snow-covered lump, and then moving on to another. There: the shadow of a tree. There: a car covered with snow, only a single window exposed. Darkness within. Was there motion?

The stalled bus was a Goliath Tours special. With a bus that big, no chains, it was perfectly reasonable that it had slid across the road, crashed into the car . . .

Except that there wasn't enough damage to the car. The two vehicles were linked too carefully, leaning into each other, blocking the road.

The southbound lane of the freeway was on the west side of a divide, the north lane a hundred yards east, across a ravine. Piranha looked toward it, ruefully. Was it less crowded? Would it make any sense to back all the way down the mountain and try the northbound lane? Should he make the suggestion to Terry?

"I'm going in," Piranha said instead. "Watch my six."

"Got it," Ursalina said, and her voice gave him confidence. Ursalina had training, not just good intentions. "Watch yourself. Check the seats."

The bus's door was a standard accordion. It was closed, but Piranha doubted it was locked. He wiped snow from the glass and peered in. No one in the driver's seat. And as far as he could see, no one in the bus, dead or alive.

"Crowbar," he said, and Sonia handed over their standard equipment for road clearing. He twisted the flat edge in the doorjamb. The door sighed and then opened enough for him to get his fingers in. He set his feet and pulled.

It opened. Piranha climbed up and shone his flashlight back into the passenger section. *Nothing.* The bus was empty except for blankets and a few empty boxes. Piranha poked at the large mound of blankets on the floor behind the driver's seat.

"They must have gotten out on foot," Piranha said.

"What about the brake?" Sonia called up.

He looked. He didn't know buses like Terry, but beneath the steering wheel a long-handled red emergency brake was yanked tight. "Yeah. Someone set it. I'm taking it off, and then

214

we can get the hell out of here." He pulled up and then eased it down. "Tell Terry I'm putting her in neutral. I can steer if he pushes."

"Okay."

Footsteps as Sonia ran back to the Blue Beauty. Piranha peered to look for Ursalina, but he didn't see her and hadn't heard her go anywhere. She was checking out the bus, no doubt. Or seeing if she could start the car.

Piranha sat. The cab's air was chilly, the metal cold to the touch. The seat, on the other hand, was just a little . . . warm.

Damn.

"Don't move." The voice was quiet enough to be imaginary, and very close. Male. Piranha felt pressure at the small of his back. The gun fit through the gap in the driver's seat, some kind of hole; someone was hiding in the blankets behind him. "Keep your mouth shut. We just want a little food. A little food isn't worth dying over."

The man sounded reasonable. Maybe he was hungry. Hungry and reasonable.

Yeah, right. They just want food. Not the bus. Not the guns, gas, or girls.

Piranha glanced up at the mirror, but the stranger was out of his view behind his seat. "What do you want me to do?" Piranha said, barely moving his lips.

"I like that question, son, because that's the question people ask when they want to live." The stranger had a shark's voice, seductive enough to convince a shipwrecked sailor to surrender his raft. "You're going to tell the one with the pretty dark hair to step on up into the bus."

Piranha's back stiffened. Was he talking about Sonia or Ursalina? Did it matter?

"Do it." The voice was more anxious, losing patience. Piranha looked to his left, out the open door. Sonia was already on her way back, her dark hair whipping across her cheek. Her earlobes were red in the cold. *I need you to keep me warm,* she always said.

Piranha felt the pressure of the gun against his back and smelled the whisperer's sour breath as he raised his voice. "I'm counting to three, and if you don't call the girl over here, I'll blow your spine out of your black ass."

Despite the cold, a trickle of sweat wound its way down Piranha's back.

Dive for the door? Take a chance the guy was bluffing, or wouldn't be quick enough on the trigger? He might fire and miss.

But if you get shot for real—shot ANYWHERE—we've got no doctor.

Piranha stared out of the bus's windshield. He only saw the flurries of snow, but more gun-toting pirates could be out there. He and his friends might have walked away alive if they'd only been asked to give up bus, weapons, and food. Walk for two hours south, and they'd be out of the snow and into California.

"One . . ."

The one with the pretty dark hair. On the radio, guys on pirate stations promised weapons, food, gas, you name it, for young females. Three girls were treasure. But how could he live with himself if he gave up even one of them, especially Sonia?

Piranha sighed, his hands tight on the steering wheel. His legs were tired and stiff from the cold and sitting still. A burst of fear blossomed in his gut, new and strong and terrible. Maybe Ursalina had been right: there was no way for all of them to survive.

"Two . . ."

So *this* was how he would die . . .

"Sonia . . . *RUN!*" Piranha shouted, at the same time he moved to duck.

Piranha heard the shot before he felt it, a sting of pain that was oddly nonlocalized. In his face. *I've been shot in the back. Why do I feel it in my face—*

A scream came from behind him. Piranha whipped his head around in time to see a rat-faced, red-haired man with sunken cheeks sliding down against the left wall of the bus, blood seeping from between splayed fingers pressed against his chest.

Ursalina! She must have been watching as quietly as a cat. Through the spiderweb's cracks in the windshield, Piranha saw the soldier drop into a shooter's one-kneed crouch, firing at the freeway's western bank. Snow exploded.

Piranha touched his face, expecting to find a mangled mess . . . but he was all right. The broken windshield had scattered glass shards across his face. His eyes blinked furiously as he panicked, thinking he'd lost one of his last two contact lenses, but he kept calm enough to gently brush the glass away. His eyes itched like hell, but he tested both; some of the edges were fuzzy because his contacts were old, but he could see.

If he was blinded, he was dead. This was an ambush.

Bullets cracked and whistled from both sides, but Piranha dove to get out of the bus, rolling into the snow while he held his gun clear. He was breathing through his mouth; air was suddenly hard to come by. The gunfire was muffled. Piranha shook his head to clear his ears of snow, trying to orient himself.

Where were Sonia and Ursalina now? Where were the shooters?

Piranha turned and studied the snowbank to his right, west of the road. Through the drifting snow he could make out a parked car, covered in a foot and a half of white. The car was of medium size, a Ford Taurus or something, and the top of its snow-crusted window was a slightly different shade of white. As if someone had rolled the window down just an inch or two, and then stuck a flap of white cloth over the slit.

And something on the ground, between the tree and the car. With a narrow shadow to guide his vision, he saw a lump . . . with a hole in it . . . and something black, like a pipe, just sticking out a little bit. Hunting blind, his uncle in Georgia would have called it. Trying to pincer them.

Bullets kicked up powder on all sides of Piranha. He had no clear targets. He couldn't see Ursalina or Sonia, or where they were shooting, and he was under heavy fire from people who could see him fine.

Piranha leaped back into the stalled tour bus, keeping his head low. A *ping* across the bus's nose missed him as he ducked inside. He gasped for air.

Separated.

Freaks would be easier, he thought. Freaks couldn't pin you with gunfire.

TWENTY-FIVE

The side window behind Kendra erupted, showering her with icy glass.

She'd always thought the roadblock looked phony. It was a little too neat, a little . . . staged. It didn't capture the wild I've-got-an-infected-hitchhiker-in-the-backseat-let-me-the-hell-out-of-here turmoil she saw in most of the other cars. Or even one of the Oh-my-God-I'm-sleepy . . . let-me-just-pull-over and get a nap-and-then-I'll-be-fine cars tumbled at the breakdown lanes. Why hadn't she said something?

"Get down!" Dean yelled.

Kendra threw herself to the floor of the bus hard enough to slam the breath from her lungs. A second shot, and then a third. She scuttled back along the aisle until her feet were pressed against one of the dried food boxes. Hipshot stood over her, barking like mad at the sharp, ugly snaps of the rifle. She was afraid he might jump up on the seat, so she wrapped her arms around him and held him down.

Above her, the Twins fired through opposite windows. Terry was still in the driver's seat, his eyes trained on the windshield. The bus's engine growled, idling.

"Easy on the ammo!" Terry yelled. "Don't shoot what you can't see." He opened the bus's door, yelled toward the tour bus up ahead. "Piranha!"

But Kendra was sure Piranha couldn't hear him over the gunshots.

"We gotta move," Terry said. "We can't sit here and—"

A glass explosion.

Terry cried out *Ugh* with a bewildered look on his face. He clapped at his chest like a mosquito had bitten him. Terry had been shot!

Kendra immediately saw all the ways it could end: tumbling down the ravine in a tangle of limbs, trapped in flames, marched out one by one, rendered naked in the snow. She vowed that nothing could surprise her, and nothing short of death would destroy her. And if she didn't survive, at least she'd met people who had made her want to try.

Kendra had no more room for fear.

She scrambled toward Terry, keeping low, ignoring the pinch of broken glass across her knees and elbows.

Terry fell from his seat, nearly on top of her. He smelled like blood.

"Hold still," Kendra said. "Let me see it."

Carefully, she peeled away the bloodstained shirt to try to see how badly he was hurt. She blinked with relief when she saw his chest was clear, and the bleeding was from his shoulder. Their faces were so close that their heads bumped.

"Am I shot?" Terry said.

A large sliver of glass was caught in the wound in the meat of his shoulder, and she yanked. Terry let out a strangled yell, but she didn't think any had broken off.

"Glass got you," Kendra said. "Not a gun."

Terry examined himself, looking shocked and relieved. "*Damn,* I don't ever wanna get shot."

"Too bad," Darius said. "Might've been your lucky day."

Ursalina had just saved Sonia's life—not once but twice. She'd shot the man behind Piranha, then she'd pulled Sonia up against the Blue Beauty when the gunshots started, slamming her hard against the tire. Ursalina had pointed silently, telling her to hide beneath the bus.

Then Ursalina was gone. Sonia had seen Piranha's feet when he jumped out of the tour bus, before he scrambled back for cover. *At least Piranha's safe . . .*

But where was Ursalina?

Sonia's eyes were sweeping the snowdrifts in search of Ursalina when something sharpened to focus in the shadows: a snow-covered car was hidden beneath a grave-shaped mound of white. And a rifle poked a few inches out of that mound. God, she could see it so clearly now, even before the blip of light from the rifle's bore.

A sound like a ball-peen hammer thumped Blue Beauty's side.

An answering shot came from inside the bus, but the distant rifle didn't move. Waiting again. Sonia couldn't see anything but the rifleman's gun, but she tried to visualize where he'd hidden his body, estimating his size and length in the snow. *Center of mass.*

Why was it taking her so long to pull the trigger? She'd

wanted to shoot Ursalina over nothing, and now she was having trouble shooting a pirate? A slaver?

But she was drenched from crawling in snow, and she was shaking, her breath ragged. Sonia's finger curled around the trigger and squeezed. She was so numb, she barely felt it when the trigger broke and the stock of her rifle bucked against her shoulder.

The snow across from her shuddered, rose up a few inches like someone breaking the top of an undercooked biscuit, and then sank down again. The rifle barrel wobbled, and then aimed up at the sky, almost as if someone was lying across the stock.

She'd gotten him.

Sonia waited for horror or excitement. Her mind was empty, but her fingers were shaking, electrified. Eager to keep shooting.

"Good shot!" Dean called from the window above her.

Sonia took a deep breath, exhaled, and looked for another target. No time to celebrate. A vivid sound caught her ear in the wind.

Unless it was her imagination . . .

"Snowcats!" Terry said.

Death sounded like the burr of snowmobiles, and Ursalina Cortez hated the cold.

Her family tree had roots in Miami, Puerto Rico, and the Dominican Republic, so cold wasn't in her DNA. That was the first thing she'd told Mickey when she moved to Washington: *Next time, we're living somewhere sunny and hot.* When Ursalina Cortez had left the tropics, the order of the universe had been destroyed. Instead of dying on her beloved planet Earth, the sunny one she knew, she was stranded here in this frozen hell.

With snowmobiles.

Suddenly, Ursalina wanted to talk to God, although believing in God enraged her. If God gets the glory, who gets the blame? God was on an Old Testament rampage, and Ursalina was on the wrong side of history. God must be a man after all; no woman, no mother, could behave like this. And God was clearly pissed off, that was clear—there were too many reasons to choose from, so she'd stopped trying to guess months ago.

But it was time to make peace and try to bargain.

You gotta admit, I did pretty right by you. I almost never took your name in vain like Abuela *said, even when you deserved it BIG-TIME. I lit candles. I thanked you for Mickey. I thanked you for bringing that baby girl into my world when I didn't know I wanted a kid, how much I needed one. You saw all this was coming, you were setting me up just to lose everything, and you let me thank you anyway.*

Her prayer was turning angry. Ursalina had avoided praying because she always ended up cussing out God, and she didn't want to dig any deeper into hell.

Ursalina crawled away from the stalled car, the snow high enough that she was wading chest-deep. But her adrenaline burned away the cold. She was caught closer to the driver's side of the Blue Beauty, away from the door. Her best bet was to get under the Beauty with Sonia.

Soon, their bus would be dead to them. If the shooters got bored, they would start aiming for the gas tank.

The kid had to get the bus moving.

Ursalina's prayer went on: *We've had our ups and downs, so I hope you appreciate the significance of me crawling to you on bended knee. I would cross myself if I could take my finger off this trigger. I'm asking you for just one thing and you will never hear from me again.*

Do.
Not.
Let.
Me.
Die.
In.
This.
Goddamn.
Snow.

Snowmobiles were bearing closer, coming from north. And south. Two, maybe three. And there were two or three shooters hidden in the snow. Terrible odds.

On the ridge, Ursalina saw a flicker: shadow, light, shadow. Running.

A shot, from somewhere to her left, spanged against the Beauty, fifteen yards from her. This was a heavier caliber, military grade, and something inside their transport hissed. Another shot, and the snow a foot from Ursalina's shoulder exploded.

But Ursalina had decided not to die running like Mickey. She knelt like a statue, training her eye where she'd seen the shadow, ignoring the approaching engines bringing death of a different variety. The Twins and Sonia would have their hands full with the snowmobiles, and one hidden sniper could kill them all.

Another shot kicked the snow, eight inches right. Ursalina felt a brief flash of fear, rolling a foot to the right . . . and lost her aperture. *Dammit!* Another shot, and this one sparking off a rock under the snow. She took a chance, rolled back to the left.

There.

Ursalina squeezed the trigger, twice. A scream, a thud of a falling body, and—

A shot answered from behind her, close enough to flick snow

into her hair. Ursalina cursed, curled into a ball, and rolled to the right until she was on her feet. She stumbled for a few inelegant steps, nearly pitching forward into the snow, before she made it to the cavern beneath the tour bus. She was running the wrong way.

And she'd missed the door.

"You okay?" the kid, Piranha, called down.

Ursalina banged twice against the undercarriage with her rifle stock. "Make sure this is in neutral. Steer right."

"I'm ready when he's ready," Piranha said.

"When are you gonna jump out?"

"First chance I get after he's clear," Piranha said.

She didn't mention that Terry might knock the second bus over too far or block Piranha in. It might work, it might not. Ursalina wanted to see the kids make it, but she wouldn't live long enough to ride with them. She wouldn't know them long enough to memorize their names. Names were a waste of time.

The night baby Sharlene died, Ursalina had forgotten how to pray. After what happened to Mickey—*what HAPPENED to Mickey, you mean how freaks bit off pieces of her until there was nothing left, at least you HOPE that's what happened*—Ursalina's head was a blizzard of curses. She shouldn't have tried to pray. No wonder she'd blasphemed when she tried even a small request.

Now God was going to shoot her down.

In the snow.

"Where are those snowmobiles?" Terry shouted.

Dean was pressed hard against the bus's rear wall of boxes, nursing a cut on his cheek. Glass fragments dusted his clothes.

But Dean went back to his window post, squinting to see

outside. A snowmobile was hazing them, moving too fast for him to target, pausing when it was out of range or behind another corner, and then coming at them again.

A two-man ride. Bright red. Dean had no idea of the maker, but whoever it was, they'd made 'em fast. The riders wore bulky coats and goggles, a passing blur. The passenger held a sawed-off shotgun with one hand, aiming directly at the driver's side window.

"Duck!" Dean called out.

Boom!

The Beauty shuddered as a fistful of iron pellets slammed into the side. Dean peeked back out and saw the snowmobile disappear uphill, around the bulk of the tour bus. Thank God the shooters had to move in close with a shotgun. Dean wasn't riding a snowmobile, so his aim would be steadier—if he could shoot fast enough.

"We gotta move," Terry said. He sounded scared. He shifted gears, a tug-of-war. The Blue Beauty bellowed a complaint while the tire's chains dragged across the asphalt, clanking to life.

Everything was too loud, too fast. No thoughts, only instinct.

Kendra was holding a 9mm from Ursalina's backpack but hadn't fired it yet. She might do more harm than good with her gun; the shapes she saw through the windows were moving quickly. Her impotence clouded her eyes with tears. She was letting her new friends down.

The bus moved, hitching forward. Trying to drag itself.

"Sonia's *under* the bus!" Kendra shouted.

Terry shook his head. "She's gotta move!" he said. "I'm starting slow."

Kendra crawled down to the door well to yell outside. She

expected to see Sonia's lifeless legs crushed red beneath her, but found only white snow. From the corner of her eye, something bright sped toward her like a ray of light. A snowmobile.

"Sonia!" Kendra screamed.

Sonia rolled from behind the front tire, red-faced. She'd picked her moment and rolled free of the bus.

The snowmobile was louder, drawn by their movement.

Sonia thrust her gun toward Kendra, trying to gain her footing. "Take this!"

Kendra took the gun, flinging it behind her. Sonia leaped, reaching for her, and Kendra caught her hand. Sonia's bare hand was as damp and cool as ice, but Kendra held on, bracing her foot against the door when she slid.

Kendra's anchor helped bring Sonia to her feet. Two running steps, and she was on the bus, clinging to Kendra when her numb hands slipped from the metal bars.

The snowmobile was so close that Kendra saw the driver's face speeding toward her: a windblown man, jaw set hard, teeth bared with determination, or a lopsided leering grin. In that instant, it seemed he could drive straight up to them and pull them both out of the bus. *Was* it a grin, full of anticipation?

Kendra's blood crawled.

Deafening staccato gunfire from inside the bus changed the driver's mind. Both of the Twins were firing at them, standing upright at their windows. The driver veered sharply away before his shooter could answer.

Sonia didn't seem to have noticed the grin or how close the snowmobile had come. "I got one," Sonia told Terry. Her teeth were chattering, but she didn't seem to notice that either. "Piranha's in the bus. He's ready to help you get clear. Just honk."

Kendra was heartened by the hope she saw flicker across Terry's face. This was how they had survived, she realized. They fit together. They filled each other's gaps. They had moved cars dozens of times.

The bus's chains clanked louder as the Beauty picked up speed, climbing toward the tour bus. Kendra thanked God for sparing their bus long enough for the Beauty to drive away. If only their bus could move fast enough to push the larger one.

Abruptly, the gunfire went silent; like the end of a nightmare, or the new one waiting. The snowmobile was out of range, and the Twins had to conserve their bullets.

"I'll give Piranha time to jump on," Terry said. The plan sounded neat and ordered, as if it didn't factor in the people shooting at him.

"You'll try," Sonia corrected him. Terry gave her a look but didn't dispute her.

"Where's Ursalina?"

Gunfire crackled from somewhere near the tour bus.

"Follow the noise," Sonia said.

The giddiness snuck up on Ursalina. It was the last thing she was expecting.

Her right nostril and ear were plugged with snow; she'd buried herself in it a few yards from the bus. She'd timed her scurrying dig just as she'd heard the snowmobile winding around the far side of the bus, ready for another approach.

Now she was hunting, not running, and she liked it.

Sure enough, while one snowmobile had flanked the Beauty and the other circled the tour bus, she'd had enough time to make herself as close to invisible as she needed to be for the driver speeding up from the left, his eyes studying the Beauty's windshield. The triggerman had picked his spot, and he

228

was going for the driver—Terry. It was exactly what Ursalina would have done.

So she was ready for him. She was so sure of the shot, she barely had to look to squeeze the trigger. She visualized the shot-gunner falling like a rag doll, and he did exactly that. The snow-mobile plowed spumes of snow into the air as it wheeled around. The driver wasn't the sentimental type. He barely slowed. He took another bead, raising his own gun—only a pistol, but he had first shot.

A bullet whizzed past Ursalina's head, but she didn't bother ducking. He was moving. She braced herself on one knee, drawing a bead even as the driver took another shot back over his shoulder, kicking up snow to her left. She squeezed the trigger.

The report was sharp. His head snapped back as if someone had slammed a two-by-four against his teeth. The snowmobile abruptly banked left, out of Ursalina's view. Then a mechanical groan, and the engine died down.

One snowmobile left, one or two snipers. The odds were getting better.

Ursalina jumped to her feet and waved to Terry, unmistakable: *Move.*

Another snowmobile was coming around, heading back north to get behind them and swing around for another go. Kendra jerked her head back into the bus as the crimson flash careened along the western bank. A rifle shot. She swore that she could hear the supersonic whine as the bullet zipped past her head. The crash of gunfire in the confined space was deafening, ringing her to her bones.

She needed her gun.

As Kendra crawled back for her gun, images flashed to her sight: Hipshot's nails scrabbling for purchase against the Beauty's metal floor. Shell casings falling as the Twins fired, precious spent shell casings rolling at their feet. The gleaming of the glass as another window exploded.

"Ursalina needs cover!" Terry said. "She's running for the bus!"

Kendra glanced through the windshield, and Ursalina was in a full run . . . from what seemed a football field away. She wasn't waiting to catch her ride. She didn't want the bus to slow down for her.

"Stay at the door," Sonia told Kendra, tossing her gun to her. Sonia took a window post, sticking her head up to survey their predicament.

"Eyes open," Dean said.

"I see her! Damn!" Darius said, and ducked back as a box next to his head evaporated into a shower of corn flakes.

Explosions filled the bus as they returned the gunfire. Kendra waited in the door well, holding the door open with one hand while she gripped her gun with the other.

Was it getting dark? It was so hard to make out shapes in the whiteness. The bus was still crawling, but picking up speed fast. Kendra watched for motion, kept the door propped open with her foot, her gun ready. She hoped the first face she saw would be Ursalina's but was ready either way.

Anyone who tried to pull her off this bus sure as hell wouldn't be smiling long.

The Blue Beauty shook as Terry slammed the gear, taking control.

A flap of clothing appeared at the edge of the doorway—Ursalina! She ran too far and corrected herself, stumbling. Kendra missed her hand when she reached for it, but Ursalina grabbed a metal bar to swing herself inside.

Ursalina looked surprised to be alive. "Thanks for getting me out of the snow."

She was looking straight at Kendra, but it sounded like a prayer of gratitude.

Still crouched low, Terry slammed the Blue Beauty into gear and headed uphill. The Beauty shook as the wedge-shaped snowplow made contact with the tour bus.

Terry peeked over the windshield as a bullet sparked off the hood.

He'd hit the Goliath clean, at a good angle to leverage his weight against the larger vehicle. Piranha, suddenly only a few yards away, gave him a thumbs-up. He mimicked steering a hard right, and Terry gave him a thumbs-up in return.

Terry had a driving partner.

The tour bus shuddered and made a grinding sound as the contact point with the crashed car scraped away. The long bus rotated clockwise as Piranha gave the wheel an easy turn. The bus moved like a dream on the frozen road, almost *too* well, slewing parallel with the bank of the road. The rear stopped short, but the nose had its own momentum.

A snowmobile whirred closer to Terry from his driver's side. The tour bus began its slow slide down the hill, the tires rotating, then locking and sliding on the compressed snow, now almost as slippery as glass.

"Come on, Piranha . . ." Terry whispered.

Piranha waited a moment before he let go of the wheel and jumped out. The snowdrift that swallowed him was so deep that he nearly vanished from sight, but he dug himself out to run, scrambling toward the Blue Beauty.

The remaining snowmobile raced toward Piranha from his blind side.

"Ten o'clock!" Terry yelled, and a chorus of gunfire opened up from the Beauty as the others shot in all directions to cover Piranha. They might blow the last of their ammunition here, but so far Piranha was still on his feet. He might make it!

Behind Piranha, the tour bus's wheels skidded on the snow, the bus sliding faster down the hill, a foot and a half of snow compressing into a slippery surface, spewing white plumes through the air as it careened.

Judging by the banks, Terry tried to keep the Beauty in the middle of the road. He took a chance to keep his head up and make a course correction, turning the wheel in the direction of the skid. More popping gunfire behind them—damn!

Where was Piranha? He'd lost sight of him.

"Charlie, come on!" Sonia called from the bus's open doorway. Terry had almost forgotten Piranha's given name.

There! Piranha emerged, his head bobbing in the corner of the windshield as he ran toward the bus door in a wild-eyed frenzy, spraying snow with each step.

The snowmobile's driver fell in the covering fire. His bundled passenger tried to keep control of the snowmobile, but he finally screamed and fell while it sped on, crashing into a tree stump.

Darius joined Kendra and Sonia at the door well, and the three of them hoisted Piranha up the steps. Despite the cold, his face sopped with perspiration.

"Are we there yet?" Piranha gasped.

Terry floored the accelerator and rode the gear up the incline, urging the Beauty to find strength she didn't know she had. *Ignore your holes and that hissing sound, baby . . . Just get us through today . . .*

Three cars and an SUV were parked along the ridge, safely out of sight from the northern side, crowded with at least twenty cr thirty huddling people. Men, women, and children. No one fired at them from the vehicles, watching as they passed.

Were they captives? Slavers? A kind of gypsy pirate village?

Terry wondered, but not for long. He risked a glance in his rearview mirror, which still hung in place despite a bad diagonal crack. Behind the Blue Beauty, two small figures were shaking rifles at them, cussing at them into the wind, running back and forth like confused children. The bus rocked as Piranha, the Twins, and the girls crowded at the Beauty's broken windows to shout epithets and taunts back at them.

It was probably too early to celebrate, but Terry couldn't blame them.

At least he was awake now.

"We got company?" Terry said, his eyes back to the powdery road ahead.

"Not so far," Piranha panted.

No snowmobiles. No engines but theirs. They were all right. The pirates had dead comrades to bury and something to remember.

California waited.

TWENTY-SIX

California

It took them an hour to get down out of the mountains, and they drove another arduous hour just to be certain no one was chasing them. They found a wooded turnabout with enough cover to conceal them, but not too tight for a quick escape. Terry pointed the Beauty's nose toward the road and hoped she would start in a hurry if they needed her.

He hoped she would start, period.

A quick sweep of the bus's exterior with flashlights showed them how lucky they were to be alive. The Beauty was so riddled with holes that she reminded Terry of the bus in a Clint Eastwood movie he'd seen once, *The Gauntlet*. One of the rounds had missed the gas tank by six inches, and the coolant tank had sprung a nasty leak. But the bullets could have taken the tires or sparked the gas tank.

Could have been worse.

Most of them camped on the bus, but Darius and Dean kept watch outside from strategic locations, out of sight and bundled tight. It was still cold, but the snow had stopped. Piranha and Sonia offered to share a shift with them, but they said they were too wired.

Nobody felt like trading war stories.

Terry slept the best he could, brushing glass shards from his seat while he tried to wipe away the chaotic memories. But as exhausted as he was, he barely slept, hearing gunshots in his dreams. Every time Terry woke, he noticed Ursalina staring out of her window, her gun in her lap. Almost like a guardian angel.

Speaking of angels . . .

Terry leaned over to try to see Kendra too, but her sleeping form was concealed by the darkness. He heard the steady rising and falling of her breath and wondered if she was cold. Wondered if he should have shared a seat with her to keep her warm.

Dawn came impossibly fast. There was no talk of building a fire to heat coffee, as they sometimes did. Breakfast and dinner were treasured traditions, milestones that gave their days a sense of accomplishment and routine. But in case the pirates were coming, they set out at first light. No time for a camp circle.

In daylight, the Blue Beauty looked like a rag. Dark liquid puddled in the melting snow beneath the engine block, something Beauty had puked up overnight. Terry couldn't identify the scent.

When he turned the key in the ignition, she only choked and sputtered. How could he have thought she would start?

Terry didn't think anyone was breathing behind him. Waiting.

He tried again, and this time the choking was in concert

236

with a wounded whirring. Terry refused to panic. There'd be plenty of time to panic later. He could almost hear snowmobiles buzzing in the quiet morning.

"She needs to heat up," Terry said.

"Or a body bag," Darius said.

Before he tried the third time, Terry told himself they could make it on foot if they had to. The snow was already melting, so they could send Darius and Dean on to Domino Falls for help. Or they could hide the bus, carry only what they needed, and try to walk to Domino Falls until they could come back for their supplies. It didn't mean death. That was what he told himself.

Terry turned his wrist, and the Beauty coughed to life. Weak life, but alive nonetheless.

"That would've been our asses," Ursalina said.

Like she was resigned either way.

Someone had cleared the roads, and there was no more snowfall once they were out of the mountains. Kendra was so grateful, she wanted to cry.

Stalled and abandoned cars and trucks lined the shoulders or sat in the fields, but the lanes were mostly clear. Unfortunately, most of the cars didn't have gas either, so Terry broke into their supply of gas cans to keep them moving. No matter what they found in Domino Falls, they would need gas and ammunition to keep going.

Kendra hoped they hadn't made a mistake when they crossed the border. But the radio kept promising them paradise, the signal growing stronger with each passing mile. California was also growing warmer, so the blown windows weren't as bad.

After ninety minutes of driving south, Kendra spotted a pickup truck parked awkwardly at the trunk of an old oak tree, doors wide open. Empty. The truck was battered across the hood and doors, windows shattered. It looked worse than the bus.

Pale clothing flapping from the tree made Kendra look higher, and she gasped. Three freaks were nestled in the tree's craggy branches! Could they climb trees, too? "What the—"

Not freaks, she realized. She saw three limp corpses—two big, one smaller—that might have been a family, nearly skeletal, their features eaten away by time. A dangling end of rope told her they had been bound up in the tree, or bound themselves. She blinked, confused.

"Looks like they climbed up to get away," Terry said, as if she'd spoken aloud. He slowed the bus as he gazed at the tree too. "Damn freaks stopped the truck, maybe. They couldn't get up there, but looks like the freaks might've waited them out. They sure beat that truck to hell."

"Maybe they ran out of gas," Piranha mused. "Or too many freaks in the road."

"How long were they up there?" Kendra said, horrified at the idea. One of the bodies, sagging slightly left, seemed to be staring straight down at her. Kendra looked away. They easily could have been trapped too.

"Maybe days," Ursalina said. "Maybe weeks. You can live a long time without food. But no water? Two weeks at best. Probably less."

"Would freaks wait that long?" Kendra said.

Ursalina gave a sour chuckle. "Why not? Nothing better to do."

Now the road was empty, as if to mock the fallen for their senseless deaths.

"I wonder where the freaks went," Kendra said, as soon as she noticed a smell wafting through the bus's shattered windows. The pervasiveness of the thick scent reminded her of the vast oceans of cattle and steer manure along the I-5 corridor between Los Angeles and San Francisco, back when her parents drove her to the bay in summer. Back when she'd had to pinch her nose to block out the stench of so much death, so much rich, thick fecal stench. This wasn't the same smell—it smelled rotten, all right, but more like fruit than flesh. Had acres of orange groves withered?

Kendra tapped Terry's elbow. She was relieved when he didn't pull away. "You catch a whiff of that?" Kendra said.

"Yeah," Terry said, "I was just thinking—"

Hipshot barked once, sharply. He stood up on two legs in one of the front windows, as if scenting a distant rabbit. Dean and Darius made their clicking code, readying their guns.

Oh God, what now? Kendra thought. She was more weary than afraid.

The smell wasn't new to her—it was eerily familiar—although it was much more pronounced now, altered slightly. When Grandpa Joe had carried her out of her house in Longview, she'd noticed the odor on her street. The stench of freaks.

Ursalina walked to the front of the bus, staring through the cracked windshield, but her handgun was still holstered. "Relax," Ursalina said. "Must be a freakfield. Smells like a big one, too."

"A what?" Piranha said.

Ursalina cast a rare smile, looking at them over her shoulder. "What happens to freaks when they can't run anymore, if nobody puts a bullet in their head?"

Blank silence on the bus. Hipshot whimpered; Kendra thought even the dog sounded confused.

"You must not be hanging out with enough freaks," she said, gesturing to the window. "Check it out."

Empty fields spread out on either side of them, neglected by growers who had fled or died. But up ahead . . .

What *was* that? One of the fields was crowded with a dark mass Kendra couldn't make out in the distance, but it seemed to take up acres.

"If that's a herd of cows, we're having steak tonight," Darius said.

"Ain't no cows, kid," Ursalina said.

Kendra's heart was pounding before she knew what she was seeing, because everything about the mass—the *gathering*?— looked wrong to her. Piranha raised his binoculars and stared out of his window while Sonia crowded beside him to try to get a glimpse. Piranha's mouth dropped open. "You have *got* to be kidding me . . ."

Kendra squinted and made out a sole figure upright at the edge of the mass.

A freak! They were all freaks in ragged, weatherworn clothes, enough to fill her yard in Longview and spill into the street. As many as they had faced at the armory!

Gooseflesh crawled across Kendra's arms and the back of her neck. If the herd of freaks saw them coming and broke into a run, could they block the road enough to slow them down? Even stop them cold?

"Terry, go *faster*!" Kendra said, at the same time as Sonia let out a warning yell.

Inexplicably, Ursalina was laughing. Kendra stared at her with disbelief.

"Run from those guys?" Ursalina said. "Forget it. They're planted. You could go out there and torch them with a flame-thrower and they wouldn't move. Speaking of flamethrowers, I wish I had one of those babies right now . . ." All joviality left Ursalina's voice as she stared at the field of freaks standing shoulder to shoulder like cornstalks. Her face turned stormy with loathing.

Kendra was horrified by the mass of freaks, but Ursalina was right: they weren't moving, except to sway in the wind. As the bus rattled by, she could see a few of the freaks who were within yards of the road. Their faces were nearly unrecognizable as human, caked with . . . what? Something reddish, but more pink than the color of blood. It looked . . . fuzzy. Had these freaks chased the family up the tree?

They all gaped. Terry swerved, bumping slightly onto the shoulder as he swiveled his head to keep staring as they passed. Hipshot barked only once as he stared out his window.

Then, as if they'd just driven past a forest, the freaks behind them were gone.

"What in the holy hell did we just see?" Piranha said.

"That's what happens after a few months," Ursalina said. "They're like windup toys that just . . . stop. They're planted."

"I don't get it," Terry said. "Hippy hates freaks, even when one was his own master. Now there's all those freaks out there, and . . . almost nothing." As if to confirm the observation, Hippy wagged his tail when Kendra pet his head. The dog had already forgotten the field of freaks.

"Dogs don't care about planted freaks," Ursalina said, shrugging. "Maybe they know they can't hurt anybody. He could trot up and piss on their legs and they wouldn't blink."

"What happens to them?" Dean asked.

"They just . . . wither away, I guess."

Dean moved to the rear of the bus to take in the bizarre sight as long as he could, peering over the stacked boxes. "They smell different," he said.

"The smell is *stronger*," Kendra said.

"Not exactly lemony goodness," Darius said.

"Is that how they find each other?" Sonia said. "The smell?"

Terry turned over his shoulder to look straight at Ursalina. "Teach us," he said. "I want to know everything you know about freaks."

"Then I'm the right person," Ursalina said. "Just call me a freakologist."

Over the next hour, with only a few stoic pauses when she was overcome by memories, Ursalina told them what she had learned after weeks at the Barracks.

"If you took that diet mushroom *and* took the damned flu shot, you turn into a freak. That was why everything went to hell so fast. There were thousands of freaks, in every city, all over the country, and by the time anyone could figure out what was happening, there were millions. Hell, yahanna was popular in the military—helped desk warriors make weight, killed appetite on maneuvers. We were just screwed.

"Anyway, once you're a freak, you can pass it with a bite. Get bit by a freak, you go to sleep—everybody does, no exceptions, no matter what. The only question is, will it be fast or slow? A bad bite, if the freak juice hits a vein, you've got a couple of hours max. If it's not so bad and you make it past the first two hours, hell, you might have three, four days if you overdose on caffeine. I knew a captain who stayed awake *five* days. But sooner or later everybody goes to sleep."

Kendra shivered, remembering how Grandpa Joe had been bitten at Mike's and how Mike's sons had chased their truck like madmen down the road. Grandpa Joe had turned fast; Dad had been slower, but not by much. Kendra realized that she and Ursalina might be the only two people on the bus who had seen someone they loved bitten by freaks. They hadn't been squirreled away at a camp in the woods.

Fingers shaking, Kendra dug her notebook out of her backpack to take notes. No doubt smart people in well-fortified crannies were studying the freak outbreak. Maybe one day she could learn what they had learned, even if it only made a difference to her.

Ursalina went on: "Once you're gone, you're gone. You wake up mad as hell . . . and fast. Those are the runners. Man, you get a pack of runners after you, those SODs will chase you for miles. Some of them can talk, a little. And they move in packs, so if you see one, bet your ass there's a nest nearby."

"We've figured out that part pretty good," Terry said quietly.

"Then there's the shamblers, right?" Darius said, moving closer. "Like out of the old Romero movies."

Piranha and Sonia scooted up to closer seats too, everyone gathering around Ursalina like it was story time. All they needed was popcorn.

"Yeah," Ursalina said grimly, "but don't be fooled. They're slow, but they're vicious. They hang on like pit bulls. The runners take a quick bite and move on—at least you have time to say goodbye, hug your kid, eat a last meal, whatever. But when a shambler gets you, they don't just bite you once—they're hungry. Those are the ones that eat you. If you're lucky, you bleed out and die. If you survive, you wish you hadn't. I saw a chick fall asleep on her feet *while* she was kissing her boyfriend. One second she's sobbing and crying, the next second . . ."

Ursalina stopped, shaking her head. "I put a bullet in her head, but it was too late. That's how fast it was. She bit his tongue off."

Stone silence. Kendra saw Sonia squeeze Piranha's hand and gaze at him, as if to try to fathom how anything could make her behave that way.

"They can go on like that for months. Shamblers wander, but they remember a good hunting ground, or places they used to go, so they come back again and again.

"Then, something happens. Just when you're like, 'Dang, you're not dead *yet*?' you might find a few of them in the woods, or in the grass—just standing there. Those are the rooters. That red crap grows out of them, all over their faces, over their skin. We used to go out on rooter shoots, before we figured out it was a waste of bullets. They don't come out of it, so they're not the problem." She paused, thoughtful. "I've never *seen* one come out, anyway."

"What's the longest time you saw a rooter like that?" Kendra said, fascinated.

Ursalina shrugged. "Maybe a month. There were six of them the medic kept out back just so we could see what would happen. We called it the Freak Garden. None of the other freaks mess with the rooters, not even the shamblers. Doc thought . . ." She stopped suddenly.

"What?" Terry said, anxious.

"Our medic thought once someone gets bitten, it's like they're hosting something. In their bodies, you know? The freak juice, the red crap, whatever it is, takes over because they're . . . evolving. Doc was taking notes just like her"—Ursalina nodded toward Kendra—"studying it all the time, but we couldn't find his notes after he got bit on a sweep in Portland. The jerks had Grandma in the basement and didn't tell us. I guess they were afraid we'd shoot her, and they were right. She was a shambler when she got Doc, so . . . we never could ask where his notes were." Ursalina's voice wavered.

"Did you have to shoot him too?" Dean said.

Ursalina met his eyes squarely. "Yeah," she said finally. "A good guy too. Like a brother to me. Saved more lives than I can count, and went out like a bitch. I don't give a damn about the infection—if we all dropped dead, so be it. But being forced to shoot good people? Friends? Family? It's not right. It's straight-up evil."

They all murmured their agreement, but Kendra suspected that only Ursalina and maybe Dean really *knew*. Dean might have learned what evil was the way Grandpa Joe had learned when he'd seen Mom at the house.

Kendra stared at her notebook to keep her thoughts quiet. "So that's four stages," she said. "Sleepers. Runners. Shamblers. Rooters."

"May be even more. Things we don't know about. Haven't seen," Terry said. "Maybe the worst hasn't even happened yet."

That idea brought more silence to the bus. A cold stone seemed to settle deep in Kendra's stomach.

She suddenly realized "Josey" Wales had been working himself into a radio frenzy in the background.

"—and while man's sins caught up with him, sex and violence and the illusion that love can be bought and sold like jujubes, the truth is that we are all connected in a web of threads, connecting our souls, and that there is nothing any of us can do, anywhere, to anyone, that will not one day return to haunt us. That is the curse, and the blessing, of our existence. We inherit the sins of our fathers, and curse grandchildren unborn with our lusts and depravity. But what you need to know is that there is salvation. Not in the sweet by-and-by, but here and now. That this terrible plague, visited up the world because some of us are so disconnected from our bodies that we needed mushrooms to sate our appetites—"

"He seems pretty sure about that," Kendra said behind him.

"Yeah," Terry said. "I'm betting that whatever is left of the CDC has bulletins all over the place. What do you know about yahanna mushrooms?"

"Yahanna?" Kendra asked. Not a question, really. She didn't have to search her mind very far. " 'Bout two years ago was the first time I heard about it. An African mushroom, I think. I heard somebody found it in the Congo. I know it wasn't formally imported—someone snuck a spore print in. I think. And grew it, and liked it and shared it. There were probably a million people using it before I heard of it, but I was just a kid."

"You're still just a kid," he teased.

"Really?" Kendra said, and leaned closer to him. "Is that what you think? A kid?" She was breathing those last words into his ear, at a range close enough for him to feel the warmth of her breath.

"You're going to get me arrested," he said.

"There aren't any more cops," she said, her hand resting lightly along the top of his thigh. She was astonished at her own daring. Terry damn near ran the bus off the road.

"Hey, guys?" Terry said, breaking the spell. "You won't believe this . . ."

Kendra was almost afraid to look through the windshield, and when she did, she wondered if she was only dreaming what she saw. A small billboard painted neatly with stenciled lettering stood on two wooden posts by the side of the road. It was a new sign, unlike any others they had seen on the freeway.

OFFICIAL CHECKPOINT 2 MI. AHEAD. BE PREPARED TO STOP, it said.

In each upper corner of the large sign was painted a California flag, with its red star and big brown bear. At the bottom of the sign, dead center, was an unmistakable six-pointed sheriff's tin star, like something from a western.

No pirates had painted that sign. Tears crept to Kendra's eyes.

One lone sign looked like civilization.

246

TWENTY-SEVEN

An hour came and went with no sign of a checkpoint. They passed only stalled cars lining the roadway, so stripped that Terry didn't bother stopping to search them. The gas tanks yawned wide open, already drained. *Last to the party,* he thought.

He had been slightly nervous about the checkpoint but was disappointed when it never appeared. Had it been overrun? He'd imagined a string of towns thriving along the I-5, maybe something like army or police, someone to whom they could report the pirates and warn others.

So far, nothing. They were as alone as those people trapped in the tree had been. In his mirror, Terry saw Kendra quickly wipe her eye. He tried to think of something comforting to say, but no words came to his mind.

Terry was bone tired, but he drove on without stopping in case someone was tracking them to retaliate. Piranha'd said that the bus pirate had demanded the girls. Who knew what else they'd been after? It was time to start imagining the worst of anything and everything.

"You okay?" Terry said softly to Kendra.

She made a sound like a laugh, but there were tears close behind it.

"Let's get out the map," Terry said. "Staying focused on what's next helps."

Kendra sighed, but she pulled out the maps. With her consultation, Terry drove as far south as Yreka, only forty miles deep into California, and then cut west on a bendy, twisty road called the 96. They traveled through the Six Rivers National Forest area, which was deserted . . . mostly.

A few houses were set way back from the road, and they could detect tiny wisps of smoke from a few chimneys. Twice they passed dirt roads with handmade signs: RESIDENTS ONLY. OUTSIDERS WILL BE SHOT ON SIGHT!!

And he believed it. He also hoped that the people in those little walled-up townlets had found some peace and safety, had not been overrun by pirates or freaks. That thought gave him hope that they might find safety too.

The signal from the Bay Area was stronger now, the Reverend Wales inviting people with skills to come to their New World. It was played on a loop, rebroadcast, he supposed, by someone picking up a low-wattage AM signal.

"And if I'd ever known where the world was going, I would have known, more than any instinct could have told me, that there was something special about those films, something that went beyond their B-movie aspirations . . ."

Their AAA road map said it was about a hundred miles to a town called McKinleyville. They were losing daylight but making good progress. The road ahead had been plowed of cars.

248

Kendra was sitting on the seat just behind him, as usual. She liked to hang close, and he didn't mind. They didn't talk much, but conversation was hard. Any talk about the past—movies, concerts, family—always led to long silences and a dull stomach-ache. Once the story had been told, it didn't bear repeating.

Ten miles outside of Yreka, a barricade appeared up ahead, brightly painted sawhorses protected by three men with shot-guns.

A spray-painted sign on the sawhorse read SLOW DOWN & STOP.

The shotguns made it official.

"What do we do?" Terry said.

"Pretty self-explanatory, if you can read," Ursalina said, walking to the front of the bus, swaying with the rocking as it slowed. "We back up, they might fire. Might be friendly. Prob-ably as scared of us as we are of them."

The men wore work shirts and heavy jackets, damp with the cold rain. One of them walked forward as the others watched. Terry had no doubt at all that they were being observed from the sides. The men didn't seem scared.

"They look like pirates with a big sign," Dean said. "To me."

Piranha stared out of the window while Sonia clung to his hand, a pistol in her lap. "Nobody do anything crazy," Piranha said, probably talking to Sonia.

Despite his misgivings, Terry slowed to a crawl and then stopped. The Blue Beauty's engines growled like a bear chew-ing bones. Terry pulled even with the stout, bearded man in the lead position and opened his door. His hunter's cap was brown camo. Unkempt salt-and-pepper curls fell in a tangle across his shoulders.

"Hello," Terry said when the man didn't speak. "Just pass-ing through."

"You look like bad news," the man said, his grip tight on his shotgun. He had a hard, practical face, a voice to match, and a Yosemite Sam mustache. He didn't seem hostile, only cautious.

"We didn't start it," Ursalina said. She sounded a little too combative, although Terry was glad she had left her rifle at her seat.

"Whatcha looking for?" the man said.

"The coast," Kendra said. "Southern California. Maybe an island called Devil's Wake."

Ursalina shot Kendra a look: *Dream on.* The guy's right eyebrow raised like a fuzzy caterpillar. "Long way, little lady."

"We'll try Domino Falls first," Terry said. "Threadville. We've heard the broadcasts."

The guy nodded his head. "Yeah, I've heard 'em. Heard rumors too."

"What kind of rumors?" Terry said. The others gathered in the doorway and front windows to hear better. "We'd appreciate knowing anything that'll help."

"I'll bet you would," he said with a small smile. "That'll cost you. Pull over."

Yosemite Sam stepped away and waved toward a narrow turnabout near the signs. Terry saw tire tracks from other vehicles that had been turned away. With a sinking feeling, he rolled the Beauty to the shoulder to idle. Three more men and one woman had emerged from the woods, just as he'd expected. The bus was surrounded.

"If they're pirates, haul ass," Piranha murmured.

"We'll be lucky if she doesn't stall," Terry said. They couldn't afford any illusions about a quick getaway in the Blue Beauty. Their first checkpoint was likely to be very good or very bad.

The man with the shotgun didn't step inside the bus, but he

stayed close to the door. He scratched the back of his neck with what looked like weather-hardened fingers. "We're regular folks here. Some say there's government back east, but Texas broke away, and there's folks in the Idaho territory say different. Not really sure about any of it. But we'll take care of our own until the victory parade." He had a slightly wild dance in his eyes. "Our only business with strangers is trade. One of the things we trade is information. Where you folks from?"

He'd probably already checked out their Washington plates, but he was looking at them as if he had no idea.

"Seattle," Terry said.

Yosemite Sam nodded. "Well, welcome to California. Here's the way it's gonna be. I have a couple of pieces of information might do you some good. You got supplies?"

Terry nodded. "Yeah. For trade."

"Whatcha got?"

"MREs," he said. They had far more than MREs, but why volunteer that?

"What kind?"

Terry rattled off the menu, and he could almost see Sam's mouth water as he nodded enthusiastically. "I'll take a case of each, you got it," the man said. "Then you'll get through here and go on your way with good intel. That's the trade."

Terry glanced back at the others. Piranha wasn't hiding his incredulous scowl, and the Twins didn't look much more convinced, arms folded. There was a thin line between trade and blackmail, apparently.

"So what's the intel?" Ursalina said.

"You first," Yosemite said. His voice was friendly enough, but backed with steel.

Terry didn't like the situation or the guns tilted in their direction, but any intel was better than none, assuming it was true. He might do the same in their position. Behind him, the others murmured complaints.

"We just got ambushed yesterday," Terry said. "Guns make us nervous."

"Comin' across the Siskiyous? Damn, you're lucky. It was the Yreka boys. Any of you get killed up?"

"No. But two of them did. Maybe more." Terry wondered if he should feel guilt or pride. He only felt pain from his cuts and shaky fingers longing for a trigger.

Terry looked for signs that the gatekeeper had any loyalties or loved ones lying dead back in the Siskiyous. Hell, the Yreka boys might be feeding their whole town. But the man's grin looked genuine, and he hadn't so much as blinked.

"Damn raiders got what they deserved," one of the other men called.

The guy's eyes crinkled as if their bus had landed smack atop the Wicked Witch of the East, although he didn't bother with a song and dance. "We take care of our own. Didn't have to go as crazy as some folks—our roads were small enough to string with razor wire. I understand how you feel. How about I come up there into the cab with you, sort of hostage while we sort out the trade?"

Terry squinted. "What do I call you?"

"Reverend Meeks will do fine," he said. And held his hand out. "Round here, a shake's better than paper."

Reverend Meeks. Reverend Wales. Was everyone a reverend now?

"Sometimes all we've got is our word," Terry said, and shook hard. Reverend Meeks might have been a preacher and might not, but that grip didn't come from flipping through Bibles. Judging from the strength, the tan, and the calluses, Meeks had done plenty of hard outdoor work. Suddenly, and irrationally, he almost wanted to beg to stay and be a part of this man's flock.

But it wasn't going to happen. If they had a chance, Meeks would have said so.

"All right," Terry said after one more glance at the others. "Let's get the stuff."

While Reverend Meeks helped himself to the seat opposite Kendra with a polite nod of his head, Piranha and the Twins climbed out to open the bus's bay door. Even without a Council, they knew it was a good idea to keep the girls inside the Beauty. Sonia looked like she was holding her breath.

Here it is, Terry thought. *If this is a shakedown, here's where we find out.*

Of course, maybe they would all just be shot dead.

Terry kept glancing at Kendra, measuring her reactions, so she kept her face calm to let him know she wasn't nervous. Not *too* nervous, anyway. Meeks smelled like he hadn't bathed in two or three days, maybe more, but his face and teeth were clean . . . and nothing in his eyes reminded her of the pirate who had leered through the bus door at the mountain pass.

Ursalina sat next to Kendra, directly across from Meeks. She didn't say anything, but she didn't have to. Ursalina could look plenty menacing without a gun.

Whining, Hipshot approached Meeks and licked his hand. Meeks scratched his muzzle. So far, they were all still friends.

"Crazy world, ain't it?" Reverend Meeks said, glancing each of them over before turning back to Terry. If he saw the gun in Sonia's lap, he never said so. "Take it none of you kids had the flu shot, took that mushroom?"

Kendra's heart raced. She wasn't fooled by the casual tone of his query. She wished her parents had listened to her warnings about that damn flu shot.

"Is that what they're still saying?" Kendra said. She tried to sound casual too. "Freaks came from the mushroom and the flu shot?"

"That's what I hear," Reverend Meeks said. "Seems that every one of the early cases, somebody's done both. After that . . . maybe you're a freak, maybe you get bit. Either way, you're pretty much screwed."

"We're all clean, if that's your question," Ursalina said.

"They got plenty to trade!" a man called outside.

Meeks didn't only look pleased; he looked relieved. Kendra suddenly realized that his thin, fit build might be due more to starvation than careful eating.

"What's your situation?" Terry asked Meeks suddenly. He even glanced at her in his mirror again, and she felt a surge of electricity to realize how much they thought alike.

Reverend Meeks sighed. "Winter's coming. There's a little trade, but we don't get much traffic. We've got no idea how bad things are going to be."

No homes were visible from this road. Depending on how many supplies they'd had in the beginning, they were probably hunting for their food.

"How many of you are here?" Kendra said.

"Enough," Reverend Meeks said.

Terry turned to call out of his window. "Piranha!" he called out. "Can you guys double down? Two boxes of each."

Kendra felt Ursalina bristle, but she kept quiet.

Piranha poked his face around the corner. "Why?"

"Courtesy," Terry said.

Piranha's sour expression lingered a moment before he

smiled. "Gettin' soft, T," he said. Out of Meeks's view, Terry gave Piranha the finger.

"We're grateful," Meeks said, "but we still can't let you stay."

"Wasn't asking to," Terry said.

Kendra almost asked if they could just rest for a couple of nights, but she didn't want to force Meeks to be impolite.

Meeks studied Kendra's face, eyes gleaming. "Hell of a world," he said.

"What part?" Sonia said with gentle sarcasm.

Meeks sighed. "Well, here's my end. Up a ways on this road, about ten miles, you'll get stopped again. Tell those men 'wildfire,' and you'll get right through."

"Wildfire," they all repeated. Like a magical incantation. Although a sappy 1970s song by that name used to make her mother cry, Kendra reached for her notebook, scribbling it down. She would write down everything he said.

The men and woman outside were carrying away stacks of boxes, smiling and laughing. Maybe Reverend Meeks had once had a thriving congregation and was now reduced to a couple dozen families. The food in those boxes would feed that many . . . for a day or so. A hard way to live.

"You're going to get going now," Meeks said, with a touch of genuine regret. "Few weeks, maybe months, things will change around here. You'll see. But we have to do things this way, protect what we have, understand? Maybe down the road we'll— "

"That's it?" Ursalina said. "We give you all that chow, and we get one word? No way. That's not enough."

"What's waiting up the road?" Terry said, more gently.

"Call it fragile order," Meeks said. "People who are good, but scared. Like everyone. Without a password, they'll turn you back. Might not be polite about it. You might've already figured out you don't want to be near the Five."

True enough. "Then one word is plenty," Kendra said.

Reverend Meeks took off his hat, shook his hair, slapped it back on. "Dammit, sweetheart, you're too reasonable. Make me feel like I'm not a good shepherd."

Her parents had taken her to church twice a month, and Kendra hoped God was still watching out for her now that the churches were gone.

Piranha grinned. "These days, Rev, if you don't take care of your own flock first, you'd end up hip deep in sheep shit."

Kendra goggled at him, but Meeks laughed. "I like you kids," Meeks said. He hitched his chin toward Ursalina. "And this young lady is right. So I'll tell you more than maybe I should . . ."

Piranha, Dean, and Darius had come back from the storage bin, listening from the bus doorway. Reverend Meeks hushed his voice, as if to keep his own people from hearing. "Nobody's gonna give you sanctuary between here and the Bay. That's a fact. Threadville's taking folks in, and they're about the only ones I'd count on. That's the good news."

Terry grinned. "Great."

But Kendra was waiting for the bad news.

"On the other hand," Meeks went on, "Wales is a crazy SOB. Make no mistake. Those Threadies are a nutty lot, and never tell yourselves otherwise. If anybody ever says it's time to toast with Kool-Aid, I'd decline if I were you."

"So it's a cult?" Kendra said.

"If it ain't, I don't know what is," Meeks said. "Wales calls himself a reverend, but we don't belong to the same church, if you know what I mean. That said . . . crazy as he is, he's keeping his people safe. It's a bona fide town, and it's growing fast. People trade, mosey on through. Some stay, if they pass the sniff test. As long as they can work."

"Once people go there, are they allowed to leave?" Ursalina said.

Meeks frowned and shrugged. "Listen, me and Wales ain't Facebook friends, so I can't say for sure. Not all of the whisper stream is good, but the complaints I've heard are from folks who were put out. Say they were falsely accused of stealing or drunkenness, or some such. Threadville knows it has a right to be picky."

And how do they choose who stays? Kendra wondered.

Wales went on: "My guess is, they've got maybe a thousand there, and they're still standing when a whole mess of other would-be towns have fallen. Seems like you get a certain size, things fall apart. But if you were my flock?" His eyes rested on Kendra with almost a wince, probably because she looked youngest. "If you had anywhere else to go, I'd say head there instead. Anyone else knows you?"

Devil's Wake was on the tip of Kendra's tongue, but Terry beat her.

"I have a sister in Los Angeles," Terry said.

Meeks shook his head, emphatic. "Don't even think about it. L.A. was a war zone before Freak Day, and it's hell and gone now. L.A. was one of the first cities to fall. And not just because of freaks."

"Pirates?" Piranha said.

"Plenty of those too, but even the pirates avoid L.A. Problem is, it's a big desert—and once the water stopped running . . . no more trucks and trains, well . . ." He sighed. "Good luck with your sister." From his voice, he was giving condolences.

Terry was silent. Kendra thought about her cousin Jovana and uncle in L.A. She'd always assumed they had fled, or had died, but the details made it worse. She and Jovana used to pretend they were sisters.

"What about Devil's Wake?" Kendra said softly. "I might have a relative there."

Meeks's face brightened. "The island? Hey, that's much better. I had some folks come through, trading from Redding. They said that they'd swapped goods with another outpost . . . gone now . . . but they had regular trade with Devil's Wake. Fish, maybe. So they've got a little security, and maybe their city government survived the change. Sounds pretty solid to me. Only problem is, it's maybe five hundred miles of hard driving."

Kendra's heart fell before it could fully stir. The Blue Beauty was already coughing and gagging. How could they make it so far?

"So we have options," Terry said. "Threadville first. If we don't like it . . ."

"We'll see what's next," Piranha said.

"One day at a time," Ursalina agreed.

"I vote for Vegas," Darius said.

"Vegas!" Meeks said, and laughed deep from his belly. A couple of the other men outside laughed too. Kendra didn't want to hear horror stories about Sin City.

Meeks swallowed his chuckles. "But seriously, one more thing: You get past the first roadblock, take the Ninety-six all the way to McKinleyville. Call it thirty miles. You'll run into another roadblock around Blue Lake. Tell 'em Reverend Meeks said 'Blue Thunder,' trade 'em some of that corned beef, and you'll get through fine. They trade on the coast, and they cut a fair deal. They're not taking in outsiders, but they've got patrolled camping grounds, and you might draw an easy breath for the night."

"Yes!" Sonia said, and the Twins whooped and high-fived.

Terry didn't seem as excited, and Kendra wondered if they were sharing thoughts again: Could they make it that far?

"Just remember: be polite," Meeks said. "The Golden Rule is the only rule left these days, and a bad attitude can get you shot. They're decent folks, but times are hard."

Kendra wrote it down, every word.

Reverend Meeks paused. "They'll give you twenty-four hours to move on, or you might end up on a work gang, understood? You don't want to be trimming brush back from the fences, burning free-fire zones, none of that. There are still freaks around. We lost a town just last week, thought it was clear. Trinidad." His voice cracked slightly.

"North or south of here?" Terry said.

"Ten miles northeast. Pirates hit 'em first. Freaks did the rest."

They all sat in a moment of silence for Trinidad.

Meeks's smile was tinged with regret and sadness. "Wish we could keep you kids. I surely do. You hold on to each other, you hear? You may not be the family you were born to, but you're all the family you've got now."

They all nodded, murmuring. Kendra whispered, "Amen."

Ursalina leaned over Kendra's seat to whistle toward the woman who stood guard near the front of the bus, her rifle readied. The woman was in her thirties, tired and a little dirty, her hair windswept, her face red from the sun despite the cold.

"McKinleyville's okay?" Ursalina called through her window. "Woman to woman?"

Kendra felt herself leaning closer too, her ears primed for guidance. A good town for the guys might not be a good town for all of them. Once anyone had guns on you, they could take more than MREs.

"Reverend Meeks's word is gold," the woman said. "McKinleyville's okay if you are. But rapists get shot you-know-where."

Sounded like Kendra's kind of town. Ursalina smiled. The

boys chuckled with rounds of *Damnnnnn,* making sixth-grade jokes about family jewels and singing soprano.

The woman laughed as if their playfulness had made her week. It couldn't be fun to stand in the road and listen to people's tragedies.

Meeks stood to climb out of the bus, moving as if his joints hurt.

"Reverend?" Kendra said. "Will you pray for us?"

"Already am, sweetheart," he said hoarsely. "Have been since you drove up. The good Lord hasn't been happy with us lately, just like the Flood. But never stop praying. Maybe one day he'll be ready to open back up for business."

TWENTY-EIGHT

La *playa*.

When Ursalina Cortez's mother talked about what she missed most about living in Puerto Rico, she whispered the words with reverence: *La playa*.

The beach. She'd said it like the sand and surf were alive—sister, mother, friend. As if the Atlantic might have kept her safe from heartache. And hell, maybe she was right. If her parents had been on the island instead of in Miami when the infection hit . . .

"For you, *Mami*," Ursalina whispered. Long before the beach was in sight, the scent of saltwater, brine, and sea breezes filled the bus. There had been one phone call—only one—and then she'd lost her parents to a void of questions. She hoped they were safe, or dead. It might be better if her parents were dead.

All of them noticed the smell, sitting up straighter, craning to see through the darkness as the bus drove alongside the ocean.

No gunfire rang. No screams in the night. Nothing to be

on alert for. Ursalina lay her gun on the seat beside her and stretched her fingers, which were half numb from holding it so tightly. Her body sagged, resting.

Grief came in a stomach cramp so sharp Ursalina nearly cried out. One of the last promises she had made to Mickey and Sharlene was that she would take them to the beach. She had hidden the memory from herself, but the ocean brought it back.

Ursalina realized she was crying, but she didn't try to cover her face.

In darkness, no one can see your tears.

The ocean rolled against the beach to their right, as it had since before the first human being stood upright, and would even after the last of us shuffled red-eyed through the sand.

Somehow, defying all odds, the Blue Beauty had made it through two checkpoints and thirty miles. Terry found himself stroking the steering wheel almost sensually, wondering if it was wrong to fall in love with a bus.

The password had worked just as Meeks had promised. A single case of MREs had brought them driving instructions to the camp and a living miracle: the ocean. It was concealed in shadows, but it was there.

It was nine o'clock, dead night and dead dark, and the Beauty felt like a space shuttle lifting into orbit. All Terry could make out at first was the openness, an absence of trees. Then, suddenly, they were close enough to see glowing bonfires dotting the beach from campers who kept a careful distance from one another.

The headlights illuminated a few more signs now: TRADING TODAY, said one. And WOOD AND FISH FOR TRADE, said another. Here, along the coast, life endured. They passed a car going north, and each vehicle moved as far to its own side of the road as possible. The other car was a station wagon, crammed with possessions and guns. Three adults and maybe two kids. A big, beefy woman, perhaps two. A guy with a beard turned to glare as he glided past.

Terry wanted to yell out to him that there was nothing up north but death.

The sun had long set, but the moon's shadow danced like a dolphin on the waves, shimmered, bringing back memories of other times and places that sent Kendra rushing to the right side of the bus, pressing her face against the glass.

"I haven't seen the ocean in a year," she said to no one but her reflection.

"Washington beaches suck," Darius said. "This is *way* better." He and Dean slapped hands and broke into song simultaneously: "*'Wish they all could be California giiiirls.'*" Impressive harmony. It was odd, and reassuring, to hear Dean singing.

Something had changed. Even Hipshot moved to the right side of the bus, fogging his seat's window with his tongue. He barked at the night-dark waves.

A guy with a powerful flashlight guided them to the sand with a dead-eyed reminder that McKinleyville would only host them for twenty-four hours, warning that dawdlers might be conscripted into work crews. To some travelers, Kendra thought, forced labor might not be a bad trade for food and protection.

The bus jounced along shallow dunes. Invisible waves marched across the shoreline with steady growls and whispers that seemed to stretch from one end of the earth to the other. The moon showed her flashes of cresting white from the waves, and the back of Kendra's neck glowed with the unnameable joy of knowing that something was still the same.

There were a half-dozen other campers out there, and three campfires. The fires might not be as warm as they looked, but it was still good to see the guards patrolling the sand, those guns pointed not at them but out at the road itself, or toward the surf.

They parked several yards from a campfire that was home to three people: a man about fifty-five, a woman a little younger, and a kid who looked about thirteen. The group had been watching them race out of the Blue Beauty onto the sand, keeping an eye on them while they stretched, chased each other like puppies, and drank in the ocean air.

"It's freezing," Ursalina said sourly, comparing it to beaches in her memory.

"Fire," Darius said. "Great invention."

"True," Piranha said. "Let's find driftwood."

The Twins and Piranha had just started combing the beach when the man at the fire rose and began walking toward them. Kendra tensed, but not for long. She saw none of the fearful caution of the others they had met on the road. The man probably had a handgun hidden somewhere, but he didn't carry himself with that one-wrong-move-and-I'll-shoot-you posture that was all the fashion since Freak Day.

The woman walked closely behind him, leaving the boy at the fire. She wore a brace on her right leg and moved like a broken Slinky. She was pale-haired and pretty but looked as if she hadn't slept in a month.

Hipshot greeted the couple with a friendly bark and wagging tail.

"Hi," the woman said. "We're the Lamphers, and my name is Sharon. Might take a while to build a good fire, so you're welcome to share ours."

"I'm Joe," the man said. "That scrawny kid tending the fire

is our son, Adam. Think we might have a beer or two to spare. These days, we're willing to bribe for company."

Kendra might risk her life for a Coke, but beer tasted horrible and only made her sleepy. But the offer was miraculous, and the others whooped.

"Sir," Ursalina said. "You've said the magic word. You can even check my ID."

The couple laughed at her joke, the idea of checking a driver's license quaint and long-ago. The woman hung very close to her husband, holding the crook of his arm. It was only after they started moving toward the fire that Kendra realized she was blind.

Joe had run a liquor store in Sacramento before Freak Day and had loaded up the camper with all the beer and booze they could hold, figuring to trade. The figuring had been pretty good. The tepid cans of Newcastle Brown Ale he offered hadn't come from their store: it had been traded a hundred miles east for a case of Chivas, Joe figuring that cans of beer might be better small change than a fifth of whiskey.

Kendra knew plenty about their story before she heard the details.

When their neighborhood had fallen to infection, they'd risked packing up to stay with friends who owned a farm. That sanctuary had lasted a week, and then the farm had been overrun too. Neither of them mentioned dead friends or loved ones, but their long silence said enough. Adam poked at the fire angrily with a stick, and sparks sprayed up like fireworks.

Finally, Joe sighed. "Pirates rule the roads, so everybody thinks towns are best," he said. "You hear about these towns rebuilding, and they seem fine for a while. But it's like the freaks can smell it. One day, everything is clear. The next, there's a hundred freaks at the wire, somebody's been bit, and his husband or wife won't give warning. Within a couple of days, there's freaks inside, and it's all gone to hell. We've seen it, oh, a dozen times, just here in Northern California. We've learned how to move fast."

Sharon and Adam were nodding emphatically.

Darius let out a satisfied beer belch and excused himself. "This place has a good setup," he said. "How are they surviving?"

"They know each other. Aren't taking outsiders, except to camp and work. Plenty of guns and dogs," Joe said.

"Strange how dogs can tell," Kendra said, ruffling Hipshot's fur as he settled beside her. Hipshot usually gravitated between Terry and her.

"You know what I think?" Sharon said. "I think we can all tell, but we don't let ourselves know what we know."

With a shiver, Kendra remembered her father's wild eyes after his bite. "Why would we do that?" she said.

Sharon Lampher turned her face toward Kendra with a fond, distracted expression, her eyes turned more toward the night sky. "Because they're us, darling. They may bite and tear, but when it comes right down to it, they're our brothers and sisters and mothers and cousins. They are us, if we make one mistake. And so whatever signals we get are all confused, all scrambled up. We don't want to know what we know."

Sharon closed her eyes about halfway, fluttered her eyelashes. Joe patted her knee. "Sharon . . ."

"No, it's all right," Sharon said.

"Mom used to give workshops, do readings . . . aura stuff," Adam said. "Tarot. Native American juju. Stuff like that."

Joe folded his hands. "If you believe in that kind of thing," he said.

"O ye of little faith," Sharon said. "Ask him why we went to you kids."

"Mom said you were okay," the boy said simply.

"Good auras," Sharon said.

Joe shrugged. "Sharon has great hunches, I'll admit. I don't know if 'auras' really exist outside our perception, or if it's just what I'd call a 'complex equivalent.'"

"A what?" Sonia said. She had settled in Piranha's lap, and his arms were wrapped around her as he rested his chin on her shoulder. Kendra envied their pose, but Terry was far on the other side of the fire. He kept glancing toward the Blue Beauty to make sure no one was trying to board the bus, still on alert. The Blue Beauty was Terry's more than anyone's.

Joe went on. "Let's say you have a whole lot of information you've picked up unconsciously. I went to engineering school, took psych classes. The unconscious mind is the ocean, and the conscious mind is a teacup. There's just a pinhole to squeeze information through, and most of it never makes it. Haven't you ever had a gut feeling you couldn't explain?"

Terry and Kendra glanced at each other when he said that, as if he'd tugged on puppet strings on opposite sides of the fire. Embarrassed, they both quickly looked away.

"Maybe they just smell right . . . or wrong," Joe said. "Or it's their body language. But you don't have time to run through a whole list, so you just get a feeling. Right? I think auras might be like that. We pick up a huge amount of information, can't process all of it as data, but we get a feeling."

As if to demonstrate the point, Hipshot rested his muzzle in Sharon's lap. "I saw everything about you in my head as soon as the bus drove up, no matter what he says," she said. "Everybody here is kind, healthy, and un-bit. Especially *this* little guy. He's about as un-bit as you could get!" She ruffled his fur.

"Yes you are! Yes you are!" Her *good-doggy* voice set his tail to thumping.

Then she looked at Kendra, and in the firelight Kendra thought her unseeing eyes changed from blue to the deeply green depths of the ocean. "You are especially interesting," Sharon said. "I'll be honest. You're the reason I invited all of you to the fire, young lady."

Darius made a little chuffing sound, a joke he'd decided to keep to himself.

"Me?" Kendra's voice was small.

"You." She looked not at Kendra but slightly past her. "Do you remember your dreams?"

Kendra had the oddest sensation, as if the world was focusing its way down to a tunnel, and that tunnel connected the two of them. No one else seemed to exist. Sharon repeated her question.

Kendra nodded, a shallow little dip of her chin, but Sharon seemed to see her.

"And what . . . do you dream about all of this?"

"This?"

Sharon's smile was kind but stern. "Don't pretend, little lady. We don't have room or *time* for that. Maybe once upon a time, those of us who see could pretend not to. We could hide. But if you hadn't noticed, we need every open eye we have." She leaned forward. "Every open eye."

Kendra's heart pounded in concert with the surf on the sand, with its steady rolling rhythm, the heartbeat of the planet, a love song between the earth and the moon dancing with her waves.

Kendra looked around at her friends, suddenly aware that she didn't want to answer the question. That this woman, with her blind green eyes, had peered more deeply into her than she wanted anyone to—now or ever. But they were all looking at her. Even Hipshot, gnawing on a rib bone Adam had given him, seemed to be waiting for her.

"Sometimes," Kendra began, so softly that she could barely hear her own voice. "Sometimes I remember my dreams, yes."

"And is there one that recurs? Anything that has changed since the outbreak?"

She nodded slowly, remembering the disturbing dreams she'd had when she was living with Grandpa Joe in his cabin. She didn't exactly remember images from her dreams, but they suddenly seemed like a story she told often. "I feel as if . . . I'm standing on a chessboard or something. Made out of strings of light. They connect off in the distance somewhere. Something is moving along those lines. Making the squares."

"Something?"

"Something alive."

Sharon nodded. "Anything else?"

"No," Kendra said. "But I never had that dream before all of this . . . no, wait. That's not true. I think I might have had it just a few times, but it started within a month or so of when everything fell apart."

"And did you ever dream about . . . the sick? Before it happened?"

Kendra took a moment to realize that Sharon was referring to freaks as "the sick," a term so compassionate that it sounded strange . . . but exactly right. She pulled her knees up to her chest and wrapped her arms around them. "I used to have dreams of being in a garden, and large plants grabbing me. And cities burning. I'd been having them for a couple of years. My parents said I would wake up screaming. It got bad. My mom didn't want to keep me in the city anymore, but my dad didn't want to leave. They started fighting all the time. Finally, they decided to move out of L.A. I felt so guilty, but I had to get out. Had to leave."

She looked at the group's rapt eyes and then began to cry. For a few moments it was as if they were all too shocked to move, then Kendra felt an arm around her shoulders, and then another, and then they were all hugging her.

Sharon Lampher's voice was terribly gentle. "Look at what happened to the cities," she said. "Pure panic. Breakdown of services. Millions died in the first months. You had a much better chance of survival in a small town."

"Weren't you in Portland when your father got bit?" Terry said.

Kendra nodded, surprised that he remembered. "I didn't want to go. I *really* didn't want to go. They wanted to give me that damn flu shot."

Kendra noticed something feral pass across Ursalina's eyes: the soldier making a mental note to keep an eye on Kendra.

"I never took the shot," Kendra said quickly. "Or ate the mushroom. I never had the chance. The hospital was . . . bad. I begged them not to take me."

"Had you ever been afraid of getting a shot before?" Sharon said.

She shook her head. "Not since I was a little kid."

"But you were afraid of this one."

Kendra was still, listening to the roar of her breathing, the pounding of her heart. Everything was so clear now. Her parents had moved for her. To help her. But some part of her—a part so small and weak that it could barely let itself be known, let its voice be heard—had been trying to save them.

Why couldn't she have seen more clearly? Enough to make a difference?

"But what good is it?" Kendra said. "It wasn't enough. Is there a way to make . . . that part of me stronger? Make the messages clearer?"

"Just listen for it," Sharon said. "My gift . . . it was easy. So much darkness, so little light. But you . . . with you, it was different. It will *be* different."

"Is it . . . too late?" Kendra asked. "For it to matter?"

"If you can even ask that question," Sharon said, "it's not too late at all."

After a time the conversation died away, and they made their good-byes to prepare for sleep. The Lamphers hung to one side of the fire, and they circled the rest. No one was more than arm's length away from the others, in case they needed to wake one another in a hurry. Silently.

Kendra felt more comfortable with her bedroll on the sand when she lay down to close her eyes, pretending not to hear Piranha and Sonia get up to go, hand in hand, to investigate a dune a hundred feet north of their fire. It was a big no-no to disappear without alerting the others, but Piranha and Sonia behaved like a secret. Maybe they thought pretending would keep it from hurting as badly if something went wrong.

When something went wrong, as Ursalina would say. And she ought to know.

Terry was exhausted from endless driving, and there was no reason to drag him from sleep. Kendra sat up and pulled herself out of the sleeping bag. When no one by the fire stirred, she wandered down to the edge of the surf. Hipshot, of course, followed her, his feet padding on the damp sand.

The water was liquid ice. The black water, nearly invisible in the dark, flowed up and rolled back, touching the tips of her toes, and she stared out across the quivering plane. The water swallowed her. Awed her. Mocked her.

If you looked across the water, all the way across, what was there? Hawaii? No . . . that was farther south, wasn't it? China? Japan? She was trying to remember her maps. And what was happening in those faraway lands? When Arizona and Montana had been made alien, the rest of the world was unknowable. Was there a world?

The surf hissed up and down the shoreline that stretched to oblivion.

Suddenly, Kendra needed to believe there were others standing on a distant beach, looking out at the ocean, wondering as she was. They were just as lonely and frightened, gazing east instead of west. Kendra closed her eyes and tried to feel a connection with the world. Was there something there? Anything?

All she knew for certain was that somewhere out there lay an island called Devil's Wake, where a blood relation might be waiting for her. Safety. Family. Could she hope Devil's Wake was real, that her future was real, or was Devil's Wake only another dream?

Eyes closed in the darkness, her toes sinking into the cold sand, she felt nothing. And then she realized that something was hidden within the nothing, something she could only see as . . . a deeper nothing. Like black threads against black velvet.

"Ohhhh," Kendra whispered, realizing she had been searching for lines of light.

Now, touching that deeper place of darkness, she followed the thread, almost as if she were pulling a buried cable out of the sand, with grains spilling over it as she pulled.

She drew, and then relaxed again, and it was as if she rose up high above the beach, higher and higher, but could still see herself standing on the shore, holding the thread. And the thread . . .

As if the smell and sound and motion of the timeless sea had washed away some of the confusion, some of the misty distraction, she saw it. The threads and their connecting nodes were dense with darkness, heavy with heat, and that *smell* . . .

"Kendra?"

A voice. His voice. *The* voice.

Kendra snapped as if she'd fallen asleep on her feet. She turned, fighting the urge to fall against Terry. He wrapped her in a blanket and left his arm draped around her. She sighed against him. He was so strong—not overly muscular like Piranha, but solid and steady. And quiet. She hadn't heard his approach.

He guided her a few steps away from the shore, until the sand was dry. Then, as if they had agreed on the moment, they sank down to the sand. Terry sighed.

"Do you care that you just scared the crap out of me?" he said, surprising her with the anger in his voice. "You're taking a stroll, so I wake up and you're gone?"

Seeing her disappearance through his eyes, Kendra felt ashamed. "I wanted to let you sleep," she said.

"Yeah, look at how great I'm sleeping. I couldn't sleep with you gone."

He said it so plainly, in a matter-of-fact way, that she wondered if she'd heard him right.

"Your breathing," he said quickly. "I hear you breathing when you sleep. On the bus, when we camp—your breathing's always close to me. So I know everything's okay."

"I listen to you breathe too," she said.

Then, for a long time, neither of them said anything. Kendra remembered Piranha and Sonia behind the dunes, wondering if they were still there. Wondering if Terry wanted to slip away together, and if he would be disappointed in her.

Kiss me, she thought. *This would be a perfect moment. If we were supposed to be together, if the only thing that came out of this entire horrible mess was that you and I found each other. And if*

273

this moment, here in the moonlight, by the waves, was the moment when we first kissed, and we told our children . . .

Kendra's daydream stopped cold. Children? How could she ever imagine bringing a child into the world?

"I hope the Blue Beauty can make it to Domino Falls," Terry said.

"You think she can't?"

He shrugged. "She needs a mechanic," he said. "Something in the undercarriage. Something rattling. And the gears are getting a little tricky." He smoothed his hands over his hair. "We'll see. She's always been a little temperamental, but now she's downright mean. I think we'll be all right."

By that, of course, he meant he wasn't sure they'd be all right. Kendra felt silly for fantasizing about a kiss when Terry was worried about breaking down on the road.

The moon danced on the water. Kendra picked up a stone and threw it, thinking to skip it out and right into the silver circle. Instead, it just hit a tiny wave and vanished.

The insanity hit her like a bomb again. Children! They might not live past tomorrow. But if they couldn't make it to Domino Falls, if something separated them, or one of them died, wasn't that a better reason to kiss and hold each other now?

Sonia and Piranha already knew the answer to that question. Were those their love cries, just barely audible now? Or was that the sigh of a bird?

Terry's weight beside her awakened a stirring Kendra had felt only mildly before, a sweet, heavy ache between her thighs. She wondered what it felt like to have a boy's naked flesh pressed against hers, the whole length of his body. Would she ever know?

She'd had a boyfriend for three months and necked with him in his car, but he'd never pressed for anything else. All she'd

274

seen was R-rated lovemaking in movies and little cheap images streamed on the Internet. Of course there was biology class, but rabbits and rhinos didn't count. And the time her cousin's sixteenth birthday party had turned into grinding, with neighborhood boys dancing too close in the dark, stone-faced, taut groins pressed behind her. Kendra had felt part intrigue, part revulsion.

But nothing captured the feeling of arousal Terry had planted in her.

Nothing else had ever come close.

"If she breaks down," Terry went on finally, "we'll stick together. Carry what we can. We can walk the rest of the way. Plenty do it."

He almost hid the fear in his voice.

That time, there was no mistaking the sound of Piranha and Sonia.

Terry chuckled quietly, embarrassed.

"Live for the moment, I guess," Terry said.

"I like that idea," Kendra said.

It was hard to see his face in the dark, but she knew he was looking at her.

Terry took the hint. He leaned over to kiss her, and his mouth was its own ocean. She'd never been cast about so much by a kiss, so much of her awake and wanting. Sand rained on her as she ran her fingers through his hair.

An endless kiss, ending too soon. Kendra must have forgotten to breathe while their lips met because her entire chest was beating with her heart.

Terry suddenly stood up and held his hand down to her.

"Where are we going?" she said.

She would have gone anywhere with him. To the Blue Beauty. To the dunes.

"Back to sleep," Terry said.

She didn't move at first, disappointed. Didn't he want her?

"What's wrong?" he said, although she thought he knew.

"What if . . . this is the last good night?" she said. The question sounded foolish, but they both knew there was nothing foolish about it.

"It's not," he said. "Or, anyway, even if it is, I have to do everything I can to make sure it isn't—like get rest so I can stay awake tomorrow. And one day . . . one day we'll have a *really* good night somewhere."

Despite all reason, and the bright weight of his promise, Kendra felt hurt. She ignored the feeling, struggling to make a joke. "Like somewhere we won't get sold to a work crew if we stay too long? Or we're not afraid of breaking down on the road?"

"Yeah." Terry's grin shone in the moonlight. "Somewhere like that. Like Domino Falls, maybe." He paused. "Or Devil's Wake."

Kendra didn't say the next thing in her mind: *What if we never find that place?*

Instead, she took his hand and enjoyed his strength as he lifted her to her feet.

They didn't wake anyone when they took their places back by the fire, so they shared the heat of Terry's bedroll and lay side by side. Neither of them closed their eyes until Sonia and Piranha returned, distracted and excited by their nearness.

As the firelight died to embers, Kendra and Terry finally fell asleep. The last thing either knew was the sound of the other's breathing.

Kendra dreamed.

ACKNOWLEDGMENTS

The authors would like to thank Major Jefferson Davis, for a tour of the Vancouver Barracks and for useful conversation on military arms, tactics, and training; Steve Perry, for overall sharp eyes; and Tahlia Holt, for help researching the Puget Sound area and Bainbridge Island.

It would be dishonorable not to thank the artists who created the images and ideas most commonly associated with the "zombie apocalypse" notion, and the very shift from spellbound Haitians to something far more sinister and universal: Don Siegel, Daniel Mainwaring, and Jack Finney (*Invasion of the Body Snatchers*), Ubaldo Ragona and Richard Matheson (*Last Man on Earth* [*I Am Legend*]), George Romero (*Night of the Living Dead*), and Danny Boyle and Alex Garland (*28 Days Later*). Understanding our vast affection for these tropes will hopefully explain why we were eager to tangle these speculative threads together . . . winking at an audience that, we hope, is having as much fun as we are.

Acknowledgments

The thematic . . . thread, if you will, weaving through all of these cinematic visions is that there is a force that dehumanizes us, that pits us against the very people and institutions we once relied upon. And that the only salvation is our connection to one another, and our own hearts.

In fact, that is all that has ever saved us. Or ever will.

Steven Barnes
Tananarive Due
March 1, 2012
Atlanta, Georgia